COOKBOOK FOR
REVENGE

Revenge Is a Process

GILBERT-ALAN SANCHEZ

PAGE PUBLISHING
Conneaut Lake, PA

First originally published by Page Publishing 2022

Cover illustration Aubrianna Sanchez

ISBN 978-1-6624-7376-0 (pbk)
ISBN 978-1-6624-7377-7 (digital)

Printed in the United States of America

This is a story of one life in the restaurant business.

We all go through life having been wronged in one way or another. Most of us move on and continue to go on with our lives. I chose to take a different route. Mine would be considered wrong in many people's eyes. To some, it's something that they've always wanted to do yet never had the nerve. Me, well, I began my journey down a different path—one that I hoped would satisfy my desire for revenge.

Here's how it all began...

CHAPTER 1
Let's Get Started

Aaron

When I was growing up, I could never figure out what it is I wanted to do with my life. The school of hard knocks is not the best way to go through life. As successful as I may have been at times, I would not recommend it for everyone. Then I discovered the world of cooking. It gave me an outlet for my fondness for fire, knives, and what some would consider strange, my love for the smell of blood.

But first, I had to pay those dues everyone was always talking about. I started with busting suds in the dish station and slowly worked my way up the ladder. Herlinda's was one of the more popular diners in the city. I moved from dishwasher to busing tables in a very short amount of time. It was then that I discovered that socializing was one thing I wasn't very good at. Talking to people I didn't know made me nervous. Asking them how they liked their meal didn't appeal to me. Most of them had attitudes that I despised— they did nothing but anger me most of the time, and all I wanted to do was put them in their place. I had no control over that product, so taking the heat for something I wasn't responsible for was not something that I found appealing.

Then my chance finally came to get out of the front of the house and into the back. In hotels and restaurants, there was always a battle between the front of the house and the back of the house. I never really quite understood it. I always felt the need, deep down inside, to explain to these people that what they were doing was wrong. I watched a chef put one side of the plate over the fire to get scalding hot and then hand it to the server. When the server would scream in pain, the chef would just laugh. He would be the one that helped to push me further into that dark place in my mind. The place where most people wouldn't go to.

Working half of my time in the back and half in the front was definitely a huge conflict that at times made things difficult. The anonymity that comes from working in the back of the house is what I needed. In order for me to do what I wanted, what I *needed* to do, flying under the radar was required. Before I could start down my path, I needed to learn the ropes, I needed to learn how to use the instruments that were necessary for my journey. Without them, I wouldn't be able to continue.

I'll always remember how arrogant I was when this whole process started, thinking that I knew it all. Never understanding that there were so many people before me that gave a lot of blood, sweat, and tears before I got my chance. I soon discovered that this wasn't a field that you could just jump into, either field, not if you truly wanted to create and make a difference. An older cook that was training me once asked me the question: How long do you think it will take to develop your own technique? After thinking, for a total of about five seconds, I arrogantly said, "About two weeks." I never saw anyone laugh so hard at me. I don't think I ever have since.

Even after that whole conversation, I still didn't get it, and I wouldn't for a very long time. It occurred to me that I really wasn't in this to create food but more to satisfy my need to make things right, at least in my mind. Too much drinking and drugging always has a way of getting in the way of trying to deal with reality. Still, it not only helped my nerve, but it also helped me to be more creative when it came to the actual career I was choosing, if you could really consider it a career.

I made my way to a local hotel where I thought I would learn more about cooking and develop my technique. On my first day of work, the cook who was training me asked me if I got high, and I of course answered yes. Indeed, my first day of learning new techniques wound up with me doing the same thing, getting stoned and drunk during, before and after work, all day every day, and I wonder why my cooking technique never got any better

I spent the next year or so working for a chef that had learned his technique as an Air Force sergeant. I'll always remember him finding a small mouse in the storeroom. I watched him pick it up with a pair of tongs, take it over to the commercial kitchen garbage disposal, turn it on, and drop it in. As he dropped it in, he muttered, "That will teach that son of a bitch to come into my kitchen." That was one of the coldest people I've ever worked for. I would spend so much of my time stoned, drunk, or hungover that I more than once would put the wrong ingredients into the food I was cooking—so often that he looked at me one day and asked me if he needed to start labeling the ingredients in Spanish. I didn't speak one word of Spanish, and he knew that. This was just one of many places I worked where it was pretty much acceptable to say whatever you wanted to the people that worked for you. Everything that happened was just one more thing that would help fuel my desire to strike back at people. The problem with uncontrolled rage is that you make mistakes, ones that can get you caught. I found that drinking and drugging only made those mistakes worse. If I ever wanted to be successful in my chosen career, I would definitely have to address that situation.

One of the hardest things to learn as an addict is that your way isn't always the best way. You need to kill the ego for you to be able to learn something from others who just might know more. Manipulating situations doesn't always work; and going through life drunk, stoned, and stupid is no way to do it. Unfortunately, you're the only one that can learn that. People did what they could to try to teach me that I just wasn't ready to learn. After moving to Colorado and Phoenix, I finally found the one chef and place that I feel has been the most responsible for starting me on my path to learning the best way to utilize my talents. It's where I really started building my technique. I started working at an upscale ranch that was located at the foot of a beautiful mountain range.

People that have been doing this for most of their lives were trained how to do things from the ground up, everything from scratch, you don't cut corners. Who was supposed to train me how to perfect the dark side of me? I loved watching shows and documentaries about all the serial killers that were out there, but I needed to come up with my own style, my own signature so that people don't ever forget me. There was no way that I would be able to achieve all that I wanted if my mind wasn't clear from all the outside influences, environmental and otherwise. It was time—time to stop all the garbage that made it harder for me to learn and to succeed.

I decided to check myself into a drug and alcohol place to start clearing my mind—a mind that I was going to need if I was going to be successful with my new career. Being in rehab was nothing like I thought it would be. I honestly don't know what I expected, but I figured this is where I needed to be. The fact that the name of the street it was on is also my name was way too much of a coincidence, one that I couldn't pass up.

It took some time to get used to not living my life with the things that were causing me to lose control. They, at the very least, allowed me to keep my cigarettes; without them, I truly would've gone crazy. After making my way through detox, I could start to move on with the program. We spent a lot of time talking about feelings, things that you've done while using. It helped me to dig deeper, to figure out who I was and what I wanted. They always tried to blame others for what I was thinking or what I had done. You get to a certain point in life, and you need to take responsibility for who you are or what you've done. I mean, who could I blame for all the thoughts that go through my head, I mean the really far-out thoughts?

As addicts, we tend to try to control all aspects of our lives, or at least we think we do. It didn't take long for me to realize that I was trying to control everything that I was doing in there. But after we were told that we needed to give ourselves up to a higher power, it all started to make sense to me. I figured out who that higher power was. The higher power for me was someone I called the Chef, the creator of all I was about to do. He was the writer of the recipes for all I was about to do. It's said that if you don't get things straight in your head, you will cross addict into something else. Sex, eating, it would be something else, and I think I figured out what I was going to cross addict into. There were moments when I actually felt emotion, where

I actually felt bad for all the pain that I had caused others. If I was going to carry on with my plans, those feelings were going to have to be put away. I was always good at compartmentalizing everything I felt. It was the only way for me to not truly feel because if I were to feel those kinds of feelings, I would never be able to continue. I continued with the program for as long as I felt I could fool those around me. It was easy to fool people into believing that I truly wanted to stop. It was more about giving myself up to the power because unless I stop, I will never be able to do the things I need to do with a clear head, free from any mistakes. I had no plans of getting caught. I finished a thirty-day program in two weeks. I was told I would never make it; I would never be able to stay clean and sober. I thanked them for the confidence, and I moved on. What they didn't know was that my main reason for getting clean was so that I could proceed with a clean and clear mind. It was time to get to work.

The chef I started to work for, let's call him Jimmy, was one of the hardest people I've ever had to work for. It's people like him that fueled my desires to seek the revenge I've been looking for. He didn't care if you got hurt, cut, burned, or if you even broke a bone the job needed to get done and your feelings or pain didn't matter. I remember cutting my knuckle to the bone one day. I showed it to him. He looked at me and said, "Put a bandage on it and go back to work." I think he reacted that way mostly because his pain didn't matter to him, so why should yours. I never worked for a guy that could be such a mean son of a bitch.

He screamed, cussed, yelled, and threatened to fire you every day. Back then, the only thing you could do was take it and move on to the next day. I had finally gotten to the point where I just couldn't handle it anymore. He had pushed and pushed people to the point where some broke down and cried and some just quit. He was one of my teachers, and I was taught to treat chefs and teachers with respect. You can't push people around nowadays. He's someone that I believe literally worked himself to death. He was dying from cancer, so the steps I took to get my revenge would just wind up taking him sooner than cancer would. It would be like getting executed, that lets them off easy, and I wasn't going to let that happen.

CHAPTER 2
The First Kill

Aaron

The first time was probably the hardest. I didn't know if I would be able to go through with it or not. I needed to focus and not back out. I was on a mission, and I had convinced myself that what I was doing was a service to all of us that had been abused throughout our careers. I wasn't going to give up.

We had a late party that night, and it was one he decided he needed to work. The party went the way most of them do—him screaming and yelling and treating staff and customers with overall disrespect. The customers were late in sitting down to eat, and he actually went out to the dining room and told them, in a very loud voice, that it was time to sit down and eat. I'm sure that they'll never come back as long as he was there—something they won't have to worry about again.

After serving them and cleaning up I asked him if he would stay longer. I needed to talk to him about something. I made him a drink, with a little something extra in it to help relax him. I dosed him with a mixture of Demerol and Valium. He wasn't really aware of what was going on, but he really couldn't say much. I took him down to an area where we used to do outdoor cookouts and laid him out on a table next to the grill. They never seem to understand that there are consequences for their behavior. Okay, maybe this isn't the consequences that he deserved, but it was my way of making sure that he never hurt anyone again. Being outside was so incredibly peaceful. No one would ever hear his screams, but then again, he wouldn't be feeling anything, so what would be the point? He had tried to yell out, but I reminded him that no one was around to hear him and that no matter how much he screamed, this was still going to be happening. He could either stay quiet, or I could tape his mouth shut. I explained to him all the things that he had done over time to all the people around him. The screaming and yelling, the threats, the insults, and at times the throwing of various objects at people. He still didn't understand why that was a problem. He would never understand. That's why this had to be done.

This man had taught me all that I needed to know about butchering, all the basics about breaking a piece of meat down. I had to look at him as nothing more than a piece of meat. I took an old smokebox from behind the kitchen, attached some casters to it, and brought it with me. I inserted a needle with a tube into the vein in his neck so I could slowly bleed him out into a stockpot. I started at his feet, severing the feet at the ankle. As I showed him each piece of his body, he tried to scream, but he couldn't. He didn't have the energy. With each piece I took away, the more he kept slowly passing out. I shot him up with adrenaline to keep him awake, but after a period of time, he just had no more left in him. He was finally gone. He knew that there were reasons for what I was doing, but he still didn't understand. It doesn't matter now. Unbelievably enough, none of this bothered me. I actually felt at peace with it. I took the smokebox with his body and the stockpot of blood and took it deep into the desert. I poured the blood into the box with the body parts and left it open for the animals to come and feed. That was a fitting burial for him.

I needed a signature—something that would make people remember me for what I had just done, a clue that would not only make people wonder but that some might actually find creative. This particular chef had a saying for us while we were carving for buffets, "Thin to win." I carved a nice piece from his torso, placed it on the back prep table in the kitchen, and wrote in his blood, "Thin to win." I needed some time away, someplace to go where I could recharge and rethink what had just happened. Maybe, just maybe I needed to find someone to love me that I could love back. Would that help curb these feelings and desires?

CHAPTER 3

The Big Move

Vanessa

One day, I decided I needed a change. Life as a restaurant manager had run its course. I could only deal with being taken advantage of and shit on for so long. It was time to go. It wasn't fun anymore. Hawaii was where I always wanted to live. So one day, I sold everything I had, picked myself up, and moved to the island of Kauai. It was perfect for me. Small, like me, quiet, yet more than enough for me to do day and night so I would never get bored and nothing but miles and miles for me to explore. This was only the beginning of my adventure.

I decided to splurge and fly first class to Hawaii. This is something I had never done before, but I thought why not. It's a six-hour flight, and I always felt anxious and nervous when I flew. I figured with the space they give to you in first class, as tiny as I am, I could just curl up and drift away, maybe fall asleep or watch some scary movies, something to help keep my mind off the vast ocean below. After having a drink and watching a movie, I drifted off into dreamland, not a care in the world.

The excitement that I felt when the plane landed for the first time was unlike anything I'd ever felt before. The excitement and anticipation were boiling up inside me so much I could barely contain myself. I landed in the town of Lihue, Kauai. Beautiful sunshine and ocean breezes greeted me as I got off the plane. The smell, the perfect smell of ocean and flowers, was unlike anything I'd ever experienced before. I knew at that point that this was the best choice I could've ever made. I made my way to the shuttle to take me to the resort I would be staying at. The Grand Hyatt was on the south shore of Kauai on Poipu beach. I had no idea all the adventures that were in store for me.

While I was on my way to the resort shuttle, I saw the cutest lava-red BMW i8 at the rental car place, and I couldn't resist it. This would be the perfect way for me to start on my adventure to the resort of my dreams. The thirty-minute drive to the resort is one of the most beautiful drives in the world. I couldn't believe my eyes as I passed by palm trees, birds of paradise, koa trees, and probably the most beautiful piece of road in the world, the tunnel of trees. It travels through a tunnel of trees made from five hundred eucalyptus trees that lined either side of the road.

Legend has it that you shouldn't drive through the tunnel after midnight and you should never drive through it with pork. It was said to be haunted. Now that was a piece of information that I loved to hear. Halloween was one of my favorite times of the year, and I wanted to test the legend. Kauai is considered one of the most spiritual places on earth, a place where you can really get in touch with yourself. This is something I needed to do. I needed to break down the walls I had built up for myself. Coming out of the tunnel, I arrived at the small town of Koloa. The small local shops and restaurants were everything I imagined—girls' hula dancing, old women basket weaving, and young girls and boys making flower leis.

After stopping for some food and ice cream, it was time for me to head to the resort. I climbed back in my car and sped off toward my destination. This was the most relaxed and at ease I'd ever felt. It was a great feeling, one that I hoped would never go away. I pulled up to the front of the Hyatt. I was greeted by two bellmen, one to take the car and one to take her luggage. As I walked into the resort, I was greeted by a beautiful Hawaiian woman wearing a long flowing colorful dress. She reached over and gave me a kiss on each cheek and placed a fresh flower lei around my neck. The smell of the fresh flowers was unreal, like a drug that made me feel so happy and free inside. Another never-felt-before feeling. One of many so far. All of them made my anxiety and stress just melt away.

I decided to go with one of the larger suites since I planned on being there for a while. When the doors swung open, I couldn't believe my eyes. I chose the ocean view suite, over a thousand square feet, bigger than most of the houses I'd lived in, with the most gorgeous views of the beach and ocean. The room was filled with over-stuffed chairs and couches. I walked into the bedroom, and there was a king-size four-poster bed with soft fluffy pillows, comforter, sheets, and flower leis and Hawaiian chocolates on the pillows. I walked into the bathroom, and there was the most stunning claw-footed tub and a huge marble shower.

After unpacking my suitcases, I decided to sit out on the patio and drink an ice-cold Dr. Pepper. Listening to the waves breaking on the sand and smelling the ocean air was so relaxing to me. I went back into my room and decided to climb into my bed and take a nap. The trip was long, and although time turned back three hours, I was still exhausted. I closed my eyes and fell into a deep sleep, not waking once, desperately needing sleep I'd been lacking for years. After sleeping for what seemed like an eternity, I woke to the sound of a conch shell horn blowing outside. The sun would be going down soon, and every day before the sun went down, men and women dressed in ancient Hawaiian clothes would blow a horn and dance a fast Tahitian dance, complete with twirling fire sticks to say goodbye to the sun and welcoming in the night.

I needed to decide what I was going to do for dinner. There were so many choices on and off the resort property. The resort offered the service of having a chef come and cook dinner for you personally in a cabana set up on the beach. Although it was meant for two, I decided that for my first night in paradise, I was going to have a chef come and cook just for me. Why not spoil myself for once? I picked up the phone and made the reservation for eight. It was only five, so I still had some time. I rolled out of bed and decided to take a nice warm bath before dinner.

I started the water, warm but not too hot, and poured in a Hawaiian ginger bubble bath. It had the most interesting scent.

It smelled of island flowers and ginger. I took my hair down and stripped down to my bra and panties. I walked to the closet and grabbed a big fluffy robe, walked back to the bath, took the rest of my clothes off, and slipped into the warm water. I made sure that the warm water and soap covered all my body. I was so small that the tub almost swallowed me up. I floated in the bath long enough until the water started to cool and decided it was time to get out. I stepped out of the tub and wrapped myself in the big fluffy robe. I needed to get ready for dinner. I put on some makeup and put my hair up. I decided to wear this cute red dress I had bought for my journey— spaghetti straps, low cut, the perfect amount of cleavage, just enough to make people wonder and short, showing off my perfectly toned legs. I put on a pair of leather sandals and a beautiful white woven shawl that I had purchased in town that afternoon to protect me from the cool ocean breeze. It was time for dinner. I grabbed my purse and left the room. I was getting hungry, and I couldn't wait to see what awaited me for dinner.

I made my way out of the room and started walking down toward the beach. All the artwork and flowers that lined the corridors of the resort were unreal. I was wondering why everything was so open in Hawaii. Now I knew—the ocean breeze smelled like a combination of salt and flowers. It was incredible and hypnotizing all at the same time. It had the ability to take away any worry or stress that may be going on inside you. That was something that I really needed. I stopped at the concierge desk to find out where I needed to go. I was personally escorted down to a secluded area of the beach right by the resort. There was a small table set beautifully with a single flower and candle, plates with Hawaiian flowers painted on the rims, and utensils made of silver. But the one thing that showed me how much these people paid attention to me and what I liked, there was a wine bucket with bottles of Dr. Pepper on ice.

Next to my table was a beautiful cart carved out of wood. On it was a cutting board, burners, and utensils. All the things needed to cook my perfect meal. My server came out and poured my Dr. Pepper into a wine glass and told me that the chef would be out momentarily to start my meal. After a few minutes, my chef appeared and introduced himself. He said his name was Aaron. I felt this immediate connection to him. It made it so much easier to be able to connect and talk since I was all alone. Either way, I was hungry and couldn't wait to finally eat.

My meal consisted of four courses, and it had things that I thought I would never eat. Such a variety of seafood, fruits, and meats; and the dessert, it was incredible. Throughout the entire meal, Aaron prepared each course on the cart right there in front of me. He talked about where it was all from and what it took to prepare it, creativity went behind every dish he made. He explained that cooking was one of the truest forms of science. Would a doctor or researcher cut corners on the drugs they're creating to help people who are sick? The way in which he described his process, the way he created food, the way he could taste it in his head before he even combined any flavors and put it on the plate truly fascinated me. How was he capable of creating such incredible flavors? How was he capable of actually making me feel things inside that I had never felt before? The feelings weren't just restricted to the nine thousand taste buds in my mouth. I felt them through my entire body—it was incredible. I didn't really understand how that all worked, how it could make me feel what I was feeling, so I decided to dig a little deeper.

He explained to me that he thinks of food like its art. When a musician, a painter, a writer, when they create, they draw on their past, the things that have given them pleasure or pain. You can physically and emotionally feel it in what they write, sing, and create. He asked me if I'd ever gotten chills, if the hair on my arms has ever stood up when I've heard a certain song, looked at a certain painting or drawing or read a certain line. I told him that, of course, I have. That's you feeling what that artist created. Those are the same feelings that I just had eating his food.

I decided to delve a bit further into his process. I wanted, no, I really needed to know where all that pain came from. He told me that all his life, coming up through the ranks, he had basically been abused by those who led him through his culinary journey. He told me that as wrong as it was, as much as he hated dealing with people that shit on you, to a certain degree, the abuse and pain helped him become who he is today. It has forced him to feel things he probably would've never felt before. His way of dealing with it, at least in the beginning, was through his creations of food. It was really the only way he knew how. He had gone through rehab and counseling, but the anger and pain were always still there. I told him if it's one thing I could relate to it was the abuse that you had to put up with in this particular industry. He asked where and whom I had worked for. I didn't ask why. I guessed it was just part of the conversation.

I asked him if we could get together the next day, and he could show me the island. He told me that he had to fly back to the mainland to take care of some business and that he would be gone for a while. He knew the chef at the resort really well, and when he came to the island, they would let him come in and do things like this for the guests. I told him that I was now a resident of the island and I would be here whenever he got back. We exchanged phone numbers, and he shook my hand—yes, shook my hand—and thanked me for a wonderful evening. I made my way back to my room, and I fell asleep, thinking of Aaron and all that we talked about. It was the best night's sleep I had had in years.

*****

Aaron

I walked back to my room, thinking, *What the fuck just happened…?*

I knew that I had to shake off what had just happened to me. Catching feelings for someone could be dangerous. With feelings comes a conscience, something I didn't have anymore—I couldn't if I wanted to keep doing what I was doing. Then again, she's another one that's been hurt by all the assholes that are out there. *Stop trying to negotiate with yourself. She's a drug, and with drugs come many problems. Move on.*

CHAPTER 4

Time to Get Back to Work

Aaron

I made my way back home. I always seemed to make my way back here. This is where the pain started and where I needed to end it, to put it to bed. All the people that caused me pain would pay for it. I was the fourth of four kids. It seemed like by the time they got to me, they had pretty much, let's say, run out of energy. I remember asking my dad one day why there were more pictures of the other kids and there weren't many of me. He said by the time they got to me, they were tired of taking pictures. Never really knew what to think of that.

They weren't around much when I was growing up. I was pretty much left to my own devices, not really a good thing for me. I started selling and abusing drugs and alcohol when I was in seventh grade. I got a girl pregnant at fourteen. She had a miscarriage. I wrecked my parents' car twice, stole a truck; and even though they were never around, they always felt the need to keep me out of trouble. I never paid one penny or spent one day in jail for all the things I did. They couldn't be there, but they made sure that I didn't get in any trouble—they always pulled my ass out of a hole.

I never held any of it against them. They were good parents; they did the best they could. I always had a roof over my head, food in my mouth, and clothes on my back. They loved me, never beat me or purposely hurt me, but they just weren't always there. I still loved them more than anything. When I was seventeen, they got divorced—one moved to Pueblo, Colorado, and one moved to Casa

Grande, Arizona. They asked if I wanted to go, and I said no thank you. I was working and selling drugs. I didn't need anyone, at least I didn't think I did.

My next, I guess you could say, recipe, involved using the Sargent. He was a bit more difficult to find. The hotel we worked at had since been torn down and replaced with a health-care facility. Lucky for me, he actually retired to that facility, so not as hard as I thought it would be. After finding out which apartment he lived in, I decided to pay him a visit. I needed to see if he even remembered who I was.

His apartment was located next to the main kitchen. It almost looked like they saved the kitchen and dining room and they built the facility around it. I made sure to dress in dark clothing with a cap and hoodie to help cover my identity. The ranch was easy, but this place had cameras down every hallway. I couldn't make the mistake of being noticed. I knocked on his door, and that same grizzly, gruff, and big-oted old man answered the door; and lo and behold, he knew who I was! His wife had died a few years prior, his kids lived out of town, and he said that he didn't have many friends there. Not really shocking considering his attitude. After sitting and talking for a while, I asked him if he could take me on a tour of the old kitchen. He happily agreed. I put my hoodie and cap on, and we made our way to the kitchen.

Since it was so close to his apartment, it didn't take us long to get there. There was actually a point where I was starting to feel bad for what I was about to do. I was wondering if that was because of my encounter with Vanessa while I was in Hawaii. Then Sargent decided he was going to start reminiscing about the good old times again—all the abuse and insults all started coming out again. Suddenly, I didn't feel so bad anymore. He reminded me exactly why I was doing what I was doing. Time to put another notch on my knife.

We started walking toward the storeroom, and he started talking about that damn mouse from years ago—the one that had the nerve to go into *his* storeroom. Before he turned around, I stuck a needle in his neck and gave him a dose of jungle juice—not enough to knock him out but enough to keep him from being able to fight back. He was old and not that heavy. He always seemed so much larger years ago probably because I was younger and didn't have as much experience in the real world. I brought his limp old body into the dish area and laid it up on the deck. I had an interesting idea about how I was going to do this one. A bit of a blast from the past.

He slowly started to wake up, and he discovered that he couldn't feel anything and he started to panic. He tried to scream, and he couldn't. No matter how much he tried, nothing came out. I started to explain to him all the things that I had bottled up inside all these years, all the shit that he had said and done that had stuck with me and never left. He still didn't care; in fact, when he figured out what was going on, he just got more verbally abusive. So I had brought a dead mouse with me, you know like the one he would stick in the disposal. I had no idea what I was going to do with it. The more he ranted, well, I finally figured out what to do with it. It went in his mouth. I decided that I was going to use the same cruelty that he had used on all those little mice from the past; who knows, maybe he still did that.

I started to slowly dismember his body, and I put each piece into the running garbage disposal. I found it fitting since he had treated so many other living creatures like that. He eventually died from all that was being done to him. The pain of the knife going into his body. I started with smaller pieces so he at least knew what was happening to him. I left his torso and head propped up in the dish station, and I wrote in blood, "That'll teach you not to come into my kitchen." I really liked leaving all these calling cards for people to find, but it was getting a bit messy. I was leaving too many opportunities for mistakes to happen, and I had no intentions of going to jail. I needed to just do my job and move on.

While I was walking out the door, my phone started buzzing in my pocket. I pulled it out and saw that it was Vanessa. I got in my car, and as I drove away, I answered the call and started talking. This could have seriously turned into a problem for me, but it made me feel safe and at ease talking to her—like that feeling of revenge was for a small moment put in check. I couldn't let that go. It made me feel human, but how long could I keep it going for? How long could I go without telling her what I actually was, what I was actually doing? I guess only time will tell.

CHAPTER 5

Time to Take a Chance

Vanessa

After talking to Aaron for what seemed like a very long time, he decided that he would come back to Hawaii for a while and spend some time with me. I picked him up at the airport with a basket full of food. I decided that since all he does is prepare food all day that I would make a meal for him. I drove us to Hanalei Bay. It was famous for the place where they filmed the movie *South Pacific*. We went to a part of the beach where there weren't a lot of tourists, laid out a blanket, and sat down to eat. I packed lots of different treats, all so good that he thought I could've been the chef instead of him. He forgot; I had worked in restaurants all my life, so I did know some of what I was doing.

After we ate, we decided to go for a swim. The ocean was the perfect temperature, and it was nice spending some time out here with someone. It had definitely been a very long time. I asked him how his time on the mainland had been. He was always very evasive when it came to his time away. Since we were just getting to know each other, I didn't really want to press him on anything, but I was always curious about what he did when he was away. I loved my time with him and didn't want to jeopardize that.

We finished our swim, gathered our stuff, and walked back to the car. We drove back to the hotel, grabbed a cup of coffee, and went back to my room. We took a shower, not together. He, for some reason, kept his distance from me. I couldn't figure out why, and he never told me why. I started calling him "the pleasure delayer." He started questioning me again about the place where I used to work. The boss I used to work for always pretended to be nice, but behind your back, he was nothing that he claimed to be. He would throw you under the bus to save his own skin or to make himself look better. I always thought that the fact that he lived in another state would make it easier. That wasn't the case at all because to make things even worse, he had another manager, a short little shit whose ass I could've kicked if I got mad enough. He used to feed him all kinds of lies based on his moods, whether you pissed him off or not—that was the worst kind of spy.

The place was a large facility that had multiple cafés and catering venues. I worked at one of the cafes, busting my ass on a daily basis with not even a thank you for all the hard work. I was underpaid and overworked. That asshole used to pretend he was my brother to my face, but behind my back, he was the worst. In the GM's office, there was this safe, a big safe, almost six feet tall. I dreamed every day about putting that piece of shit in that safe and leaving him there. The thought of him slowly suffocating, banging, and scratching on the inside of that safe while he slowly died made me feel, well, it made me feel way too good. I asked him why he was so curious about where I used to work. He told me that he just wanted to know what brought me here. It was a long way to travel, to just sell everything and pick up and go. I told him I was just tired of it all, and I needed to get away before I killed someone.

*****

Aaron

Having listened to her reasons for wanting to get out got him thinking. Could she, would she possibly be his partner in all this? All the anger that she had built up inside, could she possibly be someone that could help me with all this? I had to really think about it before I said anything because if I did and she displayed any kind of negativity on her face, that would be it. She would become the next victim, and that's something I didn't want to happen. I had to go about it slowly, carefully, and make it sound like it was something she thought of. Manipulate her thoughts and make them her idea.

In order for this to work, I would actually have to be somewhat manipulative with her. Part of that meant I would definitely have to get closer to her, physically and emotionally. I would start with making her a dinner that would make her feel incredible inside. I had a woman call me out to a table one time to tell me that her food was so good that she actually had an orgasm and would I marry her. Whether that's true or not, it made her feel something she had never felt before. That's what I had to do for Vanessa. I had to make her fall in love with not just my food but with me as well. I think that delaying her for as long as I have has just made her crave me more. We've had plenty of sexually charged conversations but never anything physical. It was time to change that.

The chef at the hotel let me take some food, burners, and all the things that I would need to create an incredible meal for her. I told her to fill up a tub with warm water and bubble bath and soak in it until I came to get her. I poured a nice cold Dr. Pepper for her to drink and then I went back to my work. With each dish, I planned how exactly I was going to tell her. It was like a puzzle in my head that I would assemble piece by piece. Making sure that the tub didn't have time to get cold, I went into the bathroom and helped her out of the tub. I told her to stand there while I slowly dried every inch of her body, making sure to not miss anything. You know how you can breathe warm air onto someone when you're really close to them? That's what I did while I was drying her off. You could see the goose bumps rising on her skin. I know what she was expecting, but I didn't give it to her, yet. I put the robe on her and told her it was time to eat. The look on her face, she was falling hard for me. Thing was, I was falling hard for her too. This better work…

I presented each dish to her and explained in detail what it was. I made sure to use foods that are known as aphrodisiacs—artichokes, asparagus, figs, and chocolate to name a few. Even adding a bit of spice helps to get people in the mood. With each dish, the more she ate, you could tell that she was getting more and more worked up, more in the mood, and saying no wasn't an option anymore. I didn't want to say no anymore. This was my plan, this is what I wanted, and in the end, I knew this was going to work.

We finished the dessert course and made our way out to the lanai. The room faced the ocean so no one could see us. The room was on the top floor, so it was really just us, plus you add the fact that it was dark and the lights in the room were turned off, just candles were burning. We were all alone. You could smell the ocean breeze and hear the waves crashing on the beach. I lay back on one of the lounge chairs. She stood next to me, opened her robe, and sat in my lap, facing me in the chair. For the first time in a long time, I was actually feeling something. I actually was caring for someone again. I honestly didn't know if it was safe or not considering what I was and what I was doing, but I didn't care. I liked what I was feeling. For the rest of the night, we made love to each other in every inch of that room. We made each other feel things we'd never felt before. I knew at that moment that this was going to work, that she was going to feel exactly the same as I do. We fell asleep in each other's arms, and it was the best sleep we had both had in a very long time.

We woke up the next morning feeling, well, feeling like we were different people, happy, in love, and like we didn't have a care in the world. We ate breakfast and sat on one of many couches in her room. After last night, I finally discovered how big this place really was. I decided it was time to tell her who I really was and what I really did. Just as I was getting ready to talk, I stopped. I thought of going in a different direction with this whole thing. A bit on the manipulative side, but if she didn't like the thought of my kind of revenge, she could express that and she wouldn't have to become one of my victims because of how she felt.

Before I could say anything, she actually brought the subject up again. She talked about how she wished she could've gotten some kind of revenge on these people for all the pain they had caused her. They made her uproot her life and give up everything that she loved, everything she owned, and all because they were arrogant assholes that needed to show how much control they had over people. They didn't have as much control as they thought. People hated them, and if there was a way, they could get rid of them they would.

I asked her what if we could get revenge on them, all of them, all the ones that had done us wrong over the years. She told me what was funny about what I just said was that she was going to ask me the same thing. She just didn't know how to do it. I asked her if she remembered me telling her about two of the chefs that I worked for. She remembered exactly who I was talking about, and she expressed how angry it had made her, how she wished that she could hurt them back for me. I explained to her what I had done, and she didn't bat an eye; in fact, I think I actually saw her smile.

She wanted details. She wanted to know exactly what I did and how I did it. After explaining it to her, like every detail of what I did, she said to me, "I realize that you're the chef, but would it ever offend you if I wanted to help you *write* the recipes?" I couldn't help but laugh—I mean really laugh. I told her that I would be honored if she would help me write the recipes. Then she asked me how much I got out of it. That one confused me a bit. "Got out of it?" I asked. "Do you mean emotionally, closure, something like that?" She laughed and said, "No, how much money?" Now I was even more confused.

The next part ranks up there with "Why the hell didn't I think of that?" She said that these people shouldn't just pay with their actual lives but also monetarily. Why should their friends or family benefit from all they've made making us and others' lives miserable? Before they die, we needed to get everything we could from them. If we're going to be going from place to place writing recipes, then we need a way to pay for our travels. Needless to say, this turned out way better than I had ever thought it could've. We started to plan who was next and how we would take from them what we needed.

We decided that we would never write anything down. All plans would just be spoken. This way, there would never be any evidence. We would be the only ones that knew, so unless we decided to flip on one another, we would be safe. I couldn't see us ever turning on each other—our connection was way too deep. We decided that the first person that we were going to visit was the asshole backstabbing manager. She had come up with an idea to help drain him of his money. One thing I didn't know about Vanessa was that she was incredible when it came to tech stuff. While I slept, she set up an untraceable offshore account for us. She also set it up so that it would take both of us to take money out. She used voice passwords that required both of our voices to get anything. It's not that she didn't trust me—it was more that she wanted to prove to me that I could trust her. She loved me, she was in love with me, and she never wanted to hurt me. She handled tech like I handled a knife, like an artist.

*****

Vanessa

I was going to hack into his phone. All I needed to do was send him a text with a link to open up a picture, a picture of her, telling him I was sorry for everything and then telling him it was a picture of me to make up for it all. He could use his imagination. The piece of shit, the person that claimed to be my brother, he was always making passes at me, saying inappropriate shit to me. Getting him to open a picture of me wouldn't be hard to do. The plan wasn't just to drain him of all that he had, but it was to also make him look bad. Implicate him in all kinds of things, things that would ruin whatever he had left. Now here was the other part of their plan. I also wanted to get the big boss that lived in another state so it all had to be a quick turnaround. We couldn't let him find out that this one was gone before we could get to him. Once we had him secured, we would send the big boss a text from his phone, telling him to look at what I had sent to him. He was another piece of shit that always looked me up and down whenever he saw me. He never said a word, but I could always tell what he was thinking. I was a piece of meat—that was it.

*****

Aaron

Now we needed to think about exactly how we were going to do this. Having a sous-chef to help me come up with the recipes was really incredible. She wanted to start with her "brother" first.

She really wanted to make him suffer. He hurt her really badly, he cut deep, and she wanted the same thing done to him. I have to say, it did give me some great ideas about how to do this. First, the text needed to be sent so we could get this plan underway. She sent the text, and it immediately started uploading all of his information to our account. Once we had what we needed, we started to drain his bank accounts, transferring not only money from his accounts but his wife's accounts. Before she was about to drain her accounts, I asked her if we really wanted to do that or not. She explained to me how over the years she actually enabled him—him and his dad—who both worked on the campus. They were always hearing talk about how both of them would take advantage of people, and if people went against them, he would do whatever he could to get rid of them, men or women but mostly men. I said, "Fuck it, take it all." It wasn't long, he was blowing her phone up with texts and calls, trying to find out what the text was all about. Needless to say, she never responded. Technically, she was already responding, and she was going to be responding a lot louder in a very short period.

Now it was my turn. I needed her to meet him at work because my plan was going to be to take care of him there. She asked him if she could meet him in the GM's offices after everyone was gone, and she would explain the text. I gave her the pigsticker to give to him. She knew the only way she would be able to get him to let his guard down was to dress as sexy as she could. Short shorts, bikini top, and a white linen shirt, tied at the waist with no buttons buttoned. I had her put on baggy sweats and a hoodie so she wouldn't be recognized if there were cameras anywhere. It made it even better that she could slowly strip down for him. She kept the pigsticker in her back pocket where he couldn't see it.

*****

Vanessa

We got into the GM's office, and I took off the hoodie and the sweats. My "brother" took one look at me, and his jaw hit the floor.

He'd forgotten how gorgeous I was, and he made sure to let me know that. He reached over and untied the knot in my shirt and held it open. He reached in and untied the knot from around my neck and let my suit drop forward, exposing my breasts. As he went in to hug me, he held his hands up, cupped my breasts, and squeezed them hard. As he pressed himself up against me, I could feel how much he had missed me. I reached into my back pocket for the syringe. Pissed off and with one motion, I pulled off the cap to the syringe and plunged it into his neck. I emptied the entire amount into him. I panicked for a minute. I hoped that this wasn't more than what was needed.

*****

Aaron

I gave her the right amount to inject into him, just enough to make him groggy and unable to fight back from what was about to happen to him. She sat him in the chair and called me in the office.

I remembered her telling me about the safe and how she wanted to put him in it and make him suffer. The first thing I did was introduce myself to him. I let him know what I was there to do. I made sure to put gloves on. I couldn't leave any fingerprints anywhere. I made Vanessa put gloves on as well. Some fingerprints can be explained, but she had been gone for quite a while. We couldn't leave too many behind. So many people were in and out of that place every day we probably didn't have to worry, but why take a chance? I took the money, stacks of cash, and rolls and rolls of coins out of the safe and put it in a backpack that I had brought with me. I also saw deposit slips for the business's bank account. I asked her if it was possible to get away with draining those accounts as well. She thought it was a great idea, so she taped his mouth shut and proceeded to do her magic on the laptop. After she had finished, she went back to him again and started to explain to him why we were doing what we were doing. He begged for his life, and then he got angry and tried to lash out at her because what he was saying wasn't changing her mind, and he knew it never would.

I pulled a drill out of my backpack and started to drill a couple of holes on the side of the safe. I wasn't trying to give him air. I was making them so that I could let things in. I was told that he had a more than healthy fear of spiders, so I thought that would be a good ingredient to the recipe. He didn't know what the holes were for, and I wasn't going to tell him. I was going to let it be a surprise. The poor guy looked scared shitless. I wasn't feeling sorry for him. It's just that I didn't know him. My motivation was getting revenge for the person that I love and that he had hurt, that he had taken advantage of. He used his friendship to get to her, and then he betrayed her. He needed to be punished, and she wanted it slow and painful. The fact that she was a horror movie freak, if I could throw a good dose of fear in there too, that would be even better.

I shot him up with a half dose and taped his hands and feet together and put him in the safe. The next part was interesting and the part she really liked. I took a small plastic cup and filled it up with small spiders. I put a paper towel over the top and taped the edges tight to the cup. I forced his mouth open; it was easy to do because of the drugs, placed the paper towel end in his mouth, and taped it to his head. The working theory was that the moisture in his mouth would wet the towel and it would rip. At which point, the spiders will crawl into his mouth and cause him to panic. This will all be happening with him in the safe and with the door closed. He will have absolutely nowhere to go, not to mention he would only be able to struggle so much having been drugged up. I closed the door to the safe and locked it. Vanessa changed the combination to the safe so that no one could get in it if they knew he was there. As disgusting as it sounds, they probably won't know he's there until they smell him. I had more spiders in a bucket with a lid covering it and tubes sticking out of it. I fed the other end of the tubes into the holes in the safe. The only place they had to go was through the tube into the safe. We got the spiders moving through the tube and into the safe and waited... Once we heard faint screams, we gathered up all our stuff. We left nothing behind, grabbed all the cash, and left.

As we were driving away, I asked her how she felt about what we had just done. She looked at me with a very happy and satisfied look and said, "As much as I thought it might disturb me, I feel more satisfied than I have in a long time." She actually called me an artist for the way I planned and executed the plan. She felt that people who caused this kind of pain to others couldn't wait to be judged at the end of their time when they died either through accident or natural causes. They didn't deserve to live out their lives happy and smiling. They needed to be dealt with in the harshest of ways possible. That's what we were doing for people, and we would keep doing so. Although our methods may be wrong in some people's eyes, our intentions are always good and always will be.

CHAPTER 6

A Tale of Two Assholes, Time for the Second Asshole

Aaron

We needed to get to the second asshole as quickly as possible. We didn't have any time to waste. It was a good twelve to fifteen hours away, depending on how fast you drive. We didn't want to fly, needed to keep a very low profile. No matter how much cash we were accumulating, it didn't matter. If we spend it, we could draw attention to ourselves, and we couldn't do that. We couldn't take a mode of transportation method that could record where we were at any specific time, not while we were doing this at least. Since I was already living part-time on the mainland, I had a car here. It was a dark Nissan Armada, leather seats, and all the amenities you could ever want. In the back, I had all my knives along with two shotguns an AR-15 and two Glocks. I basically lived in my SUV, so I needed the protection. Vanessa loved it. It made her feel like she was in a fortress, a place where she couldn't be hurt. The fact that she was so small, she could hop around it like it was nothing. After a bit of excitement with starting a new journey, she finally dozed off. She needed the sleep.

She started waking up when we were coming into Dallas. She couldn't believe how well she slept, and she was amazed that I drove the entire way without having to stop and sleep or switch drivers. I was extremely tired, and I definitely needed a shower and some sleep. We found a relatively nice hotel to stay in for a couple of nights.

Nothing like where she was living on Kauai, but it wasn't infested with roaches and flies either. It had everything we needed, especially since we weren't going to be there long. The first thing we needed to do was buy plane tickets back to Kauai for the day after next. I wanted an early morning flight, in first class so we could rest after working all night. After booking the tickets, we decided to take a shower. The warm water and soap on our bodies made us feel so relaxed. We felt like we washed the last couple of days away; and it made us feel really good, it made us feel like we were washing away our sins, and it made us feel closer to each other. We got out, dried off, and climbed into bed. We made love that was so intense. We admitted to each other that we had never felt that way with anyone before. We fell asleep in each other's arms, and we didn't let go of each other once the entire night. Again, another first for both of us and definitely something we never wanted to go away.

We woke up the next morning feeling refreshed and ready to get to work. We found an out-of-the-way diner to have breakfast and discuss what the plan was. The first thing was we needed to send the text message to him so we could get the info that we needed to drain his accounts. This had to be one of her better ideas because going places to do this was costing us money. No matter how cheaply we traveled, it was still costly. She sent the text from his buddy's phone using the same virus she used before telling him to look at what I had sent to him. I knew it wouldn't take him long to open it. They're both so predictable. The beautiful thing about this one, he had a lot more money than his buddy; and this time, I didn't care that we left his family with nothing. She explained the reasons to me well enough the last time to the point that I didn't care anymore. Getting to him might be a bit more difficult because he didn't have an office that he really worked out of. She knew one thing though. He liked her and he wanted her, and given the opportunity, he'd take it.

She heard that he liked the clubs and all the women that worked in them. He was a short, fat, balding man who thought a lot about himself. He figured because he had worked his way up in the company, that meant he was worth something—nothing could be farther from the truth. Women weren't attracted to him. Most hated and despised him. The only thing that he could use in his favor was that he had a lot of money, but he didn't anymore. She didn't max his credit cards because she still needed him to use them.

*****

Vanessa

I texted him and let him know that I was in town and asked if he would like to go and have a drink. Big boss jumped at the chance to get together with me. He wanted to meet me at one of his favorite strip clubs. The place was high-end, and they knew him well. No matter what he looked like, his money took him far in this place. I needed to look really high class so I dressed in a short black leather skirt, red spaghetti strap top, no bra, and stiletto heels. I wore a jet-black wig and a light-black jacket with a hood. Inside my small bag, I had the pigsticker that I was going to use on him. Again, I needed to make sure that no one would recognize me. I walked into the club and up to the stand where the bouncers were stationed. I told them whom I was there to meet, and they led me to a private VIP room in the back, which worked for me, because there were no cameras back there. The door opened, and there he was, waiting for me, looking at me like he was hungry.

He had champagne on ice waiting for me along with a cold Dr. Pepper. He at least remembered that much about me. After having a glass of champagne, he asked me what I was doing there and why I wanted to see him. I told him that since I don't work for him anymore, I thought it would be okay to get together and see each other. I had always been intrigued by him, and I wanted to dig a bit deeper into who he was. I told him I was on my way to New York because I had always wanted to do some dancing and acting, and what better place is there to do that, to get a break in the business. I knew what question was coming next. He asked if I wanted to practice some dancing on him; after all, that's what that room was for. I told him I was going to need at least a couple of shots to get in the mood for that. He ordered us four shots of tequila. I went to the bathroom, and when I got back, they had arrived.

He had already downed his shots and was waiting for me to take mine. I told him I needed to stand up and get ready. I walked behind him with the shots and tossed them in the sink without him noticing. Okay, I had to take a small sip so that the smell was on my breath and he wouldn't be suspicious. I told him to get comfortable and I would give him a sample of what I was going to be doing. I slowly unzipped my jacket. He could see that I wasn't wearing a bra, and he got the biggest smile on his face. *Fucking pig.* I shook my hips, turned around with my ass in his face, and I slowly bent over, running my hands down the front of my legs until I was grabbing my ankles. I could feel him start to run his hands over my ass and down the back of my legs. I snapped up, looked at him, and told him that if he wanted to do that, he was going to have to tip me for it, and I mean tip me a lot. After all, considering where we were, he was used to paying. He wasn't going to get off that easy with me. He said he needed to go get some money. I told him that he better get a lot, and I mean a lot if he was expecting anything out of me.

While he was gone, I called Aaron to let him know what was going on. He was getting a bit worried, but I told him I had it under control. I would let him know when we were coming out. I would have to drug him outside. I would never be able to carry him out. He was too big, and he would draw too much attention. He agreed. I told him to park next to his car and wait for me. It took him a while to come back in, but he finally made it back. He said he had issues withdrawing cash, so he had to get cash from his credit cards. I told him that I hoped he had gotten a lot. Since he was in with the club, they fronted him the cash that he wanted. So on top of getting cash from his cards, he got cash from the bar as well. He was eager to get started. I got him a couple of more shots, and I made sure he drank them.

I started dancing again for him. This time, I started dancing while I was facing him. I kept bending over in front of him so he could see down my shirt. He could see what he had been dreaming about for a very long time. He tried reaching his hand down my shirt, and I told him that it would cost him $500. He gave me the money, and I let him reach down and touch my breasts, not for as long as he wanted but for as long as I could take it without puking on him. As disgusted as it made me feel to let him do it, thinking about what he was going to get in the end made it more tolerable. I slowly pulled up my skirt, not completely but just enough for him to see that I wasn't wearing anything underneath. I turned around and started dancing again. He again tried to grab my ass, and I told him that it would cost him $1,500 this time. He gave me the money, and he started rubbing my ass with both of his hands. He tried to stick his hands between my legs, and I stopped him. I asked him how much cash he had left. He told me he had $15,000 left. I told him that it was time to leave and go outside to finish this, in a more private location. I asked him if I could leave through the private back entrance while he went out the front and I would meet him at his car. He agreed, and we both left. I couldn't take the chance of being seen leaving with him. No trace of us together.

I made my way out to his car. It was a gull-winged BMW that he was so incredibly proud of he used it as his screen saver on his laptop. I always thought he used it to make up for his small dick. He got to the car, and he got in. He didn't even open the door for me. He just got in. Such a gentleman. When we got in the car, he was on me almost immediately. I told him he needed to slow down if he wanted this to be as good as he had always dreamed it would be. We put the seats back as far as they would go. I told him to pull his pants down, and I pulled my skirt up and slipped the straps off my shoulders so that he could see my exposed breasts. It was dark, so it was hard to see anything, but he had his imagination; at least with this, he could use it for pleasure, in just a short time he would be using it for something a lot worse.

He tried to roll his fat, sweaty body over toward me, and I stopped him. I told him to lay back, close his eyes, and let me take care of him first, so easily manipulated, especially because he really felt like he was going to get something out of it. I reached into the pocket of my jacket and pulled out the syringe and pulled off the top. I bent over and acted like I was going to go down on him, and I jabbed the syringe into his inner thigh. I've never heard such a big guy let out such a high-pitched scream. I apologized and told him that I thought he would've enjoyed me biting him before I got started. He said he wasn't used to it and that it was okay to keep going. It didn't take too long for the drug, tequila, and champagne on board to take effect. He started complaining that he wasn't feeling too good. I told him that I wouldn't mind taking him home and that we could finish this the next day. He agreed. He pulled up his pants and waited for me to walk around to help him out of the car. Aaron had bought a cheap panel van from someone that needed the money, no paperwork, nothing to lead it back to us. He covered the back of the van in plastic sheeting from the top to the bottom. He even covered as much of the front as he could and placed an old mattress in the back on top of the sheeting. Aaron parked the van right next to his car. All we had to do was open his door and the door to the van and it was literally two feet to get him inside. Once I got him in the van, he realized that something wasn't right. He tried to fight to get out, but Aaron pulled him inside. He had no fight left in him because of the drugs and alcohol. We taped his mouth and then his legs and hands. He was too drugged up; he wasn't going anywhere. I went back to the car with some disinfectant wipes and cleaned every inch of the car that I could. Anywhere I was, I cleaned as thoroughly as I could—no traces.

We had scouted out a deserted area to take him to. No one was around for miles and no one to interrupt us. The van was black, so it blended into the night. No side windows, and we had something that closed off the back from the front. I wanted to ride with him in the back so I could explain why we're doing this to him. I told him about all the ways that he had acted toward me—the looks, the comments, how all of it made me feel. He didn't care. He told me that he felt he had the right to say and act however he wanted. God! Each and every time I think that somehow people will maybe, just maybe, change even a little bit, they still act the same way. Even faced with his demise, he still is unapologetic for everything that he did. When I think that I might just feel a bit bad for what we're about to do, they once again prove to me that I'm doing the right thing. I'm beginning to understand even more why Aaron does this with no remorse.

Part of me just wanted to get this done and over with, really quickly, and then just dump his body; but I knew that he needed to suffer for all the things that he had done—not just to me but to everyone. As many ideas as I thought I might have had for this one, I was at a total loss. Maybe everything that I just went through to get him here made me feel used all over again, like before we gave to him the ultimate punishment. In the end, he got exactly what he wanted. To see me and touch me, it didn't seem fair. It was like he sucked all the air, all the life out of me. Aaron could see that I was struggling, and that's when he leaned over and told me not to worry, that he would take care of this. He knew what to do. He told me to get the cash out of his pockets, go up front, and wait. I reached into to grab the $15K, and what I pulled out was double that. Fat piece of shit had more and had no intentions of giving it to me.

*****

Aaron

Vanessa went up front, and I started to go to work. One of the things that she had talked about was getting the air and the life sucked out of her by him, and it gave me an idea. I had put my toolbox in the van because, well, I didn't just use the contents for food. But inside the box, I had a handheld smoker. Basically, it was an automatic pipe. In the area where you put the wood chips, I connected the tube because it's where it sucked the air in, and I put a binder clip on the tube where the smoke came out. He had been quietly watching what I was doing, and he couldn't figure it out. He was still feeling all the booze and drugs in his system, and it was keeping him from putting up a fight.

I started to explain to him who I was and what I was doing there. I explained to him what we had done to his buddy just a couple of nights ago, not in detail but that he was gone and that he suffered for all he had done to Vanessa. I told him that we had drained him financially and that was the reason why he was having issues getting cash at the club. I told him that he could beg, fight, plead,

33

or even try to justify his behavior and it wouldn't make a difference to me. My only concern, the only thing I cared about was making sure that the appropriate revenge was taken for all the pain that he'd caused her. That was the first time I had seen actual fear in his eyes. He knew that this was going to be the end for him and there was nothing he could do about it. Vanessa poked her head in the back with tears in her eyes. She had heard everything that I had said to him, and she told me that no one had ever protected her like that. She wanted to be there for it. Whatever I was going to do to him, she wanted to be there.

There's an old saying, "The anticipation of death is much worse than death itself." This is why it didn't bother me to make people wait for as long as possible. They understand that they are going to die. They just don't know how. That's why it's like writing recipes. Nothing is ever the same. It's not just shooting them or stabbing them, but it's always something different. Eventually, someone might figure out that it's a serial killer, but it would take forever to do so. I never left anything they could use to identify me, and I never left any type of signature. It just always looked like the work of a crazy person. That was okay with me. I'm not looking for any press. I'm just trying to right the wrongs.

I explained to him what Vanessa had told me, that he and his buddy had sucked the life out of her, that they had treated her like a piece of meat, constantly making comments to her and looking at her like they were hungry. So I decided that I was going to suck the life out of you. I cut a small hole in the tape on his mouth and stuck the tube in it, making sure to secure it again so there wouldn't be any leaks. I put a binder clip on his nose so he couldn't breathe through it, and I took the clip off the other tube to let the air out. He didn't even put up a fight. I don't know whether it was the drugs or he just resigned himself to the fact that this was the end for him. I turned the machine on, and it slowly started to suck the life out of him. You could see the discomfort in his eyes and on his face. I would turn the pump off only long enough to change the batteries in it and then I would start again. After a longer than expected period, he stopped breathing. I turned the machine off and checked his pulse. The last thing I wanted was for him to come to life again. I turned the machine back on again just to make sure and when I decided he was done, I turned it off and started to clean up. I needed to remove the tape from his body and remove all traces of us. I wiped his body with sanitation wipes just to make sure. We wrapped him up in the plastic sheeting, put the barrier between the front and the back of the van up again, and drove back toward the club. It was late, and no one was around. We made sure to again pull the hoods up on our jackets so again no one could see who we were if there were any cameras around. We were careful, always very careful. We weren't going to get caught.

When we got back to the club, the lot still had a few cars in it. People that got way too drunk to drive and decided that they weren't going to take the chance. We pulled up really close to his car again, opened his door, and put him in on the driver's side. We put the seat all the way back to make it look like he passed out and just died right there. He always parked where he couldn't be seen by the security cameras at the club maybe so he could never be caught on film doing what he was trying to do to Vanessa. Either way, it worked in our favor. We drove the van to the airport and parked it far away in a long-term parking lot. DFW is a huge airport. It would take months or even longer for them to figure out that it was abandoned. We had gotten rid of the plastic sheeting in a dumpster along the way to the airport, so all we needed to do was make sure everything was wiped down again. I grabbed my toolbox; we locked the van, and I dumped the keys in a garbage can along the way to my car. I had parked my car in a long-term VIP-covered parking lot. I kept a lot of valuable stuff in it, and I couldn't take the chance of anyone getting it. We grabbed our luggage and made our way to the terminal. We made it to the gate with enough time to get on our flight. We settled into our seats in first class, and as much as we wanted to talk about what had just happened, we both realized that it wasn't safe. There are too many eyes and ears even in first class. It had been a long night. We put the armrest between us up, and she curled up into my arms under a blanket. We both fell asleep for the long journey to Hawaii. We couldn't wait to get back home again.

CHAPTER 7

Back Home Again

Aaron

The island was like a breath of fresh air, a place where the work we did on the mainland just disappeared. As we drove back to the hotel, we talked about what we had done. Neither one of us felt any remorse for what we had done, not a surprise for me to not feel anything, but I was concerned about her and if she was okay. She said she was just fine. She felt like a huge weight had been lifted off her chest, that she could breathe again, like when all the air left them it went in to her, it gave her new life. I asked her since we had finished off two of the people that she despised the most did she want to stop. She said there was still more work to do. There were a lot more people that had hurt me than had ever hurt her, and she wanted to help me take care of them. I was glad she was still on board with all this. If she had told me to stop, I would've stopped no matter what I had left undone. That's how much I loved her and needed her in my life. I made sure to let her know that as often as I could. She told me that she felt the same way. We both did agree that when the time came to stop, even if it was just for one of us, we would stop, no questions asked.

We got back to our room, unpacked, and ordered up some room service. As we ate, we started talking about getting out of the hotel and moving in together. It obviously wouldn't have as many amenities, but we would make it like our family home. We needed our own place, one that was away from so many eyes and ears. Right now, privacy mattered. We both had a lot of money, and after draining everything they had, we had a lot more. The next thing would be what part of the island did we want to live on and how big. Land and houses weren't cheap, but we really wanted a place with some land where we could have some animals and lots of space to roam.

After eating, we wanted to take a drive around the island to see what we could find. We started on the west side by barking sands beach and ended up on the north side of the island. Nestled on almost four acres, the home began down a long private drive that rolled through gradual hills as you entered the tree-lined estate. There were large fruit orchards and established hardwood groves. We walked around the grounds where there were hundreds of orchids, tropical flowers, and lush foliage. It had a saltwater pool with a flowing waterfall and lagoon where we could relax. It had a tree house with a functioning elevator that we could use to see sunset views or take hammock naps. It had three full bedrooms and three bathrooms. Two of the rooms were master suites with additional outdoor showers and a large hot tub. It had hardwood floors throughout the home and a three-car garage that divided the home, and it also provided a working shop for the home. A separate studio sat privately away from the home. One of the best parts about the house, it had an underground bunker that had a secret entrance from the master bedroom. It was finished like any other room in the house with a bathroom and electricity that ran off a separate line. It was too good to be true. We made a cash offer below asking, and they accepted. We didn't mind any of this being in our name because it was our home and it put us far from the mainland where we worked. The next step was working on making the place a fortress. It needed to be one that no one could get into.

We didn't want to infringe upon the beauty of the property with fences and walls and other obvious signs of security, so we did something a little different, a little higher-tech. We laid down fiber optic cables that could detect acoustic changes. I buried it twelve to eighteen inches deep around our property, and if someone came within thirty feet of it, it would send an alarm to us. It also can direct our cameras that have heat detection and night vision to the areas in question. All the cameras are hidden, and they use artificial intelligence and analytics to determine whether it's a falling leaf, an animal, or someone that we don't want there. We had cameras by the gate so we could see who was there, and they were high-def enough so we could make out faces and license plates. Motion sensor lights were put in, and because we lived on an island that was prone to hurricanes, we had a high-end generator hard wired into the house and satellite phones just in case. We even installed a nearly unhackable keyless entry system that worked on biometrics to detect our identities. Because Vanessa was a tech nerd, we could do all this ourselves. I was the manual labor, and she directed me with what needed to be done. All this may seem like overkill, but considering what we were doing, it made us feel safe. Because we didn't leave any signs behind and because everyone was different, there was nothing for anyone to latch onto. We thought that living on an island also made it safer because we could do what we needed to do and go home. After all we had just done, why would we want to leave? We still had work to do; eventually, we would just stay there, but not now.

It had been a long day of installing, and it was time to get cleaned up for dinner. We decided to take a shower in the outdoor shower. There was nothing like taking a shower outside. It was the most incredible feeling. The smells and sounds made the experience just that much better. We helped clean each other off, rubbing soap all over each other's bodies, and then rinsing off. We made love to each other outside with the warm water still pouring over our bodies. It was such an incredible feeling being outside, with warm water rolling over you while you're making love to the person you love more than anything. After what seemed like hours, we finished, dried each other off, and we went inside to get dressed. The first thing we needed to do is to make sure we stock the bunker with food, water, and weapons—everything that we would need to survive. Then we needed to start planning our next job. I knew exactly where I wanted to go next.

I used to work at this one hotel years ago. There were some people there that I really wanted to make suffer. They all had their own brand of issues, and usually, their thing was to make people suffer. I don't know if it's because they were so empty inside, but they needed the pain of others to help fill that void. Between them, they created one of the most toxic work environments anyone could ever work in, and we wound up losing people because of it. When you can give yourself, your trust to people and they shit all over you. That's really the worst because unlike the other shit, this was more personal. The other crap was easy to move on from—this was not, so because of that, I need to find a different way to deal with it, not a death sentence but a life sentence so they could continue to remember. Karma is a bitch, and they certainly haven't received enough of it.

One of the things that I hate the most is hypocrisy, and they were full of it. Do as I say, not as I do. When you can come down on someone for doing something and then turn around and do it yourself, that's the culture that was created there, and it caused more problems than it was worth for people to stay. I didn't want to get rid of them as much as I just wanted to hurt them. There are skeletons in all their closets, and with my help, maybe one day those would all come out. But at this point, I just wanted to ruin them. Vanessa and I were talking about what I wanted to do, and she had concerns—huge concerns. She reminded me that the reason why we were safe was because we left no traces of us anywhere. Nothing was left behind. We were always incredibly careful, and if we just tried to ruin them instead of getting rid of them, we could be taking a huge chance, one that we couldn't ever take. If this was the path I was going to go down, then we needed to be really smart about it. After some discussion, we came up with a brilliant idea—one that not only will get us the money that we wanted, but we could also ruin them at the same time. I couldn't bring myself to get rid of them. They had kids that I know, and I couldn't do that to them.

I needed a tech genius to pull this one off, and lucky I had one. She was one of the smartest people I knew, and she was exactly what I needed in my life right now for a wide variety of reasons. Like the last one, this needed to be done almost simultaneously for it to work. They need to be hit at the same time, or at the very least, it just all needs to be in place. The IT department there was very poorly run hacking into it wouldn't be an issue. The first thing to do would be to go after the money. There were certain areas we needed to hit. First would be the business, easy to access and easy to move the money. Next, we would have to access the HR files. In there are all the employee files, social security numbers, 401(k) information, account numbers, and everything else we would need to drain them. The second thing we needed to do was ruin their reputations. The fact that we could access the servers that included their emails, it would enable us to write a different story, one that would destroy them.

So when we got the information on the business accounts, what we found was quite a surprise. There was another extremely large account that was marked P&L Excess. This was incredible between the business, and that account, there was enough to buy half of Kauai. Why not, Larry Ellison of Oracle fame bought 98 percent of Lanai, why can't we buy our own Hawaiian island? I'll bet not many knew about that account. Vanessa didn't tell me that she had been investing our money, slowly, carefully and untraceable so maybe in time we *could* get our own. God, I love her. So before we pushed the button on the business accounts, we did the same to their personal ones. We found theirs and, by association, their significant others and set them all up to be drained. We were starting to make an art of doing this. One of the things that we discovered is that we don't always have to give someone the death penalty. We can give them a life sentence instead. Taking their money and leaving them alive would be the life sentence. Depending on who it was, it was much more of a pleasurable feeling for me.

The next step was to work on them personally. There were always rumors floating around about them—them having affairs, stealing, using derogatory terms to describe others, and one of the worst, targeting people to get rid of just because they don't like them, all bad and all indefensible in my book. They fucked with people's well-being just because, just for fun. It was time to bring out some of their skeletons. We started composing emails, making sure that we adjusted the times and dates to show them in the past and over a period. Some of the emails between them, they were making totally inappropriate comments about employees that worked for them, nothing was off the table with them. That was the sad part especially because everyone knew what was being said and who it was about. Their talk didn't stop at employees. It also included corporate higher-ups, and it was some pretty bad stuff. We sent emails going back and forth, talking about a lot of personal stuff concerning their spouses and their lives with them—things that no one should be talking about or saying to anyone else. We even suggested that there might be a relationship going on between the two of them but never saying that for sure. A lot of what we were writing was stories that we were making up, no truth to any of it. We just needed it to sound good. We needed to cast doubt on everything that they did. We needed people to never look at them the same or to ever trust them again, even their families. We even made it sound like they were all in on embezzling the money from work. That investigation would keep them busy for a very long time and there would be no money to pay for it.

Funny thing is, writing these emails is like writing the recipes. I was creating something out of nothing. All we needed to do was push the button and all the money would drain and all the emails would populate the site. One last little trick, we leaked some of those emails, anonymously of course, to a select group of people. We took a deep breath and put our plan in motion. It worked flawlessly. We got all the money, emails went out, and again absolutely no trace back to us. The best part, we didn't even have to leave the island. We could do all of it from home. Since we were three hours behind, we had already started to hear some talk about what we had done. Things weren't looking good for any of them, but then that was the whole point of doing what we did. They got a life sentence, not a death sentence. They were going to eventually wish for the latter.

After we finished, we went for a long walk on the beach. It's funny, it seems like each time we do this, we seem to get closer and closer to each other. We pretty much have all the money we could ever need, and we had talked about just stopping. But was that what it was all about, the money? The money was the sideshow. It wasn't the reason why we were doing it. We needed to make sure that we took care of the people that couldn't take care of themselves. We decided we still needed to keep going. We couldn't stop, but in time, we would have to. We couldn't keep this going forever. We needed to start to live our lives together. Until then, off we go.

CHAPTER 8

On the Road Again

Aaron

I began to tell Vanessa about this guy I worked for a long time ago as a sous-chef, a French Canadian guy. He taught me a lot about French cuisine, but again, it came at a huge personal cost to myself and a lot of other people. I was at the height of my drinking period, and I think he took great advantage of that. He knew I needed to work, and he knew I needed the money to supply my alcohol and cocaine habit. We would start our mornings with kalua and coffee, go through breakfast service, bourbon and coke for lunch service, and then it was off to the strip club between lunch and dinner. We would come back, screw up dinner service, and then right back to the strip club. We would drop so much money on drinks, drugs, and girls. I was shocked that not only were we still employed but that we didn't die or kill someone else in the process. This guy knew what it was doing to me, but he didn't care. He needed someone to party with. He even threatened to bust me down to a line cook or just kick me out altogether if I didn't come and party with him. Now since this was back when no one gave a shit what your bosses did to you, there wasn't much I could do about it. And even if I could complain, the GM was so involved in his own shit it wouldn't have mattered. This guy was having an affair with the controller, and he had convinced her to let the place give him a huge personal loan out of company funds. Not very smart or very hard to figure out. He was also the kind of guy that had taken credit cards out in his three young kids' names using their Social Security numbers. Needless to say, he had a huge drug problem.

On the daily, this guy used to do nothing but cause grief for everyone around him. I think he seriously got off on scaring people, threatening people, and making people feel small. He started dating the catering manager, and the two of them made quite the pair. Both drunks, both abusive, and both with absolutely no moral compass. I was in her office talking with her one day, and he walked in and sat at her desk. Back in the day, we used to wear those really bad paper chef hats, the ones that disintegrated when you would sweat. Anyway, she tells him to get up and he refuses to do it. Before I knew what was happening, she picked up her stapler and stapled his hat to his head. He jumped five feet out of his chair, screaming and yelling at her, telling her that he was through with her and what a fucking psycho she was for doing that. And in no time, they were in his office making out in front of everyone. That place was an HR nightmare; in fact, I don't remember the HR director at all—that's how nonexistent they were.

Their lives started to fall apart. The feeling of falling so fast they couldn't catch their breath, it surrounded them, and it started tightening around them like a python squeezing the life out of a rat. For all that they had done, one thing that they didn't deserve was leniency or sympathy of any kind. He used to throw things at people, curse at people, and abuse some of them so badly that many of them would leave work crying. They would go and complain to human resources, and all they got was a "Nothing we can do about it. He's the chef" or my favorite, "You know how chefs can be." Well, one day, something made it beyond the local HR or GM and made it to corporate. They sent a team down, and they systematically started to unload everyone. They started with the catering manager, made their way to the HR director, then to the chef, the controller, and finally the GM. They, along with building security, escorted every single one of them out of the building, not allowing them to speak to anyone. They cleaned the house of all the upper-tiered managers, and right behind them, they walked in temporary ones. Mostly idiots who sat around with their thumbs up their asses, never knowing what to do, and no one could ever figure out how they got to the positions they were in. They put me in charge of the kitchen, and I answered to the regional chef, a salty prick of a man from Ecuador. He was a crazy one, but that's a story for another time.

After finishing the story, she asked where we were going to find them. From what I knew, they were still married, and they were living in Seattle. My techie genius got as much information from me as she could so she could do a search on them. It took some time, but she finally found them. She was working, but he had stopped. After some digging, she found out that he had gotten fired again. Apparently, he was still drinking and drugging—that's what got him into trouble. Obtaining the needed information to take their money was easy. We just needed to get into the employee files. It was too easy. Everything that was needed was always in their employment files. We flew into DFW Airport and got my SUV out of parking. Everything we needed was there, so we loaded up our luggage and took off for Seattle. It was about a thirty-one-hour drive, and this time, we shared the driving duties. We drove through some of the most beautiful parts of this country, and the only thing more beautiful was the person driving with me. The time we spent together helped us grow closer and closer to each other. We spend a lot of time alone with each other, but every time is different, and every time, it helps us grow just that much closer.

We drove into Downtown Seattle and decide to stay at the Hilton. It was a high-rise hotel that overlooked both the downtown and the ocean. We booked a room at the top of the hotel where the views were amazing. I know that we had always said we weren't going to spend money and bring any extra attention on ourselves, but it had been so long since I had seen these people there really was no way that anyone could connect us unless we left something behind for them to do so. That wasn't going to happen. We ordered some room service and started planning the next day. Vanessa had gotten the finance part all set up, so the rest was on me. I didn't know if we should be doing both of them at the same time or if we should do them separately. I decided the best way to do this was together. They needed to be told everything they had done together although we would take them one at a time. That would be easy. He didn't work, so we could easily take him at his home. I'm sure that he would be drinking, drunk or close to it, and she would be easy to take once she got there. We climbed into bed, turned off the lights, and melted into each other's arms. It was the best place to be.

We got up the next morning, got our stuff together, and left. We made sure to again dress in dark clothing with hoodies, and this time, we were going to use ski masks so neighbors wouldn't recognize us. We couldn't use our car to get there. We didn't want anyone to recognize it. One thing I learned since starting this, the best place to find a car to steal is the long-term parking lots at the airport. I mean it's not like we're going to really steal it, but we were just going to use it for business and then return it to the same spot. Plus, the owner would seriously be making out here because when he got back, we would've paid his bill and he wouldn't owe for the entire time he was gone. Let's hope they don't come back before we're done. We found a paneled van with heavily tinted windows. We took only what we needed, my tools and one gun—in case someone gave us any problems—and the drugs and syringes. One extra piece that we got, a silencer for the gun. Definitely something you need when you don't want to be noticed. I wanted to stop and get a couple of more things. The first thing was easy. I wanted a huge industrial stapler. The second was a bit more difficult. I needed a Japanese katana sword. Vanessa was curious, but she trusted me. When it came to this stuff, she usually did. After some searching, we finally found one at an out-of-the-way knife shop. The owner was an old man that looked like he was born about a hundred years ago. He sold a lot of off-the-wall stuff that you never thought had existed. An ancient Egyptian weapon called a khopesh—a Falcata, which was used by the Celtiberian warriors in ancient Spain—and the one I fell in love with and decided to also buy, a bowie knife, fifteen inches long and beautifully forged. It was like being in a candy store for me.

We found the house just as it started to get dark. She hadn't gotten home yet, so the first part was going to be easy. We pulled down the alley behind the house, and there was actually a gate that allowed us to pull into the backyard. We couldn't have asked for a better situation; we were out of sight, and so was the van. We got our masks and gloves on and went in through the back door. He was passed out on the couch, probably had one too many drinks again. We sneaked up on him, although there wasn't much sneaking involved, and stuck him in the neck with the drugs. We didn't do the normal dosage. Considering how loaded he was, we didn't want to take the chance of killing him that quickly. Even sticking him in the neck didn't wake him up. This was way too easy; it was like shooting fish in a kiddie pool. We started taping his hands, feet, and mouth. He still didn't wake up; this was actually pretty sad and pathetic. I told Vanessa to put the finance part in motion. It actually turned out to be a lot more than I thought it would be.

After we finished transferring all the money, we started hearing noises coming from the couch. We walked over, and he had started puking. The tape kept the puke in, and he started choking on it. I've never seen anyone open their eyes so quick, and the panic that was looking back at me was like nothing I had ever seen before. Knowing who it was, it didn't affect me; in fact, it made me feel very satisfied watching the person that had spent most of his life getting others choked up was choking on his own filth and bile. I decided that since he was choking to death, I would show him who was letting it happen. I took off my mask, and the surprise, the shock that was on his face when he saw who I was. In that split second, I decided that this was the way he was going to die. No matter what I had planned for him, this was so much better. He was a sad, fucking human being, and he was dying in a way that he deserved. All we had to do was take the tape off and no one would suspect anything. He died choking on his own puke, there would be no questions asked.

We were basking in this win so much that we forgot about her. We heard the garage door open, and the car pulled in. We had just enough time to hide. We were going to have to do her quickly—nothing like I had planned. She came in and saw him, and we could tell that she knew what had happened. She went to him, sat down next to him, and started to cry, not a loud cry, not sobbing, but it was definitely the sound of someone that had just suffered a loss although one that she knew was coming. We were about to go after her, and something she did made us stop. She opened the drawer of the end table and pulled out a bottle of what looked like tranquilizers. She emptied the entire bottle into her mouth and lay down next to him. Even though I had wanted her to suffer my way, she was suffering in her own way. Not only had she lost the person she loved, but she had to endure a life with him—that should've been enough suffering for anyone. After she passed out, we came and looked at the bottle of pills that she took. It was Oxy, and she had taken at least twenty pills. She wasn't waking up anytime soon, or at all for that matter. As much as people might think they got off easy, they really didn't at all. They were suffering when they were alive, and they suffered when they died. We waited until her breathing stopped, and then we started to clean up. We made sure we had all our stuff and that we left nothing behind. We packed up the van and drove quietly away. Lights off, down the alley, and then out onto the street. We pulled into the long-term parking lot and parked the van where we found it. We had parked far enough away so that we would get lost in all the cameras on the way back to our car. We took the masks off but kept the hoodies up, looking down as we walked so no one could see us. We put our stuff in the car and drove out of the parking lot. We decided we would take a drive down the coast back to Arizona. From there, we would fly back home again. Although this didn't turn out like we thought it would, in a very different way, it was very satisfying.

We talked about what had happened while we were driving. We were kind of wondering if we had lost some of our nerves. The recipes were getting a bit boring, something that could've been written for a children's cookbook. What was happening though was actually good for us. We were doing what we needed to do, and we weren't making a mess doing it. The possibility of leaving things behind diminished greatly when the scene looks like it was an overdose and suicide. Vanessa scoured the news and social media sites. It was being called an overdose and suicide, and that was that. It definitely got us thinking. Could we start using this method to get our revenge? It doesn't always have to be so messy. Although there are some that deserve that kind of ending, this way leaves us options. I really had to change my way of thinking though because I was the one that always wanted the violent endings, mostly because of the ways in which I had been treated. Vanessa was the one that really didn't always want it that way. She figured that taking all that they had was good enough. She could take the money and trash their reputations at the same time. The problem with that, eventually, someone would be able to figure it out. There would be too many loose ends left dangling with ends to grab onto and track down. If we did it enough, people would see a trend. She reminded me that we were already doing that, to which, I had no response. We needed to rethink how we were going about all this; it wasn't too late yet, but we needed to make sure we would never be caught.

We did a lot of talking on the way back to Arizona.

"Did we just stop taking the money altogether, or was there another way to get this done? Taking the money had become part of the way we funded what we were doing. Although with all the money that we had already taken and invested, we really didn't need it. But that wasn't the point. It was like we were getting revenge two ways instead of just one, and we wanted to continue that. Or did we just take it every once in a while, not from everyone but maybe just the ones that could afford it?"

"Afford it? What the fuck! They would be dead. It's not like they would need it."

"But what about the families?" Vanessa asked.

"What about them? If we start to catch feelings for the people when we're doing this, we might as well toss in the towel because we will surely make mistakes if that happens."

There needed to be another way to close this gap, and if anyone could figure it out, Vanessa could do it. As much as she wanted to keep talking—we both loved talking—she was tired, and she needed sleep. She put the seat back and curled up with a blanket and a pillow and fell asleep. We had made our way through Washington, Oregon, and half of California when she woke up and screamed "I got it!" I nearly slammed on the brakes. "What do you have?" I asked. She said she solved the problem, and according to her, it was foolproof.

The key was not to take their money after we killed them, but it was to take it before. We could access their accounts and show that there was fraudulent activity. When they called their bank, we could reroute the calls to us and set up new dummy accounts for them. We could transfer all money and set up whatever direct deposits they had to deposit into the new accounts. We would have to give them access until the time came to end them, then we could just take the money. I asked her to think about what she just explained to me. Either way, no matter what accounts the money went into, we were still draining them after the fact, what's the difference? There wasn't really any difference. We were just going to have to be extra careful and just make sure that we left nothing to chance. She made sure that everything was so scrambled there was no way we could be traced, and maybe we didn't take from everyone, just a certain few so as not to make it a trend. We also thought that maybe instead of violently ending them and leaving someone else to pick the pieces up, we made it look like it did with the last ones, overdose and suicide or maybe they just disappeared completely. Apparently, the discussion made her tired again because when we stopped, she went right back to sleep again.

CHAPTER 9
Research and Development

Aaron

To write new recipes, you need to take some time away to help clear your head and think of some new ingredients—some new ways of writing those recipes. We got back to Tucson and decided to drive up the mountain and spend some time in a cabin to help clear our heads, to help rejuvenate ourselves. It felt like we were going forever and we needed to just take a break. The mountains were beautiful and cool compared to the desert below. The cabin wasn't fancy, but it had everything that we needed. There was a restaurant nearby that was famous for its cookies. As far as I was concerned, that was all I needed; however, Vanessa thought we could use a bit more than that. After eating dinner, we grabbed some cookies, cups of coffee, and we took a walk in the woods before the sun went down. It was peaceful, and it was exactly what we needed. We got back to the cabin and sat on the porch so we could finish watching the sun go down.

We talked about getting a house in the mountains as well. We could have one in the ocean and one in the mountains. We even talked about having a ranch in the desert with horses. Those would become good investments for us, and it would give us a place to go home to instead of always having to fly back to Hawaii. We did enough traveling on the mainland. The trip back to the island was another whole day of traveling. We decided on Tucson for the desert ranch and Park City, Utah, for the mountain ranch. When we come down from the mountain, we will look for something, but in the meantime, we need to start creating new recipes.

There are people that are out there that we still need to take care of, ones that had caused me a lot of issues, but what about the ones that were hurting others? The ones we didn't know about? I mean, we weren't going to advertise what we did to people that hurt others, but we felt the need to do something. We would have to go about it in a different way. It would be easy to go and eat or drink at places and just observe the way the staff works. You can see how the managers, on a busy day or night, interact with their staffs—you know, the bad ones. What we were going to was become gainfully employed, and then we will do what we do. It was easy for Vanessa to get a job. The way she looked, anyone would hire her in a heartbeat, and not just hire but most would want her, male or female. That's how we would be able to take care of business. Me, I would have to rely on my talents to get a job—my talents in the kitchen, that is. We would be using the same scenario. As far as taking the money, she could access all the information we needed. She could lure them to wherever we wanted them, and I would take care of the rest.

As time had gone on, the drugs that we needed were getting harder to find. If we pushed that one too hard, it would surely more attention than we needed. There were other ways of knocking people out long enough to get them secure that didn't require the use of drugs. I learned a move a long time ago called a brachial stun. You deliver a sharp blow to the side of the neck, causing unconsciousness by shocking the carotid artery, jugular vein, and vagus nerve. Done correctly, it had devastating results. She could easily distract someone long enough for me to do what I needed to do. How we took care of them really depended on what they did and who they were. Since we always made sure that no two recipes were the same so we didn't attract attention, a lot of what we did was decided prior to it happening. We were always prepared, and if I needed something else, like back in Seattle, we would just stop and get it. My stuff was never that complicated. We felt like we had accomplished what we went up there for. We hit the reset button and came up with a few new ways to do things. One thing we did figure out was that we weren't ready to stop—not yet. It was time for us to sleep. It was cooler up here than it was down on the desert floors. We bundled up under some blankets and fell fast asleep. We've never slept so well until we met each other. We had never felt safer than when we were in each other's arms. We woke up the next morning and took a long hot shower with each other. I can't think of the last time we bathed alone. We got dressed, packed up, and went to grab some breakfast before we started down the mountain. We decided once we got back down. We would start to look for the place we needed. We got in the SUV and started the short journey down the mountain.

On the way down, Vanessa researched some properties on the far east side in an area by Reddington Pass. There was a twelve-acre horse property that she found that she really thought we would both like. It had a 6,500-square-foot home that had three bedrooms and three full bathrooms. The kitchen was a chef's dream, and the dining room in the kitchen had a bay window with a bench that was perfect for sitting and drinking a cup of coffee while you overlook the desert and the mountains. There was a pool and spa out back with a kitchen area for grilling. There was a stable big enough for at least four horses and a couple of big corrals. The entire property was walled, not fenced, but walled off with twelve-foot walls. Whoever was living there didn't want anyone getting in or over the walls because there was razor wire that lined the tops of the walls. They actually dug trenches for the walls and poured concrete six feet down so it would be a chore to try to go under it. We made a cash offer for the property, which was accepted, and we started making plans to move in. We implemented the same security protocols we had in Hawaii, and because we were on the mainland, we built a two-bedroom house on the property, and we hired a full-time team of security guards for when we were gone. They were ex-military, not just run-of-the-mill guards; and ironically enough, they were a husband-and-wife team. We had Doberman guard dogs that roamed the property, Zeus and Apollo, named after the dogs on one of my favorite TV shows from back in the day. We ordered the furniture, and since Brian and Jody, the security team, were going to be there, they could accept it for us. They had a great deal going here. They could live on the property for as long as they wanted, as long as they were employed by us, rent- and mortgage-free. Sweet deal. They, of course, had no idea who we were and what we did, and they never would. Although the way Jody looked, gorgeous, blond hair, blue eyes, incredible body, and legs that wouldn't quit, she would definitely be able to lure anyone we wanted. Between her and Vanessa, we could own whomever we wanted. And let's not forget about Brian's talents. Special forces, sniper, his talents would be extremely useful. We were both seriously intrigued, and we wanted to know more about them.

We had them over for dinner the night before we left. We talked about our lives, not all our lives, of course, just the surface and what drove us and motivated us. As far as they know, we had both been in the restaurant business, but we made up some story about how both of our parents had left us money when they died and we invested wisely. They needed to believe that we were blue-collar just like they were. They met while they were both stationed in Afghanistan, and they fell in love. They were both honorably discharged, but they both had serious issues with their commanding officers while there and when they came back. On more than one occasion, Jody had sexual comments made to her by her commanding officers and by lower-ranking soldiers all of which were brushed off when she com- plained about it. She had been groped and touched, and she literally had her breasts and ass grabbed and squeezed while walking down the hall. On one occasion, two officers forced her to slowly strip down to her underwear and go down on them. When she got them both in the right position, sitting on the desk with their pants down, she grabbed them by the balls as hard as she could and reminded them how talented Brian was with a rifle and that they would never hear it coming. There was a shit ton of anger and resentment in both of them, and we could totally understand why. They were us just in a different profession. We talked for a bit longer and then said good night. Before they left, we let them know we would be leaving in the morning for a few days. We got undressed, and we made love to each other for the first time in our second new house. Each and every time, it got more incredible, and we always seemed to find a way to make it better than the time before. We talked for a while before we slept about everything that had happened in the last few days. But the one thing that really intrigued us was the conversation we had at dinner. They seriously would make the perfect partners in this with us. They're just as angry but just at a different group of people. You know when it really comes down to it, this was also a form of research and development. We researched and found a good security team, and there was the possibility that we might develop them into more than what they are now. I guess only time will tell.

CHAPTER 10

Time to Take it Back

Aaron

On the last "cook," I was telling Vanessa about a salty prick of a chef from Ecuador that I had to deal with when they terminated the chef above me. The guy was so abusive to the point that he would not only scream and yell at people, but he would threaten them with pots and pans and even knives. Making people afraid of him was something he got off on, and because of how high up he was, he figured he was untouchable. There was one day we were doing live lobsters for dinner. He had one sitting up on the pass-through bar on the cook line when a young server walked by and asked, "Are you going to drop the lobster into boiling water to kill it?" He said that was exactly what he was going to do, to which she asked, "Isn't that going to hurt it?" He picked the lobster up, tore one of its front legs off in front of her, and said, "Not any more than that does." I had never seen someone lose it like that. This server couldn't have been more than eighteen, and she totally freaked out. She literally ran out of the kitchen, screaming and crying. It was unreal, and we all thought that this guy has got to be the biggest prick we had ever met. We never had any proof, but we all believed that he had threatened that server if she ever complained to anyone about what had happened. I never understood why these guys always used their power to deceive and destroy people. They seriously got off on that power, and like I had said, back then, chefs were considered gods and they could get away with anything they wanted to. If there was one chef that needed to be taken care of, it was this one.

One of the things that he did to me, one of the many things, was he stole from me—not money but my creativity. He had asked me for some ideas and recipes for dishes for a corporate cookbook that was going to be published. I gave him a few ideas, and I never heard another thing about it. Months later, the club received a copy of the cookbook. I started flipping through the pages, and there they were—all my ideas and recipes. Problem was, they had his name on them, not mine. I was pissed, more than I had ever been with him. If someone has an idea, that idea belongs to them, not me. They will always get the credit. I will never take it from them. He never understood that. To him, it was all his, and he was going to take whatever he wanted. Well, it was time for us to take some back. We found out he was still working as a corporate chef in Phoenix, and the beauty of it was, he had a lot of money, like a lot. Vanessa got all the necessary information that she needed to take everything away from him. This one, I had no qualms about stealing from. We needed a reason to get him in there on a day when the club was closed. Private dining clubs were usually open Monday through Friday for lunch and Tuesday through Saturday for dinner completely closed on Sunday. That also meant that the entire building would be empty, which meant that with the exception of the security cameras, which we could evade, there was no one else to worry about. We discovered that he was looking for a pastry chef. It was easy enough to forge a résumé, and with Vanessa's skills, she could back a lot of it up online. She sent him the résumé and told him the only time she could meet was early Sunday evening. She even put a full-body picture on the résumé so she could entice him a bit more. It worked. They were meeting Sunday evening at 7:00 p.m., and since it was Saturday, we didn't have long to wait. We decided to go do a little clothes shopping before the interview.

We decided to get a little black dress that zippered completely up the front and a black silk hoodie to match. Always needed the hoodies to help conceal ourselves. We got a tiny red lace bra and underwear to match. She already had the shoes she wanted to wear, black leather Christian Louboutin ankle boots with just enough of a heel to accentuate her calf muscles. And just to make it more believable, we made a chef's coat with her name and title on it. We decided she would wear that over everything in the beginning just to keep him guessing. He asked her to text him when she got there so he could go down and let her in. The club was on the twenty-fourth floor of an office building. To be safe, Vanessa hacked the security system, which also included the camera system, and knocked it all off-line. No one would know that we were ever there. We pulled into the parking lot, and she texted him to come and get her. Time to go to work.

She walked partially to the door and waited in the dark until she saw him come to the door. Once she saw him there, she walked up and waited for him to open it. It took him a minute to put his jaw back in place from hitting the floor, but once he did, he opened the door for her. There were two things she had in her purse: the syringe with the drugs—we would need it for this one—and a piece of duct tape. She knew he wouldn't be the kind of person that would hold the door for her, at least she hoped he wouldn't because when he pushed the bar on the door, she needed to tape the latch bolt to keep the door open for me to get it. This was the easiest way, so I was hoping she could get it done. She was correct. He wasn't the kind of guy that would hold the door for her, so taping the bolt was easy. He had gotten older and heavier, and he had lost his hair. I guess, eventually, we all have to face that reality. I was hoping she was going to be okay. She would text me when she was ready for me to come up. If I didn't hear from her in forty-five minutes, I was to go up and make sure she was okay. I was planning on going up earlier anyway, but before I did, I moved the SUV to the back dock area behind a dumpster so we couldn't be seen.

*****

Vanessa

He led me to the elevator, walking slightly behind me, where he didn't think I could see him. I could feel him looking me up and down. Aaron was right. This guy was a total pig. He was arrogant and entitled and a complete narcissist. The ride up the elevator, all he could talk about was him and all he had done and how lucky I would be to work for him. We got to the floor, and he led me into his office. It was a large office, one small window with a shade on it, a large desk and a couch, more of a sectional in the corner. He was impressed with my chef coat, but he asked me if I wanted to take it off. I said sure, and I took it off and placed it on the couch. He took a chair that was in front of his desk, turned it sideways, and told me to have a seat. He pulled his chair out from behind his desk, placed it in front of me, and sat down. It was a big leather chair with a high back. It actually looked like a throne, which was fitting because he thought he was a king. He said he never offers this, but since this was happening in the evening, he asked if I wanted a glass of wine. I accepted, so he excused himself so he could go to the bar and get us a glass. While he was gone, I texted Aaron to tell him all was okay but that it was going to take longer than expected. I told him I was fine, not to worry, and I would text him when I was ready. He said okay, and I put my phone away. I know what it is that Aaron likes, what drives him when it comes to all this, but I sometimes wondered if luring them in with the hope of sex, was what I really got into, if that's what really drove me. It always worked on the men. I wondered if it would on women too. One day, we might find out. He came back in with two glasses of a 2016 Opus One Proprietary Red—very highly rated and very expensive. He made sure to tell me that. After taking a sip, we moved on to the interview.

He started giving me the job description, what would be expected of the position, at least according to what it said on paper. Who knows what else he would expect. All I was hearing was whaa, whaa, whaa—it was all noise to me. I wasn't really applying for the job, and Aaron had schooled me enough in the terminology so that I could answer most of the questions with ease. The rest I blamed on having not eaten all day and then drinking wine. After a few more boring minutes, I figured it was time to get this show going. I pretended that I accidentally spilled the red wine on my hoodie. When he reached under his desk to get a towel, I stood up and slowly zipped down the jacket, slow enough for him to hear it so he had time to straighten up and watch me slip it off. I threw the hoodie onto the couch, took the towel from him, and I asked him to please continue. As he was talking, I took another sip of wine, and this time, I pulled it away from my mouth a bit too quickly so that again, some would spill onto my chest. As he was continuing to talk, I started to unzip the dress with one hand while I was wiping my chest with the other, commenting how lucky it was that my bra was red like the wine so I wouldn't have to worry about staining it. You could tell by the look on his face that if he would've stood up at that point in time, it would've been pretty embarrassing for him. After all this, he told me that he wasn't sure who he was going to hire, that he still had people he needed to talk to. Part of me thought that he really had other people to talk to, and part of me was wondering if he was trying to see how far I would go. So why not call his bluff and see which one it was. I said that I was disappointed, but I understood. He needed to make sure he was hiring the right person for the job and that working for him would be a great opportunity. I stood up from my chair and bent over in front of him to grab my purse. I could seriously feel his hands so close to my ass that he wanted to grab it, so I thought, you know what, I'm going to push this just a bit further. He already thought I was tipsy from the wine, so when I bent over, I wrapped the strap from my purse around the zipper on my dress; and as I stood up, I pulled down really hard. It actually worked out better than I thought it would. It took the dress all the way down to the point where he could see my tits in the tiny red bra, nipples peeking out of the top, and my matching red underwear. I played like I was so embarrassed. I zippered my dress up really fast, grabbed all my stuff, and started heading toward the door of the office. As I did, he stood up, grabbed my arm, and asked me to sit down again. He said that he wanted to talk about the job some more and that he thought he could probably make a decision tonight. I knew right then and there that I had him.

I sat back down in the chair again, and he started talking to me about salary. He told me that the job paid in the low six figures but that he could take it to that as long as we could add some other things to the job description—things that we could just keep between the two of us. I believe he was offering me money for other things besides a hard day's work—in the kitchen, that is—so I would basically be his whore. I asked him what would be on his second job description. He told me that there would be work that would need to be done on Sundays, you know prep work, and of course, he would be there to supervise me. I told him I'm sure that an occasional Sunday wasn't the only addition to the job. What else would be expected? He looked really nervous when I asked that question, like he was probably used to hitting on someone or harassing someone, but this was right in his face. I was right there asking him what he wanted, and he didn't know what to say. The power just shifted to me, and he didn't know what to do. This was going to be easy. I stood up, unzipped my dress, and asked him if this is what he wanted. All he could do was nod. I walked behind his chair, grabbed my purse, pulled out the syringe, and plunged it into his neck. It didn't take long for him to pass out. I texted Aaron to come on up. It was his turn.

He walked in and looked around at everything. He asked me what had happened. I told him exactly what had happened, and he looked angry. I asked him if he was jealous of what had just happened. He wasn't jealous. He was just angry that I had to go through this every time we needed to set people up. I told him that, like him, this was my part and that, for some reason, I really loved doing it, especially for him. I also loved the control that I had over these people. For so long, I had no control over anyone. I was taken advantage of for so long, and to be able to do this now, to be able to take control and power over people, especially for someone that I love, that I'm *in* love with, that's the best feeling in the world. I went ahead and took care of taking the money. It was a lot, more than we ever thought there would be. A look of calm came over him. He gave me a hug and a kiss, and we moved on with what we had to do.

*****

Aaron

We duct-taped his mouth, hands, and feet so he couldn't move and rolled his chair into the kitchen next to a hundred-gallon steam jacketed kettle. I filled it with water and slowly brought it to a boil. We slowly started to wake him up. It may sound strange, but the look of panic that people display is always different. Some just totally panic, some look confused, and some look like they knew this was coming sooner or later. His look was the latter. He figured that with all the things that he had done in his life, it was probably time for him to pay for it. It took him a moment, but he finally realized who I was. I removed the tape so he could speak but told him if he yelled, I would cut his throat—not like anyone would hear him anyway. He didn't understand why I was doing this after all the things he had done for me. I reminded him of all the crap he put me through, all the threats, the abuse of all the employees, the stealing of my ideas, and the harassment of all the female employees.

"I mean, look at what you were trying to do with Vanessa? You had no issues doing that to an employee you didn't know. What about the ones you do know?"

Now it was time for the pleading and begging to begin. He kept going on about all the good he had done in this world.

"Sorry, you couldn't possibly outweigh all the bad you had done."

Because of what I was going to do, I needed two things. I needed his arm to be numb, and I needed him drugged up enough so he couldn't fight me. I shot him up with both drugs, and he was in and out of sleep. I asked Vanessa if she wanted to be here for this. It was going to be a bit on the bloody side. She said that if it got to be too bad, she would step out. I put the tape back on his mouth and got started.

I decided to use exsanguination to drain the blood from his body. I would slowly drain the life out of him, like he had done with so many other people. I suppose I could just cut the femoral artery, but what would be the fun in that? He would bleed out in five minutes. I needed him to be somewhat conscience for what was about to happen.

Fun fact: steam-jacketed kettles work with steam being injected between two walls of metal to heat things up, like a jacket—well, it requires large floor drains to drain all that water from steaming and cleaning.

Great thing about that, I can drain his blood right down the drain. No cleanup necessary. I put the needle and the hose in one arm, and the other end of the hose, I put directly down the drain. I opened the clamp and slowly started draining his blood. After a period, the color started to drain from his face. He again started pleading with me. Well, he tried as much as he could with the tape over his mouth. This is where it was going to get a bit messy. I told Vanessa if she wanted to leave, she could. She refused the invitation to do so. I asked him if he remembered the story about the young server and the lobster. He shook his head no. After refreshing his memory, his eyes got huge, and he started trying to move but he really couldn't. Between the drugs and the blood draining from his body, he had no energy. I reached into my backpack and pulled out the fifteen-inch bowie knife that I purchased in Seattle but never used. I cut away his sleeve, and I shot the arm up again to make sure it was numb. I started to cut through the skin and muscle and cartilage until I got to the bone. I made my way through the socket just like you would on any animal and out the other side. He knew what was happening, but I don't really know how much he could feel considering all that he had in his system. His eyes were still open. I held up his arm to his face and reminded him of what he said to the server. I saw a tear go down his face—yeah, doesn't work. Too little too late. I took his arm and tossed it in the kettle. I looked up, and Vanessa was gone. That's not a good sign. I lifted the rest of his body and lowered it slowly into the water. The kettle overflowed a bit, but that's what the floor drains are for. I tossed in an entire container, five pounds of peeled garlic so that it would help mask the smell of cooking chef. I rinsed off all the things I brought to use and placed them in my backpack. I washed down the entire line of all the blood and body matter that may have been around, bleached the entire area, and washed it down again. I put his chair back in his office, and I made sure to clean everything up. I grabbed everything that was connected to Vanessa, wineglass, everything. I sprayed the area with a cleaning solution and wiped it completely down. I looked under the desk, the couch, everywhere. I even took the towel that she used to wipe herself off. Everything went in my backpack for disposal elsewhere far away from here.

I walked into the dining room, and there was Vanessa, sitting in a booth. I asked her what was wrong, and she told me it was nothing. She just decided to take me up on my offer and leave. I asked her if she was changing her mind about what we were doing. She said no, not at all, to never worry about that. When that time comes, she'll tell me.

I asked her, "Have you changed how you feel about me?"

She looked at me, like really looked at me, and said she's never been more in love with anyone to never worry about that. She understood why I was doing what I was doing. That's why she got involved in it. She did say that if it was just random people, that she would never understand. We got up, wiped the booth down, got in the service elevator, again using hoodies to disguise ourselves, and out the back door to the dumpster area. Looked around the parking lot, no one was there, so we got in the SUV and drove away.

CHAPTER 11

Getting to Know the Neighbors

Aaron

One of the things that we always said was that we were going to be honest with each other, always say what's on our mind. As we were driving back down to Tucson, she was really quiet. I asked her again if everything was okay. I reminded her that we were always supposed to say what was on our minds. She looked at me and asked me if the reasons why I was doing this were real. I asked her what she meant by that. I stated all my reasons to her truthfully. I was abused as I was coming up in the system, and that's what I was trying to avenge. It was as simple as that, completely black and white. If I can help others along the way, I will. She told me the reason why she walked out was because she saw the look in my eyes when I was doing what I was doing, and it scared her. She said she didn't see anything there. They were empty, no feeling. I told her that these people had done some pretty horrible things to me, and I have no feeling for them. The other reason was that I can't get close to any of these people or their stories. If I do, I'll never be able to carry anything out. She made me promise that if I ever got to the point where all feelings were gone and I felt that they weren't coming back, we stop. Her fear was that my feelings for her will disappear, and she wouldn't be able to handle that. I told her that will *never happen*. She keeps me grounded, and because of her, my feelings will never go away, at least not for her. I'm glad that we talk and that we got this out of the way.

We got back home in the early morning, opened the gate, and drove up to the house. Brian and Jody were up already, tending to the horses and working out. We waved to them as we passed by, parked the SUV, and started unloading our stuff. There was a fifty-gallon steel drum outside of the garage area that I like to start fires in. I was seriously fascinated with fire almost to the point of being scary. I put the backpack full of stuff in the drum, emptied a couple of cans of Sterno in it, and lit it on fire. Sterno kept burning, and it took a long time to burn out. Everything in there would be gone before it was. We looked over, and they were both walking up to us to say hi and ask how we were doing. We told them that our trip was very successful and that we were going to go in and get some rest. We asked if they wanted to come over later and we could sit down, eat, and go over some things. We told them that we were thinking about taking them with us to Hawaii to show them the house there and would they be interested. Didn't take them long to say yes. We told them we would call them and let them know when to come back. We unpacked, lay down in bed, curled up in each other's arms, and went to sleep.

After sleeping most of the morning, we woke up feeling really refreshed. We couldn't help but think that after each and every time we grew closer to each other. I know, this all sounds a bit strange, but it's actually drawing us closer together. We took a quick shower, got dressed, and went to the kitchen. There was some furniture delivered and set up while we gone. It was exactly what we wanted. Big fluffy chairs and couches, beautiful handcrafted wood tables, and they even mounted the big screen television for me. Vanessa made some coffee, and I cooked us something to eat. Scrambled eggs with green chilis and cream cheese folded into them, served on some toasted wheat bread with a salad of avocado, tomatoes, cilantro, lemon juice, and olive oil.

We sat down at the table and looked out the bay window as we ate and drank our coffee. Jody was riding one of the horses around the corral, and Brian was fixing one of the fences. If it's one thing that neither one of us ever felt, it was jealousy. We were both in love with each other, and we were extremely comfortable with ourselves and our relationship. Any comments that we made about others, it just didn't bother us. We started talking about whether or not we wanted to bring them in to help us. We could trust us, but bringing in two more people was definitely a risk. Vanessa had done a thorough background check on them both, credit and criminal as well. She even went as far as to get their bank and medical records. They were who they said they were, so if they were hiding something, they would have to be hiding it deep. I texted Brian and asked if they wanted to meet for dinner at our house around four. We could go swimming and have some dinner. We watched him call Jody over, and he showed her the text. They both smiled, and he texted back and said that yes, they would love to come over. He asked if they could bring anything, and I told him, "Just your swimsuits. That's it." I asked Vanessa if she wanted anything special, she said yes. She wanted a couple of bottles of 2016 Opus One Proprietary Red. She said she really liked it but didn't get the chance to really drink it the other night, she got kind of busy. Even though I knew she was being a smart-ass, I told her we could look when we went to the store for food.

We decided that we were going to smoke a side of salmon. I rubbed it with Dijon mustard and a variety of spices, let it marinate for an hour or so, and then I would throw it in the hot smoker. Side salad, asparagus, and steamed jasmine rice with a little soy, and butter and yes, her red wine just not the one she missed out on. They showed up at four on the dot. Since they were both ex-soldiers, being on time was not shocking. Vanessa and Jody hit it off immediately. They both had experienced some really bad situations. The difference is, Vanessa had gone through therapy for it, even if it was our kind of therapy. Brian and I got along well enough although I was always more skeptical of people. It's the nature of the business, trust but verify and some people I just never trusted. We decided that after tonight, we would determine how far we would take it with them. We decided that no matter what, we would both have to come to the same conclusion on both of them. We just couldn't take that chance. There was too much to lose. Vanessa and Jody decided to jump into the pool to cool off. It was a hot day, and it wasn't a bad idea. Brian was talking to me about things that were going on with the property, the horses, things that needed to get done or repaired. I liked to keep a tight rein on things. He needed to know that it wasn't going to be that easy with me and that his experience didn't scare me. We all have our skills. The thing is, he didn't know what mine were, not yet anyway. I decided it was time to get in the pool, so I put the salmon in the smoker, and we hopped in the pool.

We had seen the two ladies engrossed in conversation. It looked pretty deep too. We swam over, and it looked like Jody had been crying. We asked what was going on, and she apologized for what she thought was ruining our time together. I told her that it wasn't a big deal, to not worry about it. But I asked again what was wrong, what had happened, why was she crying. Vanessa told us that they were talking about all the stuff that had happened to her, but there was one situation that she didn't tell us about. She didn't even tell Brian about this one. We decided to get out of the pool and go inside for dinner. I plated the food, and Vanessa poured the wine. We all sat down, and we gave Jody some time to calm down before she started to tell her story.

It happened with an officer and another female recruit at boot camp. There was one day that they were training and it was raining hard. Everyone was down in the mud all day long; it was a really long day, and they didn't really care how long they were outside. When they were done, they all went inside to shower and get changed. There were only two females in the squad, Jody and a girl named Susan, and she always seemed like she had a problem with her. She was attractive, but she was one of those girls that wasn't very athletic, and she always had problems keeping up. For the first time, she wasn't the center of attention, and because of where they were, she couldn't do anything to get her way out of it, at least Jody thought she couldn't. No matter how much she tried to help her, she never accepted. She figured since there were only two of them, they could help take care of each other. Jody wanted to take a break, so she asked if we could go sit in the hot tub and finish our wine. We went outside and climbed inside; we forgot our suits, so we just got in with our clothes on. She continued with her story.

She started taking a shower, and as she was putting her head back to rinse her hair, Susan came up behind her, grabbed her hair, and pulled Jody towards her. She started rubbing her body, starting at her breasts and working her way down to Jody's ass and between her legs. Jody thought this was going to be some kind of lesbian encounter, and she thought, okay, she's never been here before, so why not give it a shot. She turned Jody around, and as she started kissing her, John—the commanding officer—came up behind her, grabbed her arms, and handcuffed them behind her back. They both told Jody that if she screamed or told anyone what was about to happen, they would both tell everyone that he heard screaming, came running, and he caught Jody assaulting Susan. She would be kicked out before she even got started. They both proceeded to rape Jody for the next two hours. There was nothing that she could do. When they were done, they reminded her what would happen if she said anything. She got up from the shower floor, finished taking a shower, got dressed, and went to bed.

They didn't have much time left in training camp, and Jody wasn't going to let them know that what they did was ever going to break her. I still tried to help her whenever I could. It seriously fucked with her head. She used to look at Jody like she was waiting for the hammer to drop. She wouldn't give her the pleasure. When camp was over, she said goodbye to her, said good luck, and she thanked him for all he had done for her.

When she was done explaining, she crawled into Vanessa's arms and started to cry silently. We thought Brian was going to have an angrier reaction, but he didn't. He was extremely supportive of her, always, but he knew there were things that she was dealing with and that, in her own time, she would tell him. He was glad she let it out, and he was grateful to us for helping her with it. We got out of the hot tub, dried off, and changed into some dry clothes. They didn't have any of their own, so we lent some to them. We knew where they lived, so it wasn't an issue. We went and sat down in the living room and continued to talk. Jody thanked us for being so understanding and for listening to her. We both told her it wasn't a problem; this was a safe environment for her, so never worry.

We brought up going to Hawaii again, asking them if they still would like to go. We thought it would be nice to get away from here for a bit. It would be good for them. They jumped at the chance of going with us. They asked who would care for the animals. I told them that we could kennel the dogs, and there was a place we could transport the horses to get taken care of. I told them that we would leave the day after tomorrow and to pack enough stuff for at least three weeks. They could always do laundry and buy more if needed although you really don't need many clothes there. I wanted to impress them and charter a private jet to take us there. Vanessa brought up how we didn't want to bring attention to ourselves. I told her that we weren't going on a job, that this was all pleasure. She had hidden and legally invested all the money so carefully that no one would question anything about our finances. She also had her inheritance from her family that she invested, and it was giving her a seriously healthy return. We were covered. She agreed. We climbed into bed and talked about all that had just happened. I think we both had a really good feeling about them both. We looked forward to some new adventures.

CHAPTER 12
Time for Some New Adventures

After a really great night's sleep, we finally woke up. We seriously didn't want to get out of bed. We were so comfortable and at peace with life right now. We slowly got out of bed and hopped in the shower. Every chance we get to shower with each other, we do. It's the hot water, the closeness of it all, it just always feels so good. We don't always make love to each other, not because we don't want to, but we just need to get moving with the day. We know that we're always there for each other when we need it. We got dressed and went to get something to eat at a little café down the street from the house. There was a lot that we needed to take care of before we left. Since no one was going to be here, we needed to close it up for a while. Brian got the horses to the stable that would be taking care of them, and Jody took the dogs to the doggie hotel, only the best for Zeus and Apollo. When we got back, they had already finished getting the corral closed and locked up. We told them that as soon as they got done packing to close up their house and come up to the main house to spend the night, we would be leaving early so it would make it easier. They asked again if it was an imposition to take them with us. I told them absolutely not. I told them that they've become a part of the organization, part of the family, and that if we were going to have them take care of the property in Tucson, we needed to show them the property in Hawaii because they will probably have to deal with that one as well. The smiles on their faces were wide. They felt like the luckiest people for having gotten involved with us.

I had some pizza delivered right before they got there. We put their luggage with ours by the front door, and Vanessa showed Jody the room where they would be sleeping. Brian helped me get the pizza on the table, and we grabbed the wine that was left from last night. He started telling me how happy it makes him that Jody and Vanessa get along so well, that Jody really needed someone like her to talk to. He said that after they got home last night, Jody seemed like a different person, more relaxed, like a weight had been lifted off her. I told him that I was glad that we could be there for her—well, mostly Jody but me as well. We all sat down and started to eat, and we decided to bring up our plans for a third house. We told them we wanted to buy another house in Park City, Utah. We wanted one by the beach, which was Hawaii, desert, Tucson, and mountains, which would be Utah. The plan was to do some traveling, and we didn't want to stay at resorts. We wanted a home base to go to. We wanted them to help with security at all places and make sure that things were taken care of. It would require travel, and of course, we would pay for all of it. We would give them a corporate credit card, and they would have to submit expenses at the end of the month. All pretty straightforward and easy to do. Jody was the one that handled all the finances for them, so she would be taking care of it.

The look on their faces was priceless, like they had just won the lottery. We told them that we had a really good feeling about them and that we wanted to make sure that we took care of them. Trust is big for us. We needed to make sure that we had that because if we didn't, we needed to stop right now. Jody looked at Vanessa and then me, and with tears in her eyes, she told me that she had never told anyone what she had told us, that she had trusted us enough to do that, more than she had ever trusted anyone. She said that she had grown really close to Vanessa. She was like a sister to her, and she valued that. She would never betray that. Brian had also said how much he appreciated us and what we had done for them. He said that he would never betray our trust or us. We told them that we would be getting up at six to get ready to go so we should probably get to sleep. Before we said good night, we told them to buckle up because their lives were about to change. They said they were looking forward to it.

We woke up at around six to the smell of coffee and pastries. They had gone out and picked some stuff up for breakfast. They said they didn't know what would be served on the plane, so they thought they would make sure we had what we liked. We all showered and got ready to go. We told them that a car service would be here to pick us up by eight. We got a call from the front gate that the car service was here. Vanessa called the security company and told them we would be gone to please make sure they started sending someone out on a regular basis. A black Cadillac Escalade pulled up to the front door. The driver loaded up our luggage, and we climbed in, excited and ready to start our new adventure. As we pulled into the airport, they started to get a bit confused when we didn't pull up to the departure gates. Instead, the driver pulled around to the executive terminal where the private jets are. We told them that we decided to charter a personal jet instead of flying commercial. They were shocked. They obviously had no clue what or how much we had. We told them we wanted to make the trip special for them. We were flying on an Embraer Phenom 300E. It had eight seats, two pilots, and two flight attendants. We would be able to spread out and relax, talk, and basically do whatever we want. Oh, and the food, really exceptional. We buckled up and got ready for takeoff. Jody and Vanessa sat next to each other, and we sat behind them. The takeoff was probably the smoothest you could ever imagine. No bumps, nothing, it was just incredible. I'm sure that the flight would be smooth, but I also saw it as another opportunity to get to know them better, to feel out the anger and frustrations that they had against all the people that hurt them and were they ready to fix that. We were about to find out, but we had a feeling that we wouldn't have to twist their arms.

When we got up to our cruising altitude, Brian and I went to sit in the seats that were directly across them. We asked them how they were feeling and what did they think of the trip so far. They couldn't be happier, and they wanted to know the secret of our success. We told them that when we got to Hawaii, we would explain more to them what it is we did. Right now, we just wanted enjoy the flight and relax. Brian decided to go back to the seats behind them so he could stretch out and sleep. I asked Vanessa if she wanted to come over and sleep with me. She said no. She wanted to stay with Jody. They curled up under a blanket and dozed off. It was actually kind of cute the way the two of them had connected. They really took to each other. I think that Jody really needed the connection, one that Brian or myself couldn't give to her. The closer they got, the easier this would work in our favor when it came to whether we could trust or not. I had no jealousy when it comes to any of this. I finally dozed off after watching a movie. Things were feeling really good.

I woke up to the sound of Vanessa whispering in my ear and kissing my cheek. Jody had gone back to the seats with Brian and fell asleep with him. She climbed onto my lap, facing me, under the covers, and started rocking back and forth in my lap. She lifted her shirt and mine so that we were skin to skin, the heat between the two of us was unreal. She was slowly breathing in my ear, telling me how much she loved me, how in love with me she was. She unbuttoned and unzipped my shorts, pulled her shorts to the side, and slowly inserted me inside her. After what seemed like forever, we both came together, and it was probably the quietest we've ever been. She continued to sit on my lap, holding on to me, not seeming to want to let go. She told me that she had a great conversation with Jody, and no, she didn't tell her what we were doing. I told her that I trusted her completely and she didn't have to ever worry about that. She told me that Jody was growing closer and closer to her every day. She said that when they were sleeping, she could've sworn that Jody had put her hands in places that she didn't think she would although she could've just been sleeping and it is pretty close quarters. She asked if I was jealous, and I said not at all, that I think that this could seriously play in our favor. I told her I wasn't trying to sound bad, and I certainly wouldn't ever do anything to hurt either one of them, unless they threatened our livelihoods. In fact, I told her that I think she needs to play on that to a certain degree. She asked me if I meant the way she was touching her. I said yes. I don't think that you need to have a full-on relationship with her. That would cause way too many issues just keep her close. If we ever had any issues with Brian, we might need her on our side.

One of the flight attendants came to tell us that we were starting our descent into the Princeville Airport. Because we were flying in a smaller jet, we could land on the north shore, and since the house was on that side, it made it a lot easier to get home. I thanked the flight crew for a great trip. I told them that when we were ready to travel again, we would let them know. We got a car service to take us home. We went through the gate and started to drive up to the house, and I've never seen mouths drop so far open. They couldn't believe the size of the house, the property, all of it. The beauty just blew them away, and they were intrigued even more to know what we did to get here. We showed them around the house, and they couldn't be more impressed. We showed them the master suite where they would be sleeping and the outdoor shower that went with it. They said they've never smiled this much in their lives. We told them to get settled in and we would walk them around the property, all casual, wear a swimsuit. While we got ourselves settled in, we mapped out how we were going to bring them into this. I reminded her how it all started with us, the anger and the frustration had built up so much inside that the only way we were going to get through it was to start getting revenge on the ones that hurt us. We would have to start playing on that again because that would be the only way to get them on board.

We walked into the living room, and they were there sitting on the couch, looking like they were afraid to touch anything. We asked them if everything was okay and were they having regrets about com-ing. They told us that they did not. They just didn't know exactly what to do. Everything is so nice they didn't want to do anything that would piss us off. We sat them down and told them that they don't have to worry. Consider this as their home too. Besides the fact is, it's just stuff. Stuff can always be replaced. Trust and friendship can't be. We got up and started giving them the tour. We started with the rest of the house and worked our way outside. We started with the tree house. They thought it was the coolest thing around, a place to get away and relax. They would definitely be spending some time up there. We showed them the private studio, another place for them to get away, and we ended up in the pool. They were impressed, but we told them we had a lot more to show them—things they didn't even know about. They asked us, begged us to tell them, and show them more. We agreed, but we needed to get out of the pool and change so we could get started. I suggested to Vanessa that she take Jody into our room and show her some of the clothes that she has. Maybe she could borrow something. Vanessa winked at me and took her into the room.

*****

Vanessa

We got back into the room, and I started to show her some of the different clothes that she could borrow. After looking at a lot of things, we both finally found something to wear. I had forgotten all the stuff I left behind. I forgot how much I loved being here. As we got undressed, I noticed Jody sneaking peeks at my body. I asked her if everything was okay and did she have something she wanted to ask me. She said that I had the most perfect breasts. She asked me if they were real. I told her that they were very real, and she asked if she could feel them. I thought about what Aaron told me, and I totally agreed with him. I really do care about her, a lot, but we definitely needed to make sure that she was on our side. I told her that she could if she really wanted to, so she took a couple of steps toward me; and with both hands, she grabbed my breasts, and she lightly squeezed them. You could hear her breath quiver as she was taking breaths, short, shallow breaths. I asked her if she was feeling attracted to me. She said she didn't know. She just felt really close to me right now. I gave her a hug and told her that was okay, but let's not take it too far, and let's keep it between us for now. Right about the time we were getting dressed, Aaron called back and asked if we were ready.

The first thing we showed them was all the security that we had set up around the property. They asked us why we had so much. We told them that our security was of the utmost importance, that we liked being alone, present company excluded, and we wanted to keep it that way. We liked the way things were set up in Tucson, but we wanted to work on getting the same kind of setup there as well. We would have to do the work just like we did here so that the location of things stayed within our group. We took them back into the house and told them the location of what we were about to show them had to remain a secret for now. We told them we had to put hoods on them, which caused them to freak out just a bit to the point where they asked us if they had anything to worry about.

I said, "Don't you think that if we wanted to do something to you, we would've done it by now?"

They agreed, and we proceeded. They placed their hands on each other's shoulders, and we led them to the door of the bedroom. The entrance to the bunker was behind a row of shelves in the closet. Vanessa went in to open it so they wouldn't hear where it was. It was very quiet and made hardly any noise when it moved. She came out and got us, and we led them in the rest of the way. A ramp, not stairs, led you down into the bunker that came in pretty handy considering they were blindfolded. Once we got them down far enough to the point where they couldn't see the door, we closed it and took their hoods off.

Again, the looks on their faces were priceless. They seriously asked, "How much deeper does this go?"

"Not the bunker, us, how much deeper do we go?" The bunker was as big as half the house. It had one large bedroom and one smaller one, two bathrooms, one in the larger bedroom, a kitchen, a large living area, with a locked room off on one end. It had all the amenities that one could want. Big screen TV with satellite and a surround-sound audio system. One of the best parts was that its electricity ran off a separate line, and in case we lost power, we installed a high-end generator that we could use to supply power for the entire house and the bunker. We figured since we lived on an island with tropical storms and hurricanes, it might be a good idea. We all sat down on the couches. Every couch everywhere had to be big and fluffy for Vanessa. She liked to get lost in them. So they looked at each other and looked at us and said, "What's in the locked room? Can we see?"

We told them that this is where the trust goes up 100 percent, that if we showed them the room there would be no going back.

There's a lot attached to that room, and once we crossed that threshold, if we lost trust, that would be extremely devastating for everyone concerned. So think really hard if this is something that they want to do. They can still just go back to handling security for us, and there would be no hard feelings. It took them all about one second to agree and say that we had nothing to worry about. We made our way to the door. They could see what it was that it took to open the door, biometric locks. They could both see that our security is of great importance to us, trust and security. They entered the room, and the thing that stood out to them first was all the monitors, the sensors, night-vision cameras—all of it. It was all top-of-the-line equipment that would impress anyone that knew anything about security. Inside that room was another locked area. I opened that one, and inside was an enormous amount of weapons, handguns, shotguns, AR-15s, sniper rifles, and a variety of knives and hand-to-hand combat tools. It was unreal to Jody and Brian. All this was so unreal, like they were in a fucking movie. And now for another round of questions, they wanted to know why we had so many weapons.

"What did you need them for? We understand security, but this was a bit of overkill. Yes. Is this more than just collectors' items? Were you drug dealers? That would explain all the money and properties, right? Were you going to hurt us? Do we have to worry?"

"All really good questions, and we will answer them for you, so let's all go and sit on the couch and talk. So first and foremost, you're safe, very safe. We told you that you are like family to us. You are a part of this family. You don't have to worry about us ever hurting you. No, we're not drug dealers. We don't do drugs, so we certainly aren't going to sell them."

They both asked if they could get something to drink, something strong to drink. I had some single malt scotch in the kitchen, so I brought them both a healthy glass. We asked them to take themselves back in time, back to all the people that have ever hurt them, back to the military, boot camp, and maybe before and after that, anyone who had ever hurt them. Tears were coming to Jody's eyes. Before it started getting worse, I kept going. I told them the same things had happened to us, many times over and over. We went on for hours about all the things that had been done to us. Then we hit them with the more serious part. We told them what we had been doing to get our revenge on all the people that hurt us. We told them piece by piece what we did to each and every person, the reasons why and what we did. They asked us if it made us feel better. We both told them that it did but in different ways. We never felt bad for what we did, but I had more of a drive for it, maybe because I had endured it for longer due to what my profession was or, I should say, is. But we both felt the need to protect, the need to right the wrongs that had been done to us and to others. Now that they knew pretty much everything about who we are and what we do and what we've done, we needed to know where their heads were at with all this.

It surprised us that their response came as quick as it did. They asked what they could do to help us continue with what we are doing. We told them there's a lot they can do to help us, but we were very careful with what we did, and we needed them to do the same. They would have to listen to everything we said to do and follow it to the letter. There's a reason why we're sitting where we are. I also issued one last warning, and I made sure that they understood what I was saying.

"If either of you tries to hurt us or betray us, the consequences would be great. Now that you know that we're in the business of revenge, you understand how we will deal with it."

I told them, "I'm not trying to sound bad, but it's the reality of the situation. On the other hand, if this goes on and we work together, we will take care of you both for the rest of your lives."

They understood what the consequences would be, and they considered it part of the job description.

They asked, "When are we going to start, and who are we going to start with?"

We both looked at them and said, "You tell us. Who should we start with?"

CHAPTER 13
New Blood, Big Twist

We thought about it like this. Giving them the opportunity to make the choice of who we go after next, it would really draw them in further, and it would cement their involvement in what we are doing. If we start to take down the people that had hurt them in the past there isn't much, they could say against us, right? The one part we never informed them of and that we will never inform them of is the money part. There was no reason for them to know any of that. Besides, they were being well taken care of and we would continue to take care of them, so that would never be an issue. They were paid a very good salary, and whatever jobs we did, we would give them a hefty bonus; and if they wanted Vanessa to invest it for them, she would. We told them about adding a bonus on top of the salary they were already getting paid, and they had no issue with it. We would pay them separately so it all looked legal. Jody handled the money anyway, so it didn't really matter. What we thought was really, well, interesting or intriguing, was that Jody pulled Vanessa aside and asked that she take some of the bonus money and invest it separately for just her. She said she didn't care if I knew about it. She just didn't want Brian to know. Vanessa asked her if she wanted to talk about it, and she said she would tell her soon enough. She found out a piece of information that made her really uncomfortable, that would actually piss her off if true, but she wasn't ready to share yet. She needed to dive deeper into it.

So the individuals that Jody wanted to go after first were the two people that came after her in the shower. Brian really wanted to go after them, a lot. He said those are the people, at this point, that had hurt Jody the worst, and those are the ones he wanted gone the most. Vanessa did some digging, and she found out that they had gotten married, and they were living on the island of Maui. How convenient was that? Apparently, her family had a ton of money, and he had wanted some of that. That's why he was always letting her slide on everything. Plus, they always had that encounter with Jody that connected them. Great memory for them, but not much for her. They had no kids, and they were living on Kaanapali Beach. There was an exclusive community that was built on the side of the mountain that overlooked the beach. Sprawling properties that cost a fortune to live in, but then again, she was way beyond loaded. Her parents left her their fortune when they both died in a very suspicious car accident. No one could prove that it wasn't an accident, but there still were a lot of people that thought something wasn't right. Some of those people were some pretty shady people. It was said that her dad was in bed with some people he shouldn't be in bed with. They needed to get away from all of that, so they made their way to the island to escape it all. Since they were right on Kaanapali Beach, we wanted to come in by boat. It was really quiet, and people didn't really notice. The channel between Kauai and Oahu was too rough, so we decided to take the jet to Oahu. The flight was probably about thirty minutes, and Jody had asked to sit with Vanessa in the back. She said she needed to talk to her.

*****

Vanessa

She had disappeared from the house for a long while. No one knew where she was. Aaron and I were so busy digging into these people's lives. Brian was out in the pool swimming, so we had assumed that she was with him. She was actually digging deeper into something that she had found out about and she really needed to talk to me about it. What she told me infuriated me more than I had been in a very long time.

She had told me that, apparently, Brian knew about what had happened in the showers at boot camp. That's why he didn't have a huge reaction to it, why he was so subdued. His whole reaction was an act. I asked her how, how did he know. They had actually set up cameras in the room. They actually filmed every single bit of it. They posted it on some creepy fucking website that specializes in that shit. They blurred their faces but didn't blur hers. One of Jody's friends caught her husband on the site, and when she saw what he was looking at, she wasn't just shocked by the content. She was shocked because it was her! She told her husband, "You know that's my friend, right?" He knew all about it.

"Okay, so then why do you think Brian knew about it?"

Her husband told her that Brian knew the commanding officer. The officer told him that he had shown it to Brian and that he loved it. He found out who she was, and he found a way to meet her. He thought it was a really hot video and that he had wished it was him instead of the commanding officer. After that, they never saw each other again. Neither one knew who the other was with, and they just carried on with their lives. I was fucking floored. I couldn't believe what I was hearing. I asked her if all that she had just told me was truly a fact. She pulled out her tablet, gave me earbuds to put in, and she started playing the video. I started to cry as I was watching. The fact that he not only knew what had happened to her, but it turned him on, and it enticed him to find her. Who in their right mind would do something like that? And then to start a deep and loving relationship, knowing that you've been fooling this person the whole time? I wanted to jump out of my chair and kill him right then and there. But I didn't. I couldn't right now. I needed to tell Aaron about this. She told me after this revelation. She couldn't be around this anymore, not with him. She just couldn't. I told her to not worry. Once I told Aaron about this, it would get taken care of. He was the chef, and he would come up with a recipe just for him.

*****

Aaron

When we got to Oahu, we rented a boat. Well, it was more of a yacht. A yacht that actually had a speedboat attached to it. It had its own garage where it fit nicely, so we didn't have to dock in a huge yacht. That would definitely be something that people would notice. We boarded the boat and got underway. All of us knew how to pilot the boat, so we didn't need a crew to go with us. I had actually been learning how to pilot that private jet as well. I had my license, and I needed only a couple of more hours before I could do it myself. We really didn't need and/or want pilots with us all the time, especially with what we were doing. Brian went up top to take control of the boat. We needed at least one up there, and Jody and Vanessa dragged me below deck. They told me they needed to speak to me about something. We got to the bottom, and they sat me down on the bed.

I said, "Okay, guys, what's going on?"

They proceeded to tell me everything, even showed me the video. I think that Jody was waiting for me to blow up, but Vanessa knows me. She knew that I was a very calm, black-and-white kind of person. I was sitting in between them both. I asked Vanessa to stand up and sit behind Jody and hold onto her. Jody got a really funny look on her face. I turned toward Jody, grabbed her face, and told her that I would take care of it, that I would take care of her. I told her that we loved her and that she will always be a part of us, a part of me, and anyone that hurts my family will suffer the consequences for it. I told her that it may not seem like I care, but I do, very much.

"Both Vanessa and I have grown very close to you. I'm just coming up with the perfect way to handle this, but I need to know one thing. Are you on board with what I'm about to do?"

She told me that what he did goes way beyond anything, anyone, had ever done to her.

"He watched me get raped. He enjoyed it, and it made him want to find me and be with me. He even said that he wished that it was him that was there doing it. Who in their right mind would do that or even think about doing that? What he did was totally unforgivable, period."

"Okay, so, Vanessa, tell her how we do this."

*****

Vanessa

I told her that she was usually the one that lured the people to where we needed them to be. Jody got a sad look on her face.

I told her, "No, it's not something that he's forcing me to do. We don't work that way. I actually get off on all the power that goes with it. Imagine when those people had power over you. Well, I just take it back again, and in the end, they get what they deserve. I put them in the right spot, and Aaron takes care of the rest."

She was totally on board with all of it. She asked what we needed for her to do.

*****

We were about halfway between Oahu and Maui, and I went up top to relieve Brian. Vanessa asked him if he wanted her to show him the rest of the boat, and he enthusiastically said yes. I don't know what he was expecting, but whatever it was, I'm sure it wasn't what he was about to get. Jody stayed up top with me. She asked if I was sure she was going to be okay. I told her that we've done this before, and with people that weren't nice, that didn't know us the way Brian did. I told her that I would give her some time, probably about twenty minutes, and then I would slow the boat to a stop. By then, it all should be ready to go.

*****

Vanessa

I was showing him around the bottom deck. When I got to the main bedroom, he was fascinated by how beautiful it was and that the only thing that matched it was my beauty. I can't say that I didn't expect that. Well, if it was said before Jody told me what had happened, I would've been flattered, and I wouldn't have thought anything about it. Now he was just a predictable pig. I told him how Jody had been hitting on me, that she was really attracted to me and that she asked, and I had actually let her touch me when I caught her looking at me. You could tell his mind was spinning and that he was excited. He wasn't sitting down, so it was obvious, but he didn't even notice. He asked me what I thought about that and did I tell Aaron. I told him that if I had told Aaron about it, he would've booted them out. He wasn't a jealous person, but he didn't like any drama in his personal life.

"As far as what I thought about it, how does it make you feel?"

"It excited me, but I was always more curious about you than her. I mean, the way she touched me, it felt good, but is that the way that you touched her? Had she learned from you how a woman should be touched? The way she touched me was really soft and gentle."

I showed him by demonstrating it on myself. I was wearing a thin tank top. I had removed my bra and put on a hoodie before I brought him down. I unzipped my hoodie. You could see my hard nipples poking through the shirt. I started to slowly massage my breasts the way that Jody did. I asked him if this was the way he did it to Jody, or was he rougher with her.

"Do you like it rougher than she does?"

By this point, he had no idea what to think. His head was spinning, and he was having problems forming complete sentences. I told him that he needs to sit down on the chair by the desk before he falls down. After he sat, he told me that he had always liked it rougher than she did, and every time he started, she would stop him. The chair he was sitting in had no arms. It was one of those office chairs that just had a seat and a back. His back was to the desk, so I pulled up my skirt. He could see I had no underwear on, and I plopped myself down on his lap hard.

"Was that rough enough for you?"

I started to grind onto his lap really hard, and I asked him again, "Is this rough enough for you?"

I lifted up my shirt and told him to grab my tits the way he wanted to grab hers. I don't think he knew what to do. Again, I was in control. I was taking command of the situation, and he didn't know what to do. I was like a speeding bullet from his sniper's rifle hitting him before he had a chance to think about it. I draped my arms across his shoulders, put my mouth up to his ear, and whispered, "Motherfucker, I told you to grab my tits as hard as you wanted to grab hers, and I'm not going to tell you again."

He put his hands up to my tits and slowly squeezed them as hard as he could, so hard it actually brought a tear to my eye. When he started working his way up to squeezing my nipples, I jabbed the needle in his neck, hard, and shot those wonderful drugs into his body. I stood up fast. It didn't take him long to pass out. Right about that time, they came walking into the room. Jody looked at him, then at me, no scratches or blood anywhere. She asked me how I did it.

I told her that when you look like us, we can control anything, any situation, and anybody we want, and there are not many men or women that are immune to that. Well, maybe Aaron. He would be one of the only ones, that is. She called Aaron over and gave us both a huge hug and a kiss and told us that she is indebted to us for the rest of her life, that she would do anything for us and she would never hurt us. Aaron told her this is just the first part. Now we need to get him tied up.

*****

Aaron

We took him topside, tied his hands behind his back, and tied his feet with a strong thin rope wound like a figure 8 over and over again until there was so much he would never be able to get out of it. I laid a sheet of plastic down on the boat, put a hood over his head, and sat him up on a chair by the edge at the back of the boat. In front of him, there was a small table set up with a laptop on it. I told Jody and Vanessa not to come topside until I told them to. I slowly poured some ice-cold water over Brian's head until he started to come to. The first thing he did was realize he had a bag over his head and he was tied up. He started to struggle to try to free himself.

As he was trying to get free, I pulled the bag off his head, and he looked at me in total disbelief. He asked me what was going on, what happened, and why was he tied up. I just stared at him, running one of my knives up and down the steel I used to keep them sharp. You could tell he was trying to figure out what was going on, and all of a sudden, he started saying over and over again that it wasn't his fault. He didn't do anything. It was all her fault.

I stopped what I was doing and asked him, "What are you talking about, her fault?"

He told me what had happened below deck, that it wasn't his fault, that Vanessa had come onto him. He didn't initiate it.

I started laughing, and I asked him, "Is that what you think this is about?"

"What else would it be?" he asked.

I reached over and pushed Play on the laptop, and the video started to play. The look on his face at first was, *Oh shit, I'm fucked,* then he went into total denial mode. He told me he had never seen this before and that he was outraged by it. Where did I get it, how could he show it to me, and why was *he* tied up? I told him that he needs to make really sure that what he's about to tell me was 100 percent truthful—nothing but the truth. He then went where they all go, into the totally angry, threatening mode part of the show. He told me that he didn't have to answer to me for anything and that if he ever got out of this, he would make sure he told everyone what we were doing and what we did. And after he did that, he was going to line me up in the sights of his rifle and pull the trigger. I'd never see it coming.

I said, "You mean like right now, this situation, that you never saw coming?" I stood up with my boning knife in hand, walked over to him, leaned over, and said, "The mistake you just made was to threaten me and break my trust."

I then took the boning knife and jammed it into his shoulder. He let out a loud scream. I told him we were in the middle of nowhere and that no one could hear him. All the while, the tape was still playing in the background. I asked him again, "100 percent honesty, are you going to be honest with me?"

86

He looked at me and said, "Yes, what do you want to know?"

I asked him if he was aware of this tape, and if he was, when did he know. He said he knew the officer and that he had shown it to him. He said he wanted to meet her, and the way it looked to him, she was enjoying it. I told him to look at the video.

"Tell me about what was going on, was she enjoying it?"

He said the officer told him that she deserved it, that she was always being a pain in the ass, and she needed to be taught a lesson.

I said, "So rather than being a man, you just stood by and said nothing?"

He said, "I wanted to meet her. It turned me on, and I wanted to see for myself what she was like."

It turned out that each and every time Jody had been harassed, Brian had something to do with it in one way or another. He had paid people or even just told people to do something to her, that she liked it. And even in some cases, like the two officers that forced her to strip and go down on them, he not only paid them, but he had them record it too. She had decided to go off script and threaten them, something he never expected her to do, but she was pretty fed up with all the garbage.

"So then you've basically been playing a sick, fucked-up game with her this whole time?"

He admitted that he had been but that she was really way too stupid to figure it out.

"Well, I hate to break it to you, but she's the one that figured it out. Is this the reason why you wanted to get rid of the people on Maui because they knew your secret?"

He nodded. "Yes."

"What a son of a bitch. We may have gotten rid of people, but it was for good reasons, not for self-serving reasons, not just to save our asses."

I texted them to come to the back of the boat. When they got there, it was like a switch had flipped in Jody. They had both heard everything he said, but she wasn't crying. She wasn't even angry. She had made her own kind of peace with it, and she was ready to move on. The opposite of love—that would be indifference, not hate. He had come to the realization that he wasn't getting out of this, so he just started talking. He was ugly and mean, and the things he said to her, the things he had told her that he had done to her that she knew nothing about, he didn't deserve to live. How can one person claim to love someone so much and do the things that he did and it wasn't just a couple of times, but it was years of silent abuse? It was years of making her feel like a piece of meat to others, secretly telling people that she liked what was happening, and all of it, all of it was for his own sick pleasure. So Jody decided that it was her turn to speak. She stuck a towel in his mouth and duct-taped over that, nice and tight. There would be no reason for him to speak anymore. She told him that what he did to her was unforgivable, and the fact that she had unknowingly been made part of his sick fantasy, there were no words to describe it anymore, what it made her feel like. So the time for words and emotions was done, and now it was time for action. She told him that although he may have controlled this part of her life, there were things that she controlled as well. All the finances, most of which he knows nothing about, she took total control of all them.

"You basically don't exist. No one will know or care if you're gone. We decided to wipe ourselves from everything, and since this happened, Vanessa went even further and completely wiped you off the grid. You know what that means, right? Oh, that's right. You can't talk. That means that this is it for you. You are going to end right now, and there won't be a trace of you left."

I told him that I had driven far enough offshore, that he will never wash up anywhere. The reason for the shoulder wound was because blood draws predators, mainly sharks.

"So this is how it's going to go. I'm going to hook you up to the back of the boat, and we're going to drag you for a while behind us. Eventually, with all the blood in the water, something will come and get you, but rather than reel them in, we're going to let you out. It's a fitting end to a predatory life, being eaten by another predator. Anything else you would like to say? Oh, that's right, you can't talk."

Giving him the opportunity to speak wouldn't be worth it. It would just be more hurtful words, and Jody didn't need to hear it. With the look that came over his face, he knew his time was done.

Tears started coming to his eyes, and when Jody saw it, she actually started crying. I sat her down in front of him and told her to look at him.

"Remember all the things that he had done to you and ask yourself, is he worth any tears, even one tear?"

I've never seen anyone stop crying so quickly in my life. It was like there was a vacuum inside her head that sucked the tears right back up again. She was ready. I told Jody and Vanessa to go up, start the boat, and start driving away from the island. Once the boat started moving, I looked at him, punched two more holes in his body with the knife so we could get more blood flowing, gave him a wink and a huge smile, and pushed him overboard. It honestly didn't take as long as I thought it would. Something huge jumped up, grabbed him, and took him down. I had a light trained on him so I could see it happen. It really was a thing of beauty. I cut the line, and it took him down the rest of the way. I doubt that any piece of him would ever be found, and if there was any left, we were way too far out for any piece of him to be washed up. The rest of the fish will take care of what's left of him.

I went up to the top and told them that it was done. The look on Jody's was one of relief. She was glad that it was over. She apologized for all that she had put us through, for bringing this person into our lives, and for us having to do what we just did. We told her that this is what we do. These are the people that we bring down and that we're happy we could do it for her and get her out of the mess that she was in. If she had never met us, she would still be stuck where she was with the possibility of being abused much more than she already was. She was eternally grateful to us, but I believe that Vanessa and I both actually felt something here. We didn't want to manipulate her into anything. We both felt that having done what we did, protecting her the way we did, we wouldn't need to, and most of all, we didn't want to. The three of us have a bond that will never be broken, this we're pretty positive about. I looked at them both and said that there was one thing that we forgot to do because of him, the original reason for this adventure. I asked Jody if she was still up for doing it. She asked if we had the ability to dock the boat and rest for the night.

The whole day has taken a tremendous toll on all of us, and we really needed some time to just recharge. Being tired left us open to making mistakes, and we can't make mistakes with what we do. I didn't want to dock on Maui, but I figured we could dock on Lanai. There was a small boat harbor named Manele, and we could dock there and no one would ask any questions. So we had a choice. We could sleep on the boat or stay at the Four Seasons Resort. They wanted to stay at the resort, but Jody didn't want to stay alone. I told her not to worry. We would all stay in the same room. Vanessa asked her if she was okay with that, and without hesitation, she was okay with it. She said she wanted to be with us forever.

We gathered all the things we needed and locked up the boat. We got to the resort, and I told them to wait in the bar while I got us a room. The room I got was the ALII Royal Suite. It was this gorgeous suite that overlooked the bay, big fluffy king-size bed, and a walkup wooden Japanese soaking tub. We couldn't have asked for a better place to be. We were all tired and hungry, so we went up to the room and ordered room service. We got a sushi platter that had a wide variety of rolls, some fresh sliced mango and strawberries, and a bottle of champagne so that they could toast to Jody's newfound freedom. Amazingly enough, she wasn't even sad. She was actually relieved that she was done with him. I ate some sushi, and while they were eating the rest of it, I went and filled the soaking tub with hot water and a ginger bubble bath. I told them to get their swimsuits on and follow me. I had the fruit and champagne in the bathroom by the tub, and I told them both to get into the tub. I placed a slice of mango and strawberries in their glasses and poured champagne over it. I handed them each a glass, and I got in and sat in between them. I raised my glass of sparkling water and toasted the liberation of Jody from a life of abuse and the beginning of life with just the three of us. I told Jody we were with her forever, we will always protect her, we will always take care of her, and we will never hurt her. I told her that I knew about the encounter she had with Vanessa, and it didn't bother me at all. She turned bright red and asked if I was sure. She wasn't trying to cause issues between us. I told her not to worry. We're all in this together now.

I started to say unless, and Jody stopped me and said, "There is no unless. You'll never have to worry about me, especially after what you just saved me from."

We all toasted each other and laid back in the tub to relax. I told them both that we needed to start planning the next day. They agreed that we needed to do that, but more importantly, we needed to relax for just a bit longer.

We sat relaxing for quite a while until the tub started to cool. We pulled the plug and got out. We needed to rinse off, so we turned the shower on and got in. Vanessa took her top off and started to wash her hair and soap her body. Jody asked if we cared if she did the same, and we said no. By this time, we were so tired it didn't really matter. We finished up and got out. We dried off, put on some shorts and a T-shirt, and climbed into bed. The bed was huge with lots of pillows, so we decided that this is where we would all sleep. I had no problem with it, and neither did they. I slept in the middle with each of them lying on their side under my arm. That's how Vanessa and I usually fall asleep, but we didn't want her to have her back to Jody, so we did it this way. Besides, we thought Jody could use a little attention and comfort after the day she had. They both reached up, gave each other a kiss, gave me a kiss, and fell asleep holding hands. When Vanessa felt like Jody had fallen asleep, she lifted up her shirt and pressed her warm body up against mine. She wanted to feel the closeness between the two of us. We both fell asleep, feeling like we had taken care of a huge problem that posed a great risk to us. We had asked Jody if at any point does she believe that he might have said anything to anyone about us or even what they were hired to do. She said that they were totally off the grid. They had communicated with no one and that she checked his phone and emails regularly to see if anything was there. She wasn't as tech-savvy as Vanessa, but she did have some skills. Brian had wanted to be off the grid so badly that they were completely disconnected. We felt safe.

I woke up early and decided to go get us some pastries and coffee. When I got back to the room, they were both still asleep, holding on to each other tight. I sat down at the table, stared at them—no, not in a creepy way—and asked myself if this was a good idea or if this could turn into trouble. Vanessa and I were growing closer and closer to Jody, but my cynical, paranoid self always doubted. There was only one person I didn't doubt, and that was Vanessa. I didn't care what they did from a physical standpoint, but that also draws people closer to each other, and the one thing I couldn't have was that emotional relationship coming between us. I also don't know how Vanessa would feel if it ever came down to having to deal with Jody if we needed to. I'm far from being a heartless human being, but I'm all about protecting what I've got. I started this journey on my own, and keeping it to just me, I had nothing to worry about. Now I've brought more people in, and I've already had to deal with one issue, and even though it was something that was unrelated if he hadn't decided to pull himself off the grid, who knows what could've leaked out. I had to watch all this really closely. I wouldn't lie to Vanessa about my thoughts. I will always tell her the truth.

The smell of the coffee and pastries started to slowly wake them up. They both opened their eyes and realized that they were holding onto each other and I wasn't there in bed with them. They said good morning, gave each other a huge hug and a kiss that lasted just about a second too long. They turned around and saw me sitting there, and they looked somewhat surprised and embarrassed.

My first question was, "Why did you look so embarrassed?"

They told me they didn't know I was watching them. I told them that I wasn't watching. I was just sitting there.

Jody said, "We aren't embarrassed. We just don't want to upset you with what's happening. We didn't plan it this way. We just grew closer to each other just like we have with you.

"Well, like Jody has with you. Whatever happens between the three of us will just happen, organically, and it will never be forced. The three of us have formed an unbreakable bond that will not go away, ever."

My second question was, "Do I have anything to worry about with this new budding relationship?"

They told me no, I would never have to worry. Our bond is strong and only growing stronger. Vanessa told me that she and I are loyal to each other, and bringing Jody into this doesn't change, that it only makes it stronger. We need people. We need people watching our backs for all of us.

Then they both had a question for me, something that I didn't expect. They both had a healthy fear of me and what I do. Is there ever going to be a time that they have to worry about that especially because of what has started to develop between the two of them? I had them both sit at the end of the bed, and I sat in a chair in front of them.

I looked at Vanessa and said, "I am a bit shocked that this particular question is coming out of you. We've been together for quite a bit of time, and we've been through a lot. I took care of two of the people that had done the most damage to you ever in your life. You may have gotten away from them, but they were still there, still doing it to others. They're not anymore because of me. I didn't have to bring you into any of this, but I felt for you, and I took care of you." I turned to Jody and said, "I'm shocked about you asking that question especially after what we just did. You may have been the one that discovered what he had been doing to you, but what would you have done? Would you have taken care of him who would have protected you? You might have left him, but he would still be out there taunting you and telling people all that he had done to you. How would that have turned out for you? I'll bet that it wouldn't have turned out nearly as good for you as it is now, where are you, staying at a resort in Lanai. How could you seriously ask me if I would hurt you after all I've done to protect you and take care of both of you?"

Tears started to stream down both of their faces. They didn't know what to say. They knew that what they had just done was wrong, and they felt like shit for doing it. They started to apologize to me, and I stood up, looked at them both, and said that I needed to go for a walk on the beach. I would be back later on, and we can talk about whether we want to continue with all this. That got Vanessa seriously crying. She started begging me to stay.

I told her, "Please, I just needed some time. I will be back, and we can talk."

I grabbed the room key and walked out. I got down to the beach and started to walk, and as I did, I couldn't help but wonder about the way I think sometimes. There's a part of me that sees what just happened, and I think that that was a master class in manipulation—seriously good class. I was always told that Jews invented guilt, and Catholics perfected it. I'm a Catholic, so throwing out the guilt the way I did was a great job; however, there were a lot more feelings involved. My feelings for Vanessa and my growing feelings for Jody—that's something that I need to be aware of so that I don't make any mistakes. Thing is, I do trust them, with everything, that whole questioning of whether I would hurt them just really bothered me, especially from Vanessa. That's what gets me thinking about this whole situation, and that's why I asked the question. Someone put it in her head, and there's only one that could've done that. Maybe it was because of what's started between them, I don't know, but I need to move on, pay attention, but move on.

On the way up, I grabbed a cup of coffee for me and a couple of mai tais for them. I got back to the room, and they had both cleaned the place up, and they were waiting for me. Their eyes were red from all the crying they had been doing. They were actually still crying although not as much. I asked them to sit down, and I gave them their drinks. It's time to put this all behind us.

"I won't ever really understand how this all came about, how you could even think much less ask if I would ever do anything to hurt you, either of you."

They both tried to speak, and I stopped them.

I told them, "Going forward, this can't happen anymore. We have each other, and we're in this together."

Whatever they chose to do with each other is entirely up to them. I'm sure that it's going to change the dynamics of Vanessa and my relationship, but I'll deal with it. The next question was, are we still going to go through with what we're doing, or are they done with it. Because if we continue, the same rules apply. I need total cooperation with everything that we do.

"Because your dynamic has changed, it doesn't mean that either one of you takes control. I was doing this by myself and making sure that there were no issues, and I'll continue to do so."

They both told me they didn't want control, that they would continue to take my lead no matter what. I told them that was good.

"I already planned the next one, and we would go after it tomorrow night. Just as a reminder, the people we're going after are again people that hurt you, Jody. Just keep that in mind."

I got in the shower and started to clean up, and the door opened. It was Vanessa. She gave me a hug, and she told me how much she loved me. She was sorry for what was said and that they were paranoid because of the way I was staring at them when they woke up. She told me that they had never even done anything. They were just getting closer, that's all. I told her that I believed her and that I just wanted to move forward. We made love to each other in the shower. I swear Jody was watching.

CHAPTER 14

Back to the Original Plan

Aaron

Our next job was going to be the people that started this whole mess. We got up and checked out of the resort. We got back to the boat, and I started to lay out the plan. Our best-laid plans are those that have the element of surprise—when we hit them out of nowhere and when they never see it coming.

"I want for both of you to show up at their door tonight. They won't know what to say. They'll be shocked. Here's where we have the advantage. We know that they killed her parents, and because her dad was dealing with sketchy people, we could make this as messy as we want, and they would just blame it on those people. The one thing we couldn't do was leave any traces of us behind."

Vanessa looked at Jody and told her, "Remember. it's all about taking back the control that someone used to have on you, and you know how we will do that?"

Vanessa told her that they would wear some of their sexiest out-fits—that is always a distraction to both men and women and the two of them together. People won't be able to resist them. Aaron told them that he didn't want them to spend a lot of time in there especially if they were being watched by anyone. Aaron told them he would case the place today to make sure no one good or bad was there watching. Aaron told Vanessa that he would be taking Jody with him to case the place this afternoon. Vanessa asked him why. Did he think something was going to happen between them?

I looked at her and said that unless she told Jody everything we did *before* we did this, meaning the money end of it, she wouldn't be able to take care of her end if Jody was hanging around her all day, and rarely does Jody leave her alone. Vanessa told me that she hasn't told Jody anything about the other part, and she never would. He'll never have to worry about that. I told Jody that she needed to get ready to go. They would be taking the speedboat to shore. While we were gone, Vanessa needed to take care of business, including killing all security cameras and systems at the house. If we had high-tech security, they most certainly would. I gave Vanessa a hug and a kiss, and as I was leaving, Jody wanted to do the same, but I rushed her out. I thought that even Vanessa looked a bit put off by what she was trying to do, like it was getting to be a bit much.

While we were driving to shore, Vanessa started texting me, telling me that she was getting worried about how close Jody was getting to her. Jody was getting possessive to a certain degree, always wanting to be by her side, and it was becoming a little much. Vanessa's fear was that if she told Jody to back off, she had no idea what she might do. After all the time together, she didn't know how stable Jody was. Aaron asked Vanessa how she wanted to handle it. She knows that I would do whatever needed to be done. Vanessa wanted some time to think about it. Jody and I docked the boat and headed toward one of the resorts. They usually have rental car places where they could get a car. I had decided that because of Vanessa's concerns, he would have Jody go in and get the car.

Jody didn't even question it when I told her to do it. I told Jody I wanted to drive, but I would need her to sit lower in the seat in case they were there and they recognized her. We drove up to the neighborhood, found the house, and sat on it. Jody asked me if I had done this before. I told her that, in fact, I had. I told her that it can get boring, but we can really get good information on the people that we're watching. Jody started telling me about how close she was getting to Vanessa, that she felt like she was falling in love with her. She was having feelings she had never felt before. Jody asked me how I felt about what I had just told him. I said that I felt exactly how I told them I felt before—just make sure it doesn't interfere with what

97

they're doing. In my head, I was breaking her neck. Not because I was jealous, but because I knew this was going to happen. I thought this was going to get out of hand, and it has. After sitting there for some time, Jody had fallen asleep. I texted Vanessa and told her about the conversation I had just had with Jody. Vanessa was pissed because she didn't feel the same way, and she had told her that. She swore to me that nothing had changed between her and I and that Jody has gotten out of hand and we needed to deal with it before it gets worse. I told her not to worry, that he would take care it. Just when I tell you to back away, make sure you do it. Vanessa told him she understood. She was done with this.

After a few hours, I woke Jody up and told her it was time to go. I had looked all over the place, and there was no one watching them. We made it back to the boat, and I let Vanessa know that I saw absolutely nothing that would indicate they were being watched by sketchy people or law enforcement. I also looked around to make sure there was nobody staking out the property in a van, something law enforcement usually does. I told them both it was time to get ready, that I would be packing the boat, and they would be leaving in an hour and a half. I looked at Jody and told her again that she must listen to everything Vanessa tells her to do. Jody said that she would without question. Vanessa and Jody went below deck to get ready. Vanessa told Jody that whatever she was wearing, she won't be wearing any bra or underwear, something short, and something that can easily be unzipped or buttoned down low.

*****

Vanessa

As I was putting my skirt on, Jody came up behind me, reached around, and grabbed my breasts. She softly squeezed them, ran her hands down my belly, grabbed me by the waist, and turned me around. The first thing that I thought about doing was pushing her away and putting a stop to all this right here and right now. However, two things came to mind: one, this was a huge job, the amount of money is huge, bigger than any other one we've done. In fact, it was at least twenty times more than the other ones combined. Two, Aaron told me that he would handle it, he had a plan, and that I needed to trust him. Aaron has always taken care of me, and he always will. He's shown me that over and over again. She can't blow this up. She needs to play along with whatever is going on.

I looked at Jody and asked her what was on her mind. Jody told me that she was in love with me and that she wanted to be with me forever. After this was done, she wanted me to think about running away with her, away from Aaron, away from all the houses, and away from anything that had to do with this whole life. I needed her calm and, on their side, so I grabbed Jody's head, pulled her forward, and gave her the kiss she had been waiting for. I told Jody to finish getting ready and I was going to talk to Aaron about some final details. When I got up top, the first thing I did was tell Aaron what had just happened. Aaron told me to not worry. He was going to take care of it. Aaron gave me an earbud and told me to not tell Jody. It was too small for anyone to see, and he could tell me what he needed me to do. Aaron told me it was time to push the button for the money and to eliminate the security system.

*****

Aaron

Jody came up top, and we all headed to the shore. We drove up to the house, and I dropped them off a couple of houses down. Jody asked me where I was going to be. I told her that I would be there when it was time to not worry, to just ask Vanessa, I'm always there at the right time. Vanessa nodded and said that I always was.

*****

Vanessa

Jody and I started walking toward the house. I told her to follow my lead. As soon as they opened the door, she needed to stay behind me and keep her hoodie down so it would be hard to see her face. We needed it to be a surprise. I wanted it to be a total coincidence that Jody was there and that there were no hard feelings between them.

*****

Aaron

I found a place up on a hill behind the house to set up. This one was going to be less personal for us, but it would look like a professional did it. It would look like the sketchy people did it. I fitted Brian's sniper rifle with a silencer. I was a pretty good shot, so I wasn't worried about hitting what I was aiming at; and with the silencer, it would definitely keep it quiet. I did a sound check with Vanessa. I asked her to cough if she could hear me. She let out a small cough. It was time. Vanessa and Jody had arrived at the door; it was time for the game to start. Vanessa rang the doorbell, and John answered the door. He didn't look that imposing; in fact, he looked like he had let himself go since leaving the military. You could hear some kind of game being played in the background, loud enough so that it was hard to hear Susan when she was asking who was at the door.

*****

Vanessa

After John looked me up and down, like I was a side of beef and he was hungry, he asked me what he could do for me, if I needed any help. I told him that our car had broken down, our phones were dead, and we needed to call a tow truck. We'd been partying all day, and we needed to get back to our hotel. He invited us in. I introduced myself, and as he went to introduce himself to Jody, he stepped back; and with a shocked look on his face, he asked her what she was doing there. I looked at Jody and looked at John and asked if they knew each other. Jody immediately picked up on what I was doing and quickly spoke up. Jody acted so surprised to see him. She walked up to him and gave him a huge hug and a kiss and asked him how he was doing. Jody told me that John was her commanding officer in boot camp and that she really loved being there, that he taught her an awful lot, and she wouldn't have made it without him. Susan heard all that was going on, and she came walking out. Jody screamed, "Susan!" and ran up to her and gave her a huge hug and a kiss too.

Jody said that she didn't know that they were together, but it was great to see them both.

Both John and Susan were really confused, so they had to ask her, "Why aren't you more upset with us for what happened in boot camp?"

Jody told them that she knew she was a royal pain in the ass and that she probably deserved what she got. It was all water under the bridge to her, and she moved on from it. A huge look of relief came over their faces, and with that, they asked if we wanted to have a drink before we called for a tow truck and that they could give us a ride where ever we wanted to go. I told them we'd love to have a drink, and we all went into the living room.

*****

Aaron

The living room was in the back of the house, facing the mountain. I had found a spot on a hill that overlooks that living room area. There were no houses around. It was very private, so there was no chance of anyone seeing me or seeing them in the house. I told Vanessa where I was going to need them to be. I said that I had heard the entire conversation and that Jody had done really well.

"Are you sure that you want her to proceed with taking care of her?"

I told her to cough for yes and sneeze for no. Vanessa coughed, then sneezed, and then coughed one more time. I asked her again to just do it once, which one, knowing that there would be no turning back this time. She coughed once.

*****

Vanessa

John asked me if I was okay. I said I was. My throat was just a bit dry, and I really needed that drink. I said that I would pour some wine and they could all sit down and catch up with one another. When I went back behind the bar, I found a very old bottle of single malt scotch, and I asked John since this was a special occasion, maybe we could drink that instead. John and Susan thought it was a great idea. I decided that instead of injecting them, that she would just put it in the drink, even into Jody's. I was far enough away that I could tell Aaron about the plan without anyone hearing. Aaron agreed with the change in plan. I had on a very short skirt and a button-down white shirt, no bra or underwear. I took off my hoodie, unbuttoned my shirt very low, and pulled my skirt up farther. I grabbed the glasses of wine and went into the living room to serve them. I thought to myself, *It's always funny how people react when they see me dressed like this.* My nipples were hard, and you could see them clearly outlined in the white shirt. I thought all of them were going to have a heart attack when they looked at me. I could see out of the corner of my eye that I had distracted them long enough for Jody to stand up and take off her hoodie. Jody was wearing a dress that zipped all the way from the top to the bottom. When she was unzipping her hoodie, she grabbed the zipper to the dress and zipped it down to almost below her breasts. I sat down on the love seat next to Jody, and John and Susan sat down on the one in front of us. The ones that they were sitting faced Jody and me, but they also faced the back window that Aaron was looking directly into. We made sure that John and Susan both could see all they needed to—enough to drive them crazy and enough to get what I needed out of them. Before the drugs started to take effect, I got started.

I put one of my legs over Jody's leg. When I did, it pushed my skirt more up my legs, revealing even more of what John and Susan wanted to see. I looked at them all and said, "Can we discuss the elephant in the room?"

John asked me what I was talking about. I, at this point, was hoping that Jody would follow my lead. She had so far. I asked if anyone could tell me what really happened in boot camp?

"I know that you said you were being a pain in the ass, Jody, but what really happened?"

Jody did catch on and started to follow my lead. Jody said she was always wanting to be right all the time, always trying to be the best, and she was always trying to show everyone up—male or female—it didn't matter. Jody said that Susan was always trying to be her friend since they were the only two females, and she just kept pushing her away, and not only was she harsher on her, but she probably hurt her the most. Aaron said to me that what she just said sounded like it could be 100 percent fact. It was said too convincingly, and could she have the two of them and Brian fooled into believing that she was the victim? I coughed yes.

Aaron said, "Well then, this just became way easier to do, didn't it?"

I coughed yes.

I asked, "What did they do to teach you a lesson?"

Jody went over the entire situation that happened in the shower, and when she came to the end of the story, she said that she actually enjoyed it. Jody said that, at the moment, she felt violated, but when she left and she was shaking their hands, she felt like she actually enjoyed it, that it really turned her on. Again, Aaron in Vanessa's ear, "Seriously?" Aaron said, "She's telling the truth. She did enjoy it, and she set this whole thing up, with us anyway, to get rid of Brian and to take you away from me, and who knows if maybe one day I wasn't going to wake up."

I didn't need to cough yes. Aaron could see by my body movements that I was not only pissed off but that I was ready to end this.

I said, "So then you were basically interested in both of them, correct? Like if you had a chance, would you do something about it now?"

Jody looked at me with a strange look, but she was going to follow my lead.

Jody said, "Well, it would be something like this."

Jody got up. She stumbled for a second. She said the wine must be getting to her. She grabbed Susan by the hand, stood her up, and had her stand behind John. Jody stood in front of John, grabbed his hand, put it on her zipper, and unzipped her dress all the way down. John and Susan could see that she had nothing on underneath. Jody moved John to the middle of the love seat, pulled her dress back, and straddled his lap. She grabbed his hands and put them on her breasts and told him to squeeze them as hard as she could. Jody turned around and looked at me. She asked me what I thought so far. Wanting to keep playing the part, I reached one hand up under my skirt, and I put the other hand in my shirt and started to slowly play with myself. Jody told Susan to take her clothes off and straddle John behind her. The three of them started saying that they were feeling a bit drunk. They asked me if we wanted to take this into the bedroom. Vanessa agreed.

"We could take it in there and finish what we started."

Aaron asked how much I gave them and were the drugs working better than she thought they would. I, not being able to answer, shrugged my shoulders like I didn't know. Aaron told me to not worry. He would be down quickly. I just needed to get them in the bedroom. I started helping all of them into the bedroom, and what was truly amazing, as much as we've spoken to Jody about this, she had no clue. Maybe the fact that it was scotch, mixing it with the drugs, it intensified them; and the fact that she was acting drunk as well didn't hurt. When they got into the bedroom, they all started taking off their clothes and getting in bed. Jody stopped, turned around, looked at me, and said it was my turn, that she had been waiting for this for a very long time. I told her to get in bed with the rest of them, that I would do a striptease for them and then join them. I was thinking, *God, I hope they pass out soon.* Aaron told me that he was right outside the back door, to let him know when it was time to come in.

They were all lying there, hanging onto each other. They put Jody in the middle of them, and they were rubbing her body while Jody was rubbing theirs. There was a big wooden chest at the end of their bed, so I pulled it back away from the bed a bit, hopped on top of it, and I asked John to play some music for me. As the music played, I slowly started to undo my top. It was tucked into my skirt, so I pulled it out and finished unbuttoning it. I could hear moaning coming from the bed. I didn't know if it was because of my striptease or because they were all so engrossed in stroking each other. I think it was a bit of both. My skirt had a zipper on the side, so I slowly unzipped that, and I let it fall off, taking my legs out of it as I slowly stepped off the table. As I walked toward the end of the bed, I got on my knees and finished taking my shirt off, completely nude. I started crawling toward them, and they were all passed out. Still breathing but passed out. It was about fucking time. I put my clothes on and went to the back door to let Aaron in and to close the shutters. Aaron told me while he was waiting outside, he started thinking, he thinks that there might be a problem with all this.

I told him to tell me what he thinks the problem might be. Aaron told me that the big problem was that my DNA is all over this place. You've been in here both clothed and nude.

"Your fingerprints are everywhere because you couldn't really wear gloves in here. There's just a lot."

I started getting tears in my eyes, but Aaron looked at me and said, "Stop, I told you that I was always going to protect you, and I will. Don't worry."

Aaron said, "If we were to shoot them all in the head to make it look like a hit job, the cops, maybe even the FBI, would definitely go through this place with a fine-tooth comb. However, all they had to do was inject more of the same drugs into them and make it look like they were in the middle of an orgy and they overdosed. We wouldn't have to be as thorough with the cleaning. Meaning, that I don't think they will turn the place upside down. We will leave the syringes and the vials of the drugs behind. We'll spill a bit of scotch on the bed, bring in the glasses, and we will be all set."

I thought it was a great idea, but I said that we better get the drugs in the arms before they wake up.

Aaron said, "I know that, I've asked you this already, but I'm going to ask you one more time. Are we done with Jody?"

I looked at him and said, "Do you really have to ask after all that?"

Aaron said no, but he just wanted to make sure. They were all still asleep. They both put gloves on and injected more drugs into all three of them. Nothing painful, they just wouldn't wake up. We went throughout the house and cleaned and wiped everything down. I made sure to wipe all the glasses—everything I could think of. I even wiped the toilet seat although I never went to the bathroom. We picked everything up that we couldn't leave behind and put it all in our bag. We both went to check on them. First John, gone; then Susan, gone; and lastly, they checked on Jody. As much as she had done and what she was trying to do, we didn't feel bad for what we had just done. She was gone too. They shut all the lights off, inside and out, and left through the back door. We dropped the car off on a side street and made our way back to the dock.

Once there, we made our way back to the boat. It had been an exhausting time on the island of Maui with things happening that we had never expected. Once on board, I finished taking every penny that they had. After that, I reactivated all the security systems so no one would think anyone else had been there. One of the last things I did was take everything from Jody. I had all her info, so it was easy. I made sure to do another deep dive on her to see if I missed anything. I didn't, and just like Brian, she had wiped herself from the grid so it would take a lot for them to find out who she was. If they did find out who she was, she would be tied to them through the military, nothing connecting to us. The amount of money that they just pulled was unreal. We could seriously stop if we wanted to, at least take a break for a bit. We decided to stay out on the boat and sleep. We were alone again; it had been a while, and we both asked each other how we felt about it. We both felt the same way. We loved being alone, and we were okay with it for now. Our love grows stronger, and it will continue to do so. We're the only ones we can trust. We took a shower, dried off, and climbed into bed. We fell asleep, knowing that we did the right thing.

We woke up feeling really refreshed the next morning. We got dressed, and Aaron went topside to check on things. It was all so peaceful. I brought some coffee up, gave it to Aaron, and said, "Let's go home."

*****

Aaron

I started heading back to Oahu while Vanessa packed up below. We needed one of these for ourselves just like the plane. We don't need to have to worry about always making sure things are constantly cleaned up. If we owned them, we would still worry just not as much. We caught the jet back to Kauai and went home. It was so nice to be back home again. Our next step was eliminating all signs of them from both of our houses, and we needed to start with this one. I looked at Vanessa and said, "Let's take a break and get away. We wanted to get a house in Utah, so let's take some time and go and find one." I said, "Instead of flying into Tucson, we could take the jet and go straight to Park City and start looking for another place. Let's invest in another house and maybe find some investments there. Try to grow some of this legitimately."

Vanessa agreed that it was a great idea.

"Let's get packed, and we can leave in the morning."

The next morning, we got up and started another journey. It will be nice for the two of us to get away. It's been too long, and we've been through too much. It was a long flight, so we decided to relax and try to sleep. We would be there soon enough.

CHAPTER 15

Off to Park City

Aaron

We flew into Salt Lake City, rented a car, and drove to the Montage Deer Valley Resort. It is a gorgeous resort that has an Alpine ski lodge feel to it. Beautiful rooms, huge spa, we could definitely get lost for a few days here, and we just might, depending on how long it takes to find a house. I could tell that Vanessa loved it here by the way her eyes lit up every time she turned her head. We got to the room, and we started looking at properties. This was our third and possibly final destination. With us, you never know though. We found a house on more than forty-seven acres. The best thing was this was a bank-owned property. Apparently, it had been repossessed from the previous owner, and the bank was wanting to move it quickly. Vanessa decided to go and check out the town while I went to the bank to talk about the property. It was a local bank, not one of the big ones, which meant it would be easier to deal with. There would be no one from a big corporation looking into us. I asked to speak with the person in charge of the property, and they asked me to sit down and wait and she would be right out. I heard what I thought was screaming coming from an office in the back. It was a man's voice and he didn't sound happy; in fact, he sounded like a dick. I heard a door slam shut and from across the room walking toward me was one of the most stunningly beautiful women I'd ever seen. She had blond hair, blue eyes, and she was wearing a short black leather skirt, a pink button-up shirt with a black bra that was buttoned down just enough so that you could get a glimpse of her beautiful cleavage, black silk stockings, and black high heeled ankle boots. She stopped right in front of me and introduced herself. Her name was Lizzy Cotta, and she would be the one to help me. She looked upset. I asked her if she was okay because she had red eyes, and she looked like she had been crying. She apologized for the way she looked. I told her not to worry. Everything was fine.

She asked if I wanted to take a tour of the property. I told her that yes, I would, but I needed to call Vanessa to meet me out there. I called Vanessa, and she said she was in the middle of sightseeing. She told me to go ahead and I could let her know what I thought. I asked if she was sure. It's a pretty large purchase. She said, "Don't worry." It's okay. She trusted me. Lizzy asked if she could drive us out there since she knew where it was. It would be easier that way. I agreed, and we got in her car, a new Tesla, and started our drive. It was a beautiful drive that took about forty-five minutes. We drove up to the house, and it was just amazing. The house was just amazing. She showed me the entire property starting on the outside, and we worked our way into the house.

It's a single-level home with a master suite and exercise room, an office, a recreation room, and two guest rooms with en suite baths. There is a gourmet chef's kitchen, which I love, and a second office overlooks the living areas. The family recreation room boasts a custom-designed 440-bottle wine chiller, kitchenette/wet bar, multiple entertainment screens, and opens to the covered patio. The south-facing covered patio is accessed by wall-to-wall twelve-foot glass doors. Upstairs, there's a fully equipped caretaker's apartment with a private entrance and garage door. Above, the guest suite has three bedrooms, two baths, sports/golf simulator, and views. The list goes on and on, and it was just as incredible as the rest of our homes but just in a different way.

It was funny or interesting depending on how you think about it. She was really excited about the exercise room. I asked her why it interested her so much. She said because she really wanted to open her own place someday and that she already trained people now on the side. I asked her what was stopping her from opening her own place. It was the one thing that always stopped people—money. We brought in our coffee and sat at the counter in the kitchen. I told her that I'm ready to make a cash offer on the property. Her beautiful blues eyes got huge. It's obviously going to be below asking, she said obviously. I asked her if she got any kind of a bonus for selling it. She told me under any other circumstances, meaning any other boss, she would get a sizable one; but he already said if it sold, he's taking it all. He said he would consider giving her a small percentage if she were to do some things for him. I think we all know what that means. She said the reason she dresses the way she does is because he told her that she needed to dress a little more, professionally. She just couldn't ever tell which profession he was talking about. It's not like she's some sort of conservative prude. She didn't mind dressing like that, but sometimes she felt like it was being forced on her, and she didn't like it. She stopped midsentence and said that she couldn't believe that she was telling me all this. It just all came spilling out. I told her not to worry. I didn't mind listening.

I told Lizzy that I had a proposition for her, and no, not like the ones that her boss has.

"You can see how huge this place is. There are many areas that can be turned into a gym for you to bring clients to and train them."

She said that it was a great offer and she appreciated it, but she didn't have the money for renovating anything. I told Lizzy that I would pay for the renovations on whatever is needed. She could completely design it however she wanted. The way in which she could pay it back was to live on the property and take care of it while we're not here.

"We won't be here year-round, and I will need someone to look after things."

I will make sure that there are security measures in place so she wouldn't have to worry. I explained to Lizzy the type of security that we had in place at our other properties, and she was quite impressed, not just with the security but with the properties as well. She told me that she had two dogs, both Saint Bernards, and that her sister and two nieces came to visit her a lot. They didn't live far away, so she saw them a lot and would all that be okay. There's a three-bedroom, two-bathroom guest suite that she can live in. There will be more than enough room for everyone, and the dogs would have a lot of space to roam. I had an idea where she could build out her studio. I told her that there is the five-stall barn, it had rubber paver flooring and a separate tack room with laundry and a bath. We weren't planning on getting horses here. We could enclose the barn and build up the inside walls so that it would be able to support equipment. We could expand the tack room to give it men's and women's locker rooms with showers and saunas if she wanted to add them. Laundry could stay in place because she'll definitely need that. One thing I could never understand is why gyms never had massage services on hand as well. You're beating someone's body up, so why not have that available? Aaron stopped, looked at Lizzy, and apologized.

"I'm sorry. I was just rambling on. You're the professional. You'll know what you need."

Again, those blue eyes were opened wide, but this time, tears were coming out of them. I asked her if I said or did something wrong. Lizzy looked at me and said that all this is just blowing her away, that usually when offers like this are made to her, there are a lot of strings attached, and they were usually sexual in nature. I told her that is not my intention here. I'm not asking her for anything in return. The only thing I'm asking for is exactly what I said—that's it.

I stopped and said, "Well, there is one thing."

Lizzy looked at me and said she knew it was too good to be true. Tears started welling up in her again.

I said, "Wait, I was talking about getting some training whenever I'm in town. Sorry."

Lizzy started laughing and crying so hard she couldn't stop. I asked her if she was okay, and she said yes, she was, and she apologized.

I said, "My god, it seems like you've gone through an awful lot so far in your life. You must have to be this sensitive to things."

She said, "There's not enough time to tell you."

I told her, "I have nothing to do. Tell me whatever you want."

Lizzy told me that all her life, she's never been taken seriously because of how she looks. "I'm not trying to sound like a stuck-up diva, but that's just the way it's always been. Men have always tried to take advantage of me. They have always hit on me, groped me, and some, some have even forced me to do things that I didn't want to do." Lizzy told me, "On more than one occasion, my boss has accidentally 'brushed' up against me. It's funny that when he did that, his hands were open with his palms facing me, touching my ass, breasts. It didn't matter. He would try anything. Then he decided to take it up a notch and told me I needed to start dressing more professionally. Meaning shorter skirts, buttoned-up shirts, barely buttoned, basically what I'm wearing right now. The worst it had gotten was the time he brought in clothes and lingerie for me to try on. He told me I needed to work late one night. He called me in his office to talk, shut the door, and locked it. He told me that he wanted me to try everything on, in front of him, and that if I didn't do it, he would terminate my employment. He would tell them that I came onto him and who would they really believe, him or someone that had no standing in the company."

I told her I was really sorry that she had to go through all that, but all that was about to end. Lizzy said she appreciated all it is that I'm doing for her but that he would still be running around doing the same shit to someone else if she leaves. I told her to let me worry about that part. I asked Lizzy that if her boss was gone, would she be put in charge, and if she was, could she handle running the bank and doing the gym. I said the reason I was asking was because, in my business, I need a good bank to hold and invest my money for me. Lizzy asked me if I was talking about laundering money.

I said, "No, we're not talking drug money here."

I told her that Vanessa and I had inherited a lot of money and we were just really good at investing it. I told her that this could be really good for everyone, that I would even pay her a fee, obviously off-book, for handling the money. Lizzy told me that it was a small bank and that she could easily handle both as long as she could have a manager for the gym. I said that wouldn't be a problem. I told her that this was a very productive meeting, and Lizzy agreed. Lizzy said it was time to go back to the bank and draw the paperwork up for the house.

I told her, "Then we can get started on transforming a piece of it into your dream."

Lizzy jumped up and gave me a big hug, one she might have held for a second too long, but I could see why people loved her, at least physically. I didn't quite know her personally, but from what I saw, that was pretty great too.

We got back to the bank, and Lizzy introduced me to her boss. His name was William H. Bucksacker, and he was a short chubby piece of shit. When I shook his hand, I squeezed it so hard I thought the guy was going to cry. I told him that I wanted to spend some time talking with him, one on one, that I was impressed with the way he runs everything here, including his dress code for Lizzy, and that he might have an opportunity for him elsewhere. He was so interested he immediately set up a time to talk. I told William that I was going to be making a cash offer on the house and I expected Lizzy to get the commission for it; in fact, I said I would take it out of the cash offer and give it straight to her.

I asked him, "What's the percentage here. Is it 3 percent?"

William took a deep breath, and Lizzy's eyes got wide. "That would be $600K, right?"

William said, "Yes, that would be correct."

I asked him if he had a problem with that, and William said, "Not at all."

I said, "Good, I knew I liked you, and I have big plans for you."

We left William's office and went back to Lizzy's. She shut the door, put her face into my chest, and let out the quietest scream he had ever heard. She picked her head up, hugged me, and thanked me for what I just did. I told her that it was just going to get better for her going forward. Lizzy told me that she at least had the money now to build out the gym if he would still let her do it on the property.

I told her, "No, that money is for all the crap you've had to deal with all the years you've been here. Take that money and do something with it for you. I will continue to do what I said and build it out for you. This is an investment for me, and who knows, maybe this could grow into more."

This had turned out to be an unreal day for Lizzy. She was still waiting for the other shoe to drop, for me to tell her this wasn't all true, but that never happened. I signed the offer letter and told her to draw up the paperwork. She could deliver the final paperwork to the resort where Vanessa and I were staying so we could both sign it. We shook hands, and I headed back to the resort.

I got back to the room, and Vanessa was relaxing in a chair, drinking some coffee, just looking out the window. She looked at me and told me that she hadn't felt this relaxed in a long time. I explained to her in detail everything that just happened, what the plan was, and that Lizzy would be there soon with the paperwork for us to sign. Vanessa thought that it was a great opportunity to not only help someone out but to invest in something that has the potential to grow a lot, legitimize more of the money. Vanessa also thought it was a good idea to have a small local bank to hold and invest our money, and I don't mind paying fees under the table, but it sounds like we need to do something with the asshole—that's her boss. Vanessa asked me what I had in mind when I talked to him and told him that I had something for him. I told her that I really hadn't gotten that far yet. I just wanted to work on removing him from Lizzy's life.

Vanessa looked at me and said, "I thought we were taking a break from all that?"

I told her, "I meant that when I said it, but this just kind of fell in my lap. I think you would've felt the same way if you were there."

Vanessa agreed with me. She told me that when she gets here, they can talk and she can get a feel for how she is. She did like the idea of turning part of the property into a gym. I really had no desire to have more animals, horses, or dogs to take care of. It's been so long since we've been back to Tucson, and it's not really fair to the dogs who have been in a doggie hotel since we've been gone although I'm sure they're not hurting for anything.

We decided to order some hors d'oeuvres and some wine for our meeting. Everything got there right before Lizzy did, so everything was all set to go. I let Lizzy in and introduced her to Vanessa. She wasn't dressed as revealing as she was, and that was a good thing.

Vanessa, like me, doesn't get jealous, but I still didn't want her to think that there was anything else swaying my judgment. I poured a glass of wine for the ladies, and they sat down at the table to go over the paperwork. Lizzy told us that since Vanessa needed to sign the papers as well, she had to go over everything with her that she and I went over, including the fee paid to her. It's the law. I told her that was fine. I told her everything when I got to the room. Vanessa was impressed with Lizzy's attention to detail, which made her feel confident about going into business with her. When all the papers were signed, Vanessa made a money transfer to the bank for the sale price minus Lizzy's 3 percent. Vanessa asked Lizzy where she wanted her money transferred. Lizzy gave her an account number, and Vanessa prepared the transfer. Before she did it, she looked at Lizzy and asked her if she wanted the pleasure of hitting send, and Lizzy jumped at the chance. Now that that business was all done, it was time to move on to our next order of business.

Vanessa asked Lizzy how long she thought it would take to get all the areas built out and ready for business. Lizzy had said that she has a friend in town that's an architect, and she believes that she's got some time coming up in the next month or so, and then she could help. I told Lizzy that I was not trying to be difficult, but if the person wouldn't be available for at least a month, then maybe we needed to bring someone in from Salt Lake City to do the work. Vanessa agreed with me, but she had a suggestion for Lizzy. She asked her if the friend was actively working a job or trying to get one. Lizzy said she was trying to get one, that she was putting together the proposal for the client, and she was going to make the presentation in a couple of days. I asked Lizzy if she believed that her friend could do the job that she needs for her to do. Lizzy responded that she had total faith in her ability to do the job. Vanessa told her that if she had that much faith in her, to call her and tell her that we will pay her double her normal rate but that she must dedicate herself to this project and this project only; and if this works out, we will probably have work she can do at our other properties.

We asked Lizzy if she would also consider doing some work at our other properties as well. If this gym concept worked out here, why not do the same at our other properties as well? Lizzy could not believe the day she was having; this was just really unbelievable to her. Lizzy asked them if they were being serious.

They both asked her, almost simultaneously, "Have you checked your bank account?"

Lizzy opened her laptop and looked at her account. About $800K had just been added to her account. Lizzy was shocked. She said it's supposed to be $600K—that's $200K more! Vanessa told her that she added more money because she was so impressed with her attention to detail.

"Do you believe us now?"

Lizzy was again just floored by the day. She told them both that she's beginning to believe and going forward she will have faith. Before Lizzy left the hotel room, she called her friend Roni and explained to her the situation. Roni asked if this was for real. Lizzy explained the day, including her fee, and Roni agreed to meet with them. They all decided to meet at 9:00 a.m. at the house. No need for a hotel room anymore. They were now third homeowners.

After Lizzy left, Vanesa thanked me. She thanked me for always thinking of her and always taking care of her, for always treating her like she was number one. Ever since we met and especially the last few days, I had proven over and over that I would always be there for her. Vanessa and I spent the rest of the day exploring the resort and Park City. It was all so beautiful we knew we made the right decision to be here. We went back to the room, ordered dinner, and went to bed. We had a big day tomorrow getting settled into our new home.

Vanessa was excited to get to the house. She wanted to get up and grab coffee and breakfast on the way. When we got there, Vanessa was floored. It was more amazing than she could have ever imagined. I took her on a tour of the entire property, and she loved it, maybe more than the other ones; but it's like a new toy—you always like the new toy better. Obviously, the first thing for Vanessa was furnishings. We don't need a lot, just fluffy stuff. We had seen some stores in town, and she could just get some stuff from there. The bank had left some chairs around the kitchen bar area for clients to sit and talk so we could use those when Lizzy and Roni got here. The ladies got there at exactly nine, which impressed both Vanessa and me. Being punctual was something we both loved.

We welcomed them at the door. Lizzy introduced Roni to us. She was tall, almost six feet tall, with long black hair and piercing green eyes. She was almost eye to eye with me, but Vanessa had to look up at her a bit.

We all sat down, and Vanessa said, "First things first." She handed Roni a cashier's check for $75K and told her that this was a retainer for her services. "Would this be enough to keep you working for us and only us? Obviously, when the jobs start, you would get paid on top of that, along with whatever bonuses we pay."

Like Lizzy, Roni was a bit floored. She told them that yes, that would be more than enough but could she ask some questions.

I told her, "Of course you can. Whatever you want to know."

Roni's questions were all basically the same as Lizzy's. Before I could answer, Vanessa chimed in and said, "Look, we're business people. We just bought this house with cash, and we own two more, one in Tucson and one on the island of Kauai that are just as big and just as nice. How we made our money is irrelevant. Just know that it's not drug money." (Yes, that is true—it's not.) "We have no ulterior motives here. We're just doing business, and we want to know if you all would like to get involved."

Roni apologized. She said that she wasn't trying to offend them. She just wanted to make sure that they weren't getting involved in anything that would be bad or hurt them. I said that we totally understand their hesitation and that we're not offended by the questions, but they really have nothing to worry about. Besides, we won't even be here most of the time. Lizzy will be watching over everything. Roni told them that she would love to be a part of anything that they were going to do. Vanessa told them that it was great news for everyone, but we have a different idea for Lizzy.

Roni and Lizzy looked at each other with that uh-oh look in their eyes and then looked back at Vanessa.

I stopped the conversation and said, "Look, guys, not every 'but' has something bad coming after it. Trust and believe going forward."

They both agreed they would.

Vanessa continued, "I know that I talked to Aaron about heading up the bank, but after discussing it with each other, we think that what we would like for you to do is manage funds that we give to you to invest. We would pay you a salary plus commission, and the fact that you'll be living here, rent- and mortgage-free, that will clear that monthly expense. Let's not forget that you'll be running the gym and making money from that, and once we start opening at other places, you'll be busy dealing with that as well. You're not going to have time to run a bank on top of all that, are you?"

Lizzy agreed. There would be no time for her to do all that. I told them both that they would also make sure all this is put into a contract if it made them feel better. Lizzy and Roni said that it wouldn't be necessary to do that. I started to tell them what our plan was for Roni.

"We want to have Roni go to Tucson and Hawaii and work on doing the same thing there that is being done here. Transportation for both of you will be taken care of. We have a personal jet that we've been using. All we need to do is give them a day's notice. Roni, you will, of course, be paid a salary for the jobs along with bonuses. If all this is acceptable, then let's start moving forward."

Every bit of it was more than acceptable to Lizzy and Roni. Their next question was, "When do we start?" Oh, and Lizzy had one concern or one question, what about her boss?

I said, "Don't worry about him. I will take care of him." I added, "We can start as soon as possible. Have Lizzy take you and show you the areas we were talking about." I stopped them. "One more thing. Roni, we need you to get us the best security company for an install. We know exactly what we want. When you come out to Tucson and Kauai, you can see what we have there."

Roni said she knew a great company; she could have them set something up temporarily until she can see exactly what we want.

"That would be perfect. Thank you."

After they left, Vanessa asked me again what the plan was for Lizzy's boss, especially now that I told her I would take care of it.

"Well, I'm just not feeling it right now. I'm usually getting all worked up about creating another recipe, and it's just not happening right now."

Vanessa understood where he was coming from. "Maybe we just needed to recharge and concentrate on ourselves right now, growing who we are and what we have. That's something that might help clear our heads. Let's make a list of the things that we want to get done.

1. Get this house set up the way we want it.
2. Work with Lizzy and Roni on the gym, what we're going to build out. There will be permits that will take some time.
3. Help Lizzy with the concept, name, etc.
4. Start an account and give Lizzy access to be able to invest.
5. Work with Roni on temporary security
6. Come up with a time for all of us to head to the other properties.

"That's going to be quite a bit, and it will take some time. I think we can leave workers behind to work on projects. We can also ask Lizzy if her sister can look over the property and projects while we're gone."

There was a knock at the door, and I went to go answer it. Lizzy was at the door, crying. I sat her down and poured her a glass of wine. Vanessa came over, and when she calmed down a bit, we asked her what was going on and what had happened. She went to work, and her boss called her into his office. He told her that he was really upset with the fact that she "stole" the commission from him and that he wanted it. She told him that he didn't do anything to deserve it, that she's the one that showed the property and sold the property, so she should be the one that gets the commission. Lizzy told him that she wasn't going to give it to him, that she was going to be quitting so he wasn't going to be able to take advantage of her anymore. William told her to take a look at the big screen TV on his wall. He pushed a button on his computer, and up on the screen was a video of the night he brought in the clothes for her to try on for him. There was everything on there, every single second.

Lizzy told me that there were things she didn't tell me, that she was embarrassed by. She didn't tell me that every time she changed, when she was naked, he would go over to her and grab her body.

She couldn't change into anything new unless she let him do it. He also made her touch him every single time. He made her go down on him, and then the final act, he bent her over his desk, and he had sex with her.

Vanessa said, "You mean more like raped you?"

Lizzy started crying, saying she tried to keep that out of her head, that thought.

I told her, "You can't think that way. You need to face it."

Vanessa asked her, "How did it end?"

Lizzy said he told her that unless he got the money, he was going to leak the tape. He would tell people that she forced him to buy the clothes for her and that the only way she got the commission for the sale of the property is because she did the same thing to me.

"He thinks I'm out getting a cashier's check for him. I didn't know what else to do, so I came here."

Vanessa told Lizzy to go to the bathroom and get cleaned up. Lizzy said she felt dirty after that. She felt like she needed a shower. Vanessa told her there were clean towels in there. If she needed to take one to go ahead. Lizzy told her she was just kidding.

Vanessa said, "I wasn't. If you need one, go ahead and take one."

After Lizzy got up and went to the bathroom, Vanessa turned around, looked at me, and said, "What the fuck! Can we ever get away from this shit?"

Aaron just shrugged his shoulders and said, "I guess not."

CHAPTER 16
The Gift That Keeps on Giving

Aaron

Vanessa asked me what I was going to do with her boss. I told her that I was going to need to play on the "I have something in mind for you" bullshit while not letting onto the fact that I know about what's going on.

Vanessa said, "Or we can just ruin him instead."

I asked, "How will we do that?"

She said, "Well, haven't we always used me to draw people in? Why can't I go over there? He hasn't met me. I can dress totally inappropriately and let him do his predatory bullshit. We can record him with both video and audio, then threaten to expose him with it. But turn the tables and get a huge chunk of money from him for it, then tell him he needs to leave town. On the way out of town, you can do your thing, fast and easy."

I asked her, "What will be fast and easy?"

She said, "Well, you never got to use that sniper rifle the last time. Wait for him to go around one of the mountain curves, shoot a tire out, and watch him go over the edge. Once he's gone, we can take the rest of his money. He didn't have any family, so the money would go to waste just sitting there."

I looked at her and said, "Wow, you just wrote that entire recipe yourself. I didn't think that you were the icy one."

She told me, "I've learned a lot from you. Besides, rape turns me icy."

I said I was going to go and get some things ready to go. Vanessa was going to go and check on Lizzy and get herself ready to go.

*****

Vanessa

I went into the bathroom as Lizzy was just getting out of the shower. Lizzy said she decided to take a shower. She hoped that I didn't mind.

I said, "Not at all. If I didn't want you to, I wouldn't have said anything." I was thinking to myself as Lizzy was drying off, *My god, what an incredible body she's got. It's seriously perfect from head to toe.* Lizzy had brought a pair of workout shorts and a tank top. She said she always had that with her. It was small enough to fit in her purse, and you never know when you might need it. She put them on, and I thought it just made her look even more incredible. She had a tight ass and the most perfect breasts. She would definitely be a *huge* distraction although she could also be quite motivating. She would attract a lot of clients, but the only problem was, we would have to get trainers that looked as good as she does, both male and female. That would be easy enough to do although there weren't many that look as good as Lizzy does. She explained the plan to Lizzy, minus the forced car accident and taking his money.

She couldn't believe that we would be willing to do that for her.

I told her, "If we don't do something, you will have to give him the money or run the risk of being ruined, and knowing him, even if you do give him the money, he will probably be ruining you anyway. That's the kind of guy he is. You can't trust his word." I asked Lizzy if she wanted to help me pick out something completely inappropriate to wear. "After all, you know him the best."

Lizzy told me, "No bra, no underwear, short skirt, button-up shirt with a see-through tank top underneath, like a really thin tank top. High heels, not chunky, never chunky, and always stiletto type, and if you have some frilly ankle socks, that will be perfect."

I told her I had all that. Lizzy helped me get dressed, complimenting me on how gorgeous my body was. She asked me how often did I work out.

I told her, "Thank you. I don't work out as often as I would like. Aaron and I are always traveling, so it's tough, but we both try as often as we can. We also do a lot of outdoor stuff with each other too."

I asked Lizzy how I looked. Lizzy said she would fuck me. That's how good I looked. I gave her a hug, said thank you, and told her it was time to get started. I told her, "Just stay here and work on stuff around here, work on moving in, and whatever needs to be done for the gym."

Lizzy told her there was some equipment that she wanted to look at and how would she buy it if she wanted it. I walked her into the kitchen, pulled an envelope out of the drawer, and handed it to her. It had Lizzy's name on it. She opened it, and it was a black American Express card. Lizzy couldn't believe it.

"This is mine?" she asked.

"Well, it's got your name on it, so yes, it is. You just need to file expense reports with us every month. That shouldn't be too hard considering you're a banker."

Right about then, Aaron walked in. He saw Lizzy with the card in her hand, and he asked her if she believes now.

Lizzy said, "Yes, I do. I do believe now."

I told her, "There is one for Roni as well, but please let us inform her of that."

Lizzy gave us both big hugs and thanked them again for everything. We told her it was only the beginning.

Before we walked out the door, Lizzy stopped them. She asked them if she could be involved with this; after all, she's the one that had been hurt by all of it. We both looked at her and asked her if she was positive that this was what she wanted to do. Lizzy told them that she was 100 percent sure, this guy really did a number on her, and she needed to make sure that when it all went sideways for him, he knew it was her that did it. We both agreed, but she had to follow our lead on this, with all of it. Lizzy agreed that she would do whatever we wanted.

"Well, let's go and get you dressed. We have work to do."

Lizzy had the clothes she wore over, but she needed something different, so she asked if she could borrow something from me. We were almost the same size, so that wouldn't be an issue. I had this leather jumpsuit that zipped from the front all the way down. It was so incredibly skintight, yet you wouldn't know it because it was so comfortable. I told her that it looked incredible on her. I rubbed my hands up and down to see how it felt. I stopped myself and apologized to Lizzy. I said that I didn't ask her if I could do that, and I was sorry. Lizzy told me that unwanted hands are what bothers her, but she knows that I meant no harm to her. Lizzy put on a light jacket and high heels, and we all left for the bank.

Before we got out of the car, Aaron gave me an earbud, and he had cameras in both of our purses. He told us both to set our purses down on either side of the room so we could get recorded from every angle. The feed for the cameras, audio, and video would go right to my phone I could play it back instantly for him to see. We're not getting a cashier's check. We will tell him that we need to get an account number that we can wire the money.

I looked at Lizzy and said, "Remember, follow my lead. No matter what I tell you to do or what you see, follow my lead. Do you understand?"

Lizzy said she understood, but if she's a bit slow getting it or if she's nervous to please help push her along. Aaron decided to give her an earbud and said that he would coach her along to help her. That made Lizzy and me feel better. We both got out of the car and headed toward the bank. When we walked in, we turned more than a few heads. Lizzy asked if William was in his office, and they told her yes and to go ahead.

"Go in. He was expecting you."

When we walked into his office, the look on his face was like he had just hit the jackpot. He couldn't believe what he was seeing. Lizzy introduced me and said that I was someone that was handling Lizzy's money. I told him that I would need an account number to transfer the funds too, William gave me his account number immediately. The thought of getting his hands on that money made him a happy man because he had plans for it. He had planned to take the money and just leave, go travel for a while, and just not look back. I could easily put it in and then take it out later when this was all done. So after William saw that the money was transferred, he looked at Lizzy and asked her if she still wanted to keep her job, that he would groom her to take over for him. Lizzy was about to flip out and tell him to go fuck himself when a little voice started talking to her in her ear. Aaron told her that he knew how she felt but no revenge yet. He told her to look at him in a very flirtatious way and ask him what he had in mind. Lizzy asked William what exactly would she have to do for that.

William said, "Well, why don't you go over and unbutton your friend's shirt for me? Let me see what she has on underneath."

I thought to myself, *Men are so fucking predictable. I would just get on with it, but we need for him to tell us what to do, like he's bribing us.*

Aaron told Lizzy to do exactly what he tells you to do but first ask him.

"Does this mean I can keep my job and you'll groom me to take yours?"

"Wait for him to answer yes, and if he won't, then Vanessa will handle it from there."

Lizzy asked him exactly the way Aaron told her to. William started to go back and forth, not really answering the question. I bent over the desk he was sitting at, far enough for him to see just enough cleavage, and said, "If you want to see what's under here, answer the question. Will you do what you told her if she does what you ask?"

He looked at my cleavage and then me and said, "Yes, I will. I'll even put it in writing for you."

I thought to myself, *I really doubt he would do that, but that's okay. We have it on tape. Lizzy was impressed with how I handled the situation. It was a bit empowering, extremely motivating, kind of how she motivates people to work out.*

What if no one understands? It's not motivation. It's called manipulation. We can all use different terms for it, but what it really boils down to is convincing people to do something they wouldn't necessarily do on their own.

Lizzy walked in front of the desk where I was and stood in front of me. She then started to slowly unbutton my shirt. She pulled the bottom part of the shirt that was tucked into my skirt out and unbuttoned it the rest of the way. William asked her to face me toward him, get behind me, and take my shirt off. Lizzy removed my shirt, and William was floored by what he was looking at. I looked at him and asked him if that was it.

He said, "Oh no, there's more that I want."

Aaron said to both of them, "Of course there is."

Lizzy, with some newfound confidence, said to him, "Look, I need to really know that if we do all that you tell us to, basically bribe us to do, that I will get my job back, with a raise, and I will be groomed to take your position."

William said again, "I will do all that I told you I would, including giving you a raise if you do what I tell you to do, and yes, if you want to call it bribery, then fine."

Always amazing what men will admit to when they want something. Lizzy thought it was over, but Aaron told her it wasn't.

He told her, "Just that one thing isn't enough. We need him to show us and everyone how fucked up and depraved he is. Don't worry, we will know when to stop it."

Lizzy said, "Okay, then please continue, boss. What else would you like us to do for you?"

He said he liked it when she called him boss. He said that he wanted the same thing done to her, have me take off Lizzy's coat and show him what's underneath. We stood in front of his desk again, and I grabbed the zipper to her coat. While I was zipping down Lizzy's coat, I grabbed the zipper on her outfit and zipped that down too. I stopped with the outfit zipper right at her belly button, then turned her toward her boss, and took off her coat. Her breasts were so perky and big that they just pushed up on the outfit, but it didn't let them out. I thought he was going to have a heart attack when I took the coat off. Lizzy was wondering if it was time to stop yet, and it was like Aaron was in her head.

He said to her, "I know what you're thinking, but you can't stop yet." He told her, "You know how you can get through this." She couldn't answer, but he knew that in her head, she was saying, *How?* He said that she needed to change the way she's seeing this. "Turn your attention toward Vanessa. See how beautiful she is, and think about nothing but her. The more you put into her, the more control you take over him, and it will make it just that much sweeter when you take him down."

That made Lizzy feel that much more comfortable, so she decided it was time to take his advice. Lizzy looked at him and said, "What next, boss?" Lizzy stopped for a minute and asked him, "So tell me something. With all that you're asking us to do and all that you're promising, aren't you afraid of it coming out and making you look bad?"

He said, "Who do you think people are going to believe, me or the two of you? I mean, look at the two of you. You're dressed like sluts."

This time, Aaron spoke to them both. He told them both, "Calm down, and remember, in the end, we win."

We both took deep breaths. William knew that he pissed them off, but seriously, what were we going to do about it? He had all the control. Lizzy looked at him again and asked him what he wanted them to do next. Michael sat in his chair behind his desk. He said he wanted Lizzy to stand me in front of the desk and take my skirt off but leave the socks and heels on. Lizzy unzipped the skirt and let it drop to the ground. It was obvious I didn't have underwear on. William couldn't believe it. We could both tell what he was doing under his desk. Lizzy got an idea.

She looked at him and said, "Boss, I don't know if I can do this anymore. Can we please stop?"

He looked at her and said, "You're both going to do exactly what I tell you, or I'll fire you. I'll ruin you and your reputation. You will be so screwed no one will hire you again!"

Aaron said, "Good move, Lizzy. Nothing like a little more icing on the cake."

Lizzy looked at him and said, "Okay, I get it. What's next? Let's get this over with."

He said he wanted Lizzy to walk around behind him, take off her outfit, and press her breasts up against the back of his head while rubbing his shoulders. At the same time, he wanted me standing in front of him. He'd seen Lizzy's body; now he wanted to see more of mine. We both did exactly what he told them to do. Now he wanted us to give each other a long kiss while bending over him. Once we did that, he would make sure that she would get what she deserved.

Lizzy and I started giving each other a very long, passionate kiss. While we were kissing, I could feel his mouth on my breasts and his hand between my legs. Aaron told them to pull back. That was far enough. We both pulled back and asked if that was enough.

William said, "For now, it is."

As we were putting our clothes back on, I asked him what he meant when he said for now. William told them both that this won't be the only time, that this was going to happen as often as he wanted it to, and they wouldn't be able to do anything about it. Lizzy's mouth just dropped open.

"That's not what you told us."

He said, "It doesn't matter what I told you. There are way too many things I want to do with you two. You're going to be my sex toys whenever I want you to be."

Tears started to come to Lizzy's eyes. I had had enough. I looked at William dead in his eyes and said, "Is that what you really think? Do you really think that you have the control here?"

William looked at Lizzy and said, "Apparently, your friend doesn't know who I am."

I told him to look at me, not Lizzy. I told him, "I know exactly who you are. You're just like every other piece of shit guy that thinks he's got control over every female because he's got money and power or authority. The biggest mistake that people like you make is that you don't actually have as much power as you think. You'll do whatever you can to hold onto your power, including what you just did, which was to basically bribe and threaten two women into satisfying your sexually, sick, deviant behavior. You basically just molested us both, using threats and promises of letting Lizzy keep her job."

Lizzy couldn't believe what she was seeing and hearing. Aaron told Lizzy to just let me go. I was on a roll.

"Men like you have no power, and you stay awake at night worrying whether someone's going to take it from you. But never in your wildest dreams would you ever think that a woman would take it away from you. Well, you're right, a woman won't, but two women are going to."

William looked at me and said, "You have nothing on me. No one will ever believe you, so pick your shit up and get the fuck out of my office, and oh, by the way, Lizzy, you're fired."

I looked at him and said, "Yeah, I don't think so. I have a little something to show you."

I took out my phone and started to show William the video of what just went on—every single bribe, threat, all of it. He didn't know what to say. He was lost. There was absolutely nothing that he could say to fight what he was looking at. He tried, but he had nothing. He tried to threaten us and said he would take the phone away from us. I told him that I would kick his piece of shit ass all over this office and then feed him his balls. He looked at Lizzy and tried to reason with her. She looked at him and told him to not even bother. He would never get sympathy from her.

I said to him that "I could've sworn I told you to not look at Lizzy, don't talk to her, and don't look at her. You're not good enough for her. You deal with me now."

William looked at her and asked her what she wanted. I said, "Here's how it's going to go now, boss. You still like being called boss, right?"

I continued, "You're going to get in your car, and you're going to leave. No going home to pack. No packing your office. You're going to go now."

William asked what was going to happen if he refused. I said I would release the video and he would be ruined. He said he would tell them it was all role-playing. "Again, my word against theirs."

I said, "I figured you would say that." I grabbed him by his arm, walked him to the window, and opened the curtains just a little bit. Through the break in the curtains was a red laser dot, the kind that one associated with a sniper rifle. "That person is going to make sure that you leave town exactly the way I told you to. If you don't, there will be red on your chest, but it won't be from a laser."

Lizzy's mouth dropped open. William was scared shitless. He agreed. He said that he would get in his car and leave now.

Trying to get one last dig in, he said, "That's fine. I have all of Lizzy's money, so I don't need anything else."

I said, "Oh yeah, about that." I took out my phone, pulled up my program, walked over to Lizzy, and told her to push the button. I looked at him and said, "No, you don't. I just took it back."

He was about to freak out on them when that little red light hit him again.

I looked at him and said, "This will be the very last time that I tell you to leave."

Before he left, I spoke into the mic and said, "Make sure he gets in his car right away and he leaves."

He asked who I was talking to. I just looked at him and then looked at my watch. He walked out the back door of his office, got in his car, and left. Aaron had left before he did so he could get ahead of him. They needed to finish the plan so he wouldn't be out there talking. Lizzy grabbed me, gave me a kiss and a hug, and thanked me. She said she had never seen anything like that in her life. I told her to stop talking about it. We would when we got home. We walked out the back door and started walking home.

*****

Aaron

It really was easy for me. Park City has a lot of winding mountain roads, so tracking the path out of town was easy. He was pissed, and he was driving fast, and as soon as I saw him coming around the corner, I fired, hitting the front tire that was leaning into the curve.

He lost control and went over the cliff. I watched his car tumble down the hill, and it burst into flames. All evidence of a shot-out tire was gone; it really was that easy. I texted Vanessa and told her that it was done and to take the rest of the money. She pulled out her phone, pulled up her program, pushed the button, and it was done. She told me where they were. In a few minutes, I pulled up beside them, picked them up, and took them home. Another long emotional day was done. This was really starting to take a toll, emotionally, for both of us. Could we actually go and talk to a shrink about it? Uh, that would be no. We just needed to take a break for a while.

CHAPTER 17

We Need to Talk

Vanessa

We got back to the house, and they seriously needed to take a shower to wash all his filth off them. Lizzy wanted to talk about it, but we both told her that it would wait until after we get done. Lizzy went to her new house to shower, and we started talking.

I asked, "How did we get here again? We were going to take a break, and not only did we not, but we got someone else involved with what we do. How are we going to tell her how easy it was for us to pull this off? And then when she finds out that William is dead, how are we going to convince her that we had nothing to do with that?"

Aaron told her, "That would be an easy one. The car burst into flames on the way down. There is no evidence."

I asked, "Then what about you being gone?"

"She had no idea where I was. That's an easy one, especially since I can't be five feet away with that rifle."

One thing I did tell Aaron, and I didn't know how he was going to take it, but there's a really big piece of me that gets off on what we just did. I mean, it was actually exciting for me to let him do what he wanted because I knew in the end that we were going to win.

He reacted exactly the way I thought he would.

I asked him why. "Why don't you ever get upset or jealous?"

Aaron looked at me and asked me if I loved him and if I was in love with him. I said yes to both, and it grows more so every day. Aaron told me that's all he needs.

"I believe in you, and if you tell me that, then there's nothing that can come between us."

"So if I told you that Lizzy kissing me excited me to the point of getting wet and he could feel that when he was touching me, you're okay with that?"

Aaron said, "Let me ask you a question. What was making you wet, Lizzy kissing you or him touching?"

"Lizzy kissing me."

"Okay, so he's dead. I don't have to get jealous or mad. We always get revenge, right?"

I said, "That's very true. We do."

Aaron looked at me and said, "Baby, I love you more than anything, and I will until I die. Don't ever worry if it matters to me, it does, but I trust and believe in you."

That made me feel so happy and safe when he said that. I truly believed that we will never leave each other. When we speak to Lizzy, we tell her as little as possible, at least until we know her better.

Lizzy came downstairs and asked if we wanted to talk yet. She said she would be more than happy to not discuss it anymore if we didn't want to. I looked at her and told her that we had planned on talking to her about it, and Aaron told her that we would be willing to answer any questions that she might have.

Lizzy's first question, "How did you know what to do, and why are you so good at it?"

I told her that we've helped people in her situation before. "For some reason, we're magnets for it."

Aaron told her, "When you do it as often as we've done it, you become good at it."

Lizzy's second question, "Do you ever hurt people that don't deserve it?"

Aaron told her, "We've never done anything to anyone that didn't deserve it. There are people that have done things worse than what your boss ever did to you. Not that what happened to you wasn't bad. It was really bad, and we respect that."

Lizzy's third question, "Have you all ever killed anyone?"

Aaron looked at me and then looked at Lizzy and said, "How would you like us to answer that?"

Lizzy said, "Truthfully, please. It won't change how I feel about you both especially after what you did for me."

I wanted to answer. I said, "Lizzy, there have been people that have died. Yes, some that have died at our hands, yes, but it's usually because of what they've done first. We've never killed anyone unnecessarily."

Lizzy's fourth question, "This one is for Vanessa. Have you done things like that with men or women before, and does it bother you? Does Aaron get upset?"

I told her, "I have done that before with both men and women, but it's for a reason. It's not for sexual reasons, so it doesn't bother Aaron. He knows that I love him and only him."

Aaron said, "I'm sorry, but this all sounds so strange telling you all this."

Lizzy said, "I told you that it wouldn't change how I feel about either one of you, especially after what you all did for me."

Aaron told her, "It wasn't a question of what you thought. It was a question of trust."

Lizzy looked at Aaron and said, "When you came into my life, you saw me at the lowest point ever in my life. I was being beaten down every day, and I didn't know what I was going to do next. My next step was to quit, probably go broke, and live with my sister or on the street. You stepped into that bank, and my life changed forever, not for the worse but for the better. You were my lifeline, and you saved me from certain destruction. You have my undying love, devotion, and trust."

We both believed her. It was way too sincere, and after all we've done for her, if she was lying, she's better than we are.

I asked, "Are we all okay now? No issues with anything that's going on?"

Right before Lizzy answered, she got a text from Roni, asking her if she knew that her boss died last night. Lizzy turned the phone around and showed them the text. Lizzy asked us if we did it.

I said that I was with her, and Aaron said he was on his way to get them. She said that she could tell we were lying, but it was okay, at least she knew. She texted her back and told her that she hadn't heard, but she's not sad that it happened.

She looked at us both and said, "Can we just be honest going forward?"

We both agreed that we would be, but Aaron added, "Please don't ever betray us."

She said we had nothing to worry about.

I said, "Now that we're done with this, let's move on to our plans for you and this place."

We all agreed. Lizzy told us that Roni had drawn up some plans for the different areas. She just needed for us all to look at them and approve. Lizzy said that Roni would be here soon, and we could do that. Lizzy showed them a breakdown of the equipment that she wanted/needed to make the place the way she wanted it. She had set up interviews for a manager since she was going to be gone, trainers, a masseuse, and she wanted to have a nutritionist on staff to really help people that need it. She said that she would like for her sister to be the manager since she needed someone she could trust while she's gone. Aaron and I agreed that it was a good idea. We needed someone that we could trust, and we liked her sister. She also fit the part; she was in just as good of shape as Lizzy, so that helped. I told Lizzy that I decided that all the people that she hired needed to look like her. They needed to look at that part. She needed to look at that part. And not just in shape, but they need to be just as good-looking as her. I made sure to tell Lizzy that this was my suggestion, not Aaron's; and although he agreed, this wasn't something that he came up with. Lizzy told us that she was hoping we were going to say that because she had wanted to do the same thing, but she didn't want to look bad to us. I told her that I thought we're beyond that by now. Aaron agreed.

CHAPTER 18

A New Face in the Game

Aaron

Roni arrived, and we all sat down to go over the plans for the new area. They were just amazed at how great this was going to look, not to mention the quality of Roni's work. Workout area, weights, locker rooms with showers, separate area for the masseuse, and offices for management and nutritionist. The only change was, we wanted the manager's office to be larger. We wanted it to have a bathroom and a shower, and it needed to have two rooms, one set up just like a bedroom. We wanted this because Lizzy's sister, Jenny, had two kids; and if she ever needed to be there and she needed a place for the kids, it needed to be as comfortable as possible.

I told Lizzy to make sure to add whatever else she felt was necessary for her family. Both Lizzy and Roni were just floored by our generosity and caring for people. Lizzy knew firsthand how much we truly care. We told her to get started on the job and let us know what kind of deposit she needed for the crew. The next topic would be security and what temporary fix had Roni come up with. Roni told them that she could have a temporary system installed, but instead, she wanted to have around-the-clock security while we were all gone, especially with construction crews there—at least until she can see exactly what system they're talking about.

I told Roni I wanted her to investigate one last thing—to see what it would take to have a secret bunker installed with the entrance coming in from the bedroom, but also, I wanted a secret exit somewhere else. The building of this would have to be with the security company involved. It would have to be a well-kept secret. Roni said not to worry. She would have everyone working on the project sign NDAs with a penalty of death if they expose anything. Lizzy looked at us and thought to herself, *Roni doesn't really know how much truth is in that statement.* I told them now that we all have what we're doing, the next step was to make our way to the other properties.

"Can everyone have everything started so that we can leave in two days? People will be able to communicate with you, even in the air. When we are out of range, we have satellite phones for that."

Both Lizzy and Roni agreed that they could be ready to go in two days. I told them to only bring the essentials.

"We don't know how long we'll be gone, and we can always buy you what you need."

Vanessa told them we're going from this climate to the desert and then to the tropics. She learned it was way too hard to pack for. She would just buy what she needed at each place and leave it there—bras, underwear, shoes, clothes, even makeup and toiletries.

"There will be more than enough room for you all to keep your stuff."

I told Roni that we can all leave from here. It would be easier that way. Roni walked out the door with Lizzy, asking her if this was too good to be true.

"Can we trust them?"

Lizzy told her, "I would never put you in a situation where you would get hurt, so yes, we can trust them."

Everything was all set, and it was time to go. Roni came to the house in the morning, and I had a car service come and pick us up. When we were almost at the airport, they asked us when the flight left. Vanessa told them basically whenever we want it to. We pulled into the terminal for private planes and stopped at our jet. I still wasn't going to pilot because we weren't making any recipes with them. We're trying to build a business, and we needed to talk. Lizzy and Roni were in awe of what they were seeing.

Roni asked, "Are we flying in this jet?"

I told them, "For now, we lease the jet, and even though I know how to fly them, we still have a crew on standby for when I don't want to fly it myself."

Lizzy and Roni sometimes both felt like this was all a dream. We boarded the plane and took off for Tucson. Vanessa told them that it was a quick flight.

"Only an hour and a half, so don't get too comfortable."

They both commented that it was their first time on a private jet, so it might be hard to *not* get comfortable. On the way down, I talked to them about the areas that were around the ranch.

"It's twelve acres, and there aren't as many buildings on the property. However, there is a horse barn that we can convert into what we need to do. We can also do additions if needed. We already built a two-bedroom house on the property that you and Roni can use. It was there from the previous owners. They used it for a security team that used to live there."

Vanessa went in the back and called the security company that was watching the property.

She instructed them to please go and clean out the house where Jody and Brian lived, then call in a cleaning crew to scrub it down. Burn whatever is in there. She didn't know where Aaron found these people, but every one of these people that we hired were no questions asked. They would do whatever they're told. I told Roni that she'd need to look at the security system to get an idea of what we wanted and needed. Roni said that the contractor she worked with had hooked her up with a couple of contractors in Tucson, ones that we could trust. I told her that we already had some security in place, so that's one thing she wouldn't have to worry about when it came to keeping an eye on the contractor. Both Lizzy and Roni expressed how grateful they were and how they're looking forward to starting this new project.

Roni and Lizzy had never been to Tucson, so it was a new adventure for them. An SUV picked them up at the airport, and they made their way to the ranch. Lizzy commented about how they didn't bring much, and they would need to stop to get some things. They both said that they would pay for it. I told them that we would pay for it. I already told them not to worry. I told the driver to go to this high-end mall in the foothills. We could find things for them there.

*****

Vanessa

The mall was nestled in the foothills of Tucson, high-end restaurants and shops—everything we could ever need. I asked Lizzy if she had come up with a name for the gym yet. She said that she had not, but she had a few ideas rolling around in her head.

"Well, what are they? Tell us so that we can help."

"Okay, here are the names that I came up with, Assured Results, Push Your Limits, Achieve Your Balance. These are a few I was thinking about."

We all loved them. "Now what about for the massage part?"

"Let Us Heal You, Unbelievable Touch, We Beat You, Now We Treat You."

Lizzy personally liked the last one best, but she thought it might be too much. We all laughed at the last one.

I said, "Anything is possible. Remember, this is about you and your personality. That's what we're investing in."

We went into just about every store and bought a lot of what we needed, but we missed one thing—bathing suits.

I said, "Come on, you're in the desert. You need a suit or two or however many you want."

We went in and bought three suits each. I didn't need them, but I thought, *What the hell*. When I was walking alone with Aaron, I told him that I couldn't believe how incredibly gorgeous Roni's body was. It's just as nice as Lizzy's, only taller.

We ate some sushi and started walking back to the SUV.

Aaron asked me how I felt about just relaxing and taking it easy and if it made me antsy.

I said that it did, but I still wanted to do what we're doing and get all this off the ground. The assholes out there weren't going anywhere.

"Understood, so then we will just keep going with what we're doing."

Aaron told me that his concern was money. He hasn't looked at the accounts for a while, and we're spending a lot of money. I said that he needed to look at what's going on with the accounts at least once a week.

I said, "Honey, we're never going to run out of money. It's too well-invested. It's not going to happen."

We got in the SUV and headed to the ranch.

We got to the ranch, and Lizzy and Roni's heads started spinning. They both told us that besides the beauty, the possibilities are endless as to what we can do here. Aaron told them to start working on what they needed and let's get moving. We still have another house to go to. We drove them over to their house so we could let them in and show them around. I wanted to make sure that the place was clean and scrubbed, that all traces of them were gone. Once again, they didn't disappoint. I told them to get settled in then come up to the house so we could go for a swim.

Lizzy and Roni agreed. They got all their new clothes put away, got their suits on, and headed toward the house. Once they got to the house, I gave them the grand tour. I poured them a glass of wine and led them out to the pool. Lizzy asked where Aaron was. I told her that he was taking care of some business and that he would be out soon. We all needed the relaxation time, and the pool gave them that. I asked them how far they had gotten on ideas for here. They told me that they were working on the plane, and they did some before we left. They had an idea based on what we wanted them to do.

"That's good to hear. I'm sure that Aaron is getting everyone lined up now to get out here and work. We just need to say the word."

Roni said, "Can we start anytime? I already had things drawn up at least enough to get started."

Aaron finally came out and got in the pool. He asked everyone how they're feeling and how they like the property. They both couldn't say enough about the place and how they already had a lot of plans for it. Aaron said he could have people out there in two days to get started working. They both said that would be perfect. Lizzy said she would get started working on getting equipment ordered and delivered.

Aaron said, "That is perfect. Once we get things started, we will take off for the island and get started on that property. In the meantime, let's work on this place and have some fun."

Aaron got out of the pool to get us some more wine and to start making us some dinner. We decided to go sit in the hot tub while Aaron made dinner. They asked me how long I had been with Aaron and how we met. I told them about how I left here because of how abused I was by my old bosses, so I moved to Kauai. I told them about the romantic dinner he made for me and how, from then on, we have always been together.

"We've done so much for each other that we can't see being without one another."

I asked Roni what her life had been like and was she with someone. Roni said that she was seeing someone that worked for a construction company. His name was David, and it was great. Then over time, he started to become an asshole. He was abusive both physically and mentally, and it was hard to get away from him; but she did, and she made her way up to Park City. I asked where he was. She told him that he's still in Phoenix somewhere working for a construction company. Lizzy asked her if she ever thought about getting him back for all that he had done to her. She said that she would love to, but she doesn't have that much control or power over him. She said he was such a degenerate gambler. One of the worst things he ever did to her, one night, they were at home and these two guys came to the door looking for him.

"He told me to tell them he wasn't there, so I did. They forced their way in, and they proceeded to tell me how he owed them $100K for gambling debts. I told them that wasn't her problem. They said that it was my problem because he told them if he didn't get the money for them, then they could have her for a night. I panicked, and I tried to get out, but they grabbed me, and right about then, David came out of the bedroom. I thought, *This is great, he's going to save me*. He looked at me and said that if I just accept what's going to happen, it will go a lot easier. I couldn't believe what I was hearing. He basically used me to pay his debts off.

"David sat on a chair in the corner of the room, and the two guys sat on the couch. They told me to stand in front of them and slowly strip for them. These guys had their dicks out, and they were stroking them while I was stripping, even David was doing it. I wanted to run, but I knew I wouldn't get anywhere. When my clothes were off, they made me get on my hands and knees on the couch, and one fucked me from behind while the other made me suck on his dick, then they switched. This went on for a couple of hours until they made me get on my knees in front of them while they came all over me. I got up, cleaned myself off, grabbed my shit, and I left. And I never looked back."

Roni started to cry, and Lizzy and I both went over to comfort her. Aaron came out of nowhere and asked her how much she wanted to get revenge for what they did. Roni said she would do anything. Lizzy said to count her in, and I said, "You know where I stand."

Aaron told us, "Let's eat, talk about the business we came here for, and get some sleep. Tomorrow, we will discuss what we can do about Roni's revenge."

*****

Aaron

Roni and Lizzy made their way back to their house, and we made our way to bed. While we were lying there, we discussed how we were back in this situation again. We did agree that what she told us was pretty bad, and if anybody deserved revenge, it was those guys. I told her that I was already concocting recipes for them, not to worry. We gave each other a hug and a kiss and went to sleep, thankful that we have each other.

*****

Lizzy

Roni and I made it back to the house and got ready for bed. Roni asked me if I would sleep with her. It would just make her feel better after all she just talked about. I had no problem with it and climbed into bed with her. Roni asked me what I thought he meant by revenge. I looked at her and asked her how badly she wanted to get revenge on them for what they did to her. Roni told me that if she could kill them, she would. Not wanting to give anything away, I told her that I had no idea what they had in mind. I just know that they're good people, and Aaron would do anything to take care of people he cared about. Roni asked me that if they said they would kill them, would she help them do it. I told her that I would do anything to protect her and take care of her.

"If you asked me to do that for you, I would. You know the things I went through, but what they did was bad. Anything you want, just ask, and I'm yours."

Roni gave me a hug and a kiss, and I told her it was time for sleep.

"We will see what they have to say in the morning."

As the sun started to rise, a knock came at the door of our house. I climbed out of bed, and it was Vanessa with coffee and pastries from a local bakery down the street. She asked if we were awake and if we wanted to come up to the house to talk. I said to give us about thirty minutes to get ready and we would be up to the house. I went back into the room to wake Roni. She looked so peaceful, but we needed to get up and get to the house. I gave her a kiss on her forehead and whispered in her ear that it was time to get up and go. We both got dressed and made our way up to the house.

*****

Vanessa

I brought them over to the kitchen where Aaron had made breakfast. Roni decided to start the conversation. She asked what they meant by getting revenge. Since this is something that Aaron started, I let him explain. Aaron and I agreed that we would only share a very abbreviated version of what we do—mostly just tell them how things just fall into laps and that we will always help people no matter what.

Aaron told them, "When we get their revenge, we're not nice about it. We use Vanessa and whoever else is involved to lure them in with whatever plan I come up with, and then I finish it. There's never any trace, and most of the time, it looks like an accident. If this is something that you don't want to do, just say so and we can pretend like this conversation never happened, and nothing else about our business will change."

Lizzy had already experienced the way in which we got revenge and she loved it, but she didn't know if she should let Roni know that she had been there already. Aaron and I weren't offering up that information either.

Roni looked at Lizzy. She nodded. She looked at me and Aaron and said she was in and what did she need to do.

I asked her if there was anything that she's still holding onto. "Meaning, if you're put in a situation where you're having to manipulate these guys where you're going to be getting touched by them; can you handle it, or will you freak out?"

Roni said that she hated them with all she's got. "No doubt I've been wanting to hurt them for a very long, but I never thought I would be in front of them again, so I really can't tell you."

I said, "We could practice what we're going to do, and Lizzy and I will be there too, so you won't have to worry."

Aaron added, "Based on the information you gave her, Vanessa had done some research this morning on all of them. They're all still in the Phoenix area. Andy and Flynn are still in the gambling industry although they run their own book now, and David is still a degenerate gambler and working construction."

Roni was asking what they had to practice.

I answered, "Well, we need to pick out what we're going to wear. It has to reveal as much as it can, usually covered up under hoodies so they can't see at first. The key is to always get them off-balance, to take them by surprise so they don't know what hit them. All three of them have pissed off numerous people. Andy and Flynn took business away from others, and well, David is just a bad gambler, so this might actually be easier to not have to hide it. We could make it look like someone had actually done it to them."

Aaron said, "We can take them to a construction site."

He had already picked one out that was in a very far out of the way area in Phoenix. New building construction was almost in the middle of nowhere. I found out that Andy and Flynn operated out of a bar, and it would be easy to meet them in there.

"At night, when it's dark and people are already drunk, we could wander in the bar, pretending like we didn't know they hung out there. After that, it would be easy to get them out of the bar. We can park the SUV in the back alley, get them in the back seat, start teasing them and making them feel comfortable. Aaron will be in the third row with shots that will knock them out. Then we will take them out to the site. David is usually hanging out at one of the local strip clubs."

I wanted to handle him. I had something special in mind for him.

The next task was going to be to decide what to wear.

Lizzy had a great idea. "How about lingerie?"

I asked, "How are we going to work that one out?"

"How about lingerie with light coats over it that goes down to midthigh?"

I said, "That is actually a great idea, I have a bunch of lingerie in my room. Let's go and try it on and see if we need to go and get anything."

Except for Roni being taller, we were all about the same size. We all found some really great things to wear—all of which would drive anyone crazy. All we would need were the coats and we would be ready to go. Aaron got the SUV loaded up, and we started our short journey to Phoenix. Aaron made sure that I had taken care of my part. Being bookies, they would have money stashed somewhere, and I found it. They thought they were smart but not smart enough. I checked into David, and sadly, he had nothing. Before we got too far, Aaron asked them again if they were sure this is what they wanted to do because once we start, there's no going back. Lizzy and Roni both said yes.

Aaron said, "Okay, no turning back."

We got to the bar right about when the sun was going down. It was perfect timing. We wore shorts and T-shirts over the lingerie, so all we had to do was take them off and put the coats on. Aaron gave us earbuds so he could talk to us.

He reminded us, "They were two-way radios, but don't accidentally speak back to me. That would blow the whole thing."

I told Roni to follow my lead. Roni would know what to do once I got started. Aaron told us that he would pull around to the alley and wait for us.

We walked into the club and went to a table in the corner so we could more easily scan the crowd. It wasn't a packed house, but it was enough so that they didn't stand out. Roni saw Andy coming out of the office by the bathroom in the back. Lizzy and I asked her if she was okay, if she was feeling any anxiety. She told them that she felt nothing. That was what I needed to hear. I waited for him to go back into the office and followed him to see if she could see who was in there. It was only him and Flynn. I walked back to the table and told them what I saw. Two of them, three of us, this will be easy.

"So here's the plan. All three of us go to the office. Since the bathroom is right there, we'll pretend like we're so drunk that we go through that door instead. After we're in there, just follow my lead. Roni, are you still okay? You can stay behind if you want to and just meet us in the alley."

She said she was fine and that she needed to do this. We all got up and started walking toward the office. We kept our heads down and our hoodies up. We got to the door and started laughing out loud, like we were drunk, and we burst into the office. Andy and Flynn both turned their heads like they were pissed off until they saw who came through the door—three of the hottest girls they'd ever seen although all they were looking at was our bodies.

I looked at them and said, "Oh my god, we thought we were going into the bathroom!"

Andy said, "Don't worry, mistakes happen."

They all took their hoodies off, and neither one of them recognized Roni. They really didn't recognize her. Aaron knew that Roni's blood was starting to boil.

He quickly said to her, "Do not worry. This is actually very good for us. We won't have to worry as to whether they trust us or not."

She took a deep breath and calmed down. Aaron told her to just follow my lead.

I asked them, "What are you doing in here? You all are missing a hell of a party out there."

Flynn said, "The party was way better in here," and he offered us a drink.

Andy poured us all a drink, and he and Flynn sat down. They asked us where we were from.

I told them, "We came up from Tucson for a couple of days to visit. We were thinking of moving up here, but we need to find jobs. Do you have any ideas where we can find work?"

Flynn said that we might be able to work for them. I knew this was total bullshit. They thought we were just dumb, drunk females, so why not take advantage of us, right?

"Really? What do you all do? What can we do for you? Do you own the bar?"

Andy said they did own the bar, but they also ran a sportsbook on the side. I thought that this was a perfect time to play dumb.

"Sportsbook? What's a sportsbook?"

Flynn said, "Well, we place bets for people on sporting events. We pay out to the winners, and the losers pay us."

I said, "It sounds easy enough. Sounds like it could be fun."

Andy said, "It's not fun for the people that lose a lot because sometimes they can't pay."

Lizzy asked him what they would do when people couldn't pay.

Andy said, "Sometimes people trade us things, and sometimes we have to persuade people to pay."

Roni asked them, "What kind of trade do people do with you?"

Aaron said, "Before he answers, you need to brace yourself for what he says, and don't react."

Andy said, "People have traded cars, jewelry, and one time, we actually had a guy that traded his girlfriend."

Roni said, "That actually sounded kind of hot. What was that like?"

Andy asked her if she really wanted to hear about it. She said yes, she did. All of us said we wanted to hear about it in detail. Andy told them that they walked in, and she didn't know what was going on until her boyfriend told her.

Roni asked him, "What did she do then?"

He said that she got really excited and asked if she could dance for them, and of course, they said yes.

"How did she dance for you? What did she do?"

Andy looked at her and said, "Well, hard to describe. If Andy and I sat down in our chairs, how would you dance for us?"

I asked, "How about if we take turns?"

Andy and Flynn sat down in their chairs, and Roni said, "Let me show you what I would do," and she started to dance. She asked them, "What were you doing while she danced?"

Lizzy and I went and stood behind them. We started rubbing their shoulders and said, "Yes, show us what you were doing."

They unzipped their pants, pulled out their dicks, and started stroking them. Lizzy and I walked to the sides of the chairs and opened up our coats, exposing nothing but the lingerie we were wearing. They turned their heads, let out a huge sigh, and started trying to suck on our breasts.

Right then, Roni said, "Eyes up front, boys."

She opened up her coat, undid the front clasp from her bra, and let her breasts slowly pop out. I looked at them and asked them if they wanted to take it outside. They couldn't zip their pants up fast enough. As they were getting themselves dressed again, I asked if there was a back door. Our SUV was out in the back alley, and it had more than enough room for all of us. Andy led us all out the back door. I unlocked the doors and had Andy and Flynn get in the back seat on opposite sides of the SUV. It was dark so they couldn't see in the far back. Roni climbed on Andy's lap, Lizzy climbed on Flynn's lap, and I sat between the two. We all opened up our coats and our bras and let our breasts fall out. They grabbed them on the sides of their heads and started lightly grinding on them. I had their dicks in my hands, and I was slowly stroking them. I asked them both if they liked what they were getting right now and did they want more. They both let out an enthusiastic yes.

I said, "Okay, give them more."

Aaron popped up from the back and stuck them both in the neck. They went down fast. They duct-taped their hands, feet, and mouth; put a hood over their heads; and threw them in the back.

"They will be out for a while we have time," Aaron said.

We drove them out to the construction site that Aaron had found. There was a cement truck that was on site, and Aaron thought that would be the best place to put them. We all asked him if we were just going to put them in there and leave. Aaron told them that he wanted them to gamble for their lives.

"We need to remind them why they're here. We need for them to remember Roni. Getting rid of them would be way too easy for them without ever reminding them why."

I told both Lizzy and Roni that this part was usually Aaron's thing. We pulled them out of the SUV and sat them on either side of a couch in the foreman's office. We pulled the hoods off and threw some water in their faces to wake them up.

*****

Aaron

As they slowly started to wake up, a look of panic started to fill their eyes. They started asking me who I was and why I was doing this. All the ladies were standing out of sight. I looked at them and said that I had heard they ran their own book and that there were times when they took trade in return for money owed.

"Is that true?"

They both nodded, and Andy said, "What fucking business is it of yours?"

I had this thin curved boning knife that I liked to use. I walked up to Andy and slowly pushed it into his shoulder. Andy let out a scream, and Flynn tried to jump at me, but we had duct-taped their legs to the legs of the couch. I made a slashing move across Flynn's forehead, not deep, but deep enough to stun him and make him go back into his place on the couch. I looked at them and said that it was my business because they had hurt someone that I cared deeply about.

"In one of your trades, you decided that you were going to take a human being in trade. There's something seriously wrong with people that do that."

Andy said, "She enjoyed it, she wanted it, and it turned her on."

I said, "Really? She did? Roni, do you want to come out here?"

Both of their eyes got huge when they saw her come out.

They were both like, "Wait, you were the girl in the bar. We don't even recognize you."

Roni said, "Yes, that was the problem. You don't."

Roni proceeded to explain to them in detail what they did to her, every single detail, and how she didn't enjoy any of it.

"My asshole boyfriend sold me to you both, and you basically raped me."

Andy said they had to get their money somehow.

I said, "You know, what you did was not only wrong, but it makes you both less of men than you already are."

Finally, Vanessa and Lizzy came out, and when they saw them, they knew that this was the end, they're not getting out of this, and with that comes the threats, the "do you know who I am" garbage that so many of them use.

I looked at them and said, "Yes, I know who you are, and I'm not impressed. I have no respect for guys that like to rape women, and even worse, the two of you doing it at the same time."

They asked, "What about David? He's the one that traded her to us for his debt."

Vanessa said not to worry. She had something special planned for him.

Roni looked at them both and said, "Tell me that you really don't recognize my face."

They looked at her and said they were sorry, but they didn't.

"So is the reason why you told me to show you what I would do is because you don't remember what you did to me, because you don't remember me?"

Andy said, "Yes, that would be the reason."

Roni said, "I'm going to tell you what you did to me. In fact, I might show you too. You made me strip in front of you while you sat there and stroked your dicks. You remember, David was in the back doing the same thing? Here, let me get those tiny dicks out for you."

Roni grabbed my knife and cut their pants open, then she reached in, grabbed their dicks, and pulled them out.

"Lizzy and Vanessa, can you come over and stroke them for me? They're just a bit busy."

They both started stroking them softly and then started getting rough.

"You made me get on my hands and knees on the couch, and one of you fucked me from behind while the other stuck their tiny dick in my mouth." Roni said, "Hey, I have an idea," and she walked over and shoved Andy's head onto Flynn's dick. Andy wouldn't open his mouth, so Roni put the knife to his dick and said, "Open your mouth, or I take yours right now." He opened his mouth, and Roni kept pushing his head down onto Flynn's dick, harder and harder each time. "How does that feel?" she asked. "Do you like it? Does it turn you on or make you hot because that's exactly what you did to me."

She then made Flynn do the same thing. She pulled them back and had me undo their feet. She told them, "If you try to run, I'll take your dicks before you get to the door."

Vanessa, Lizzy, and I were slightly floored by Roni and how she was handling the situation. But then again, she was angry, and to make things worse, they didn't even remember what they did to her. Roni said that she was going to show them one of the most degrading things they did to her. She made Andy get on his knees in front of Flynn and started stroking his dick.

"Looks like you need a little help. Do I need to be topless for you?"

She took off her top, and he started to get hard again. I held Andy on his knees until Roni got Flynn to cum all over his face. And then she switched and did the same to Flynn. She wouldn't allow them to wipe their faces off.

She told them, "It can sit there on your faces just like you made it sit on mine."

I was impressed. She wrote recipes almost as good as I did, but it was my turn now.

"So here's the deal, guys. I don't really know if it's worth letting you gamble for your lives anymore. You've pissed off so many people, and you hurt our friend an awful lot. That last one should keep you from continuing to survive on this planet. They begged for a chance to live, okay?" I said. "Ladies, what can they gamble on? Let them fight to the death? No, that's too easy. They'll just try to run or attack us. So then what should it be? Roni, would you like to decide since you're the one that they did this to?"

"Honestly, I'm over this whole thing. Let's gag them and bag them and get it done. I'm tired."

I said, "Okay, let's get it done."

They were both trying to get away when I stuck them again in the neck. It didn't quite knock them out, but they couldn't do much. We duct-taped their mouth and bagged their heads again and started to walk them outside. My plan was to put them in the concrete truck and turn it on long enough for them to get nice and coated and then leave them there. I had a self-loading concrete truck. I put them in the shovel one at a time and loaded them in. They were so out of it you could barely hear their screams. I put the mix and the water in right behind them and then started it up. There's a series of blades inside the drum that are used to mix the concrete. It's not going to feel too good, but the plan wasn't to keep them spinning—it was to spin them just enough and then stop. By morning, they should be set.

I asked Roni if she was satisfied with that. She said that she just wanted it to spin for a couple of minutes longer. I let it go longer and then stopped it. It was time to get going. I told them that we need to erase all traces of them being there. As soon as we were done, we took off.

Vanessa asked about tire tracks. I told her it was a construction site. There were so many of them; we didn't need to worry.

Now it was David's turn. We found him in a strip club that he liked going to. It always seemed like this was what every one of these guys was all about. Sex, nudity, abuse—they were all into it in one form or another, and it was all to control the females that were around them. We could seriously take the rest of our lives to bring all these fuckers down. What David did was worse than what Andy and Flynn did. He betrayed the person that loved him and trusted him. He let her get raped for a few thousand dollars just to pay off a debt. That's beyond evil. Vanessa had a special plan for him. Since he liked selling people, she was going to do the same to him. There were plenty of groups south of the border that were always looking for slave workers, sex, and otherwise.

"I got in touch with one of them and asked them if they needed a young white boy that they could work that needed to be taught a lesson. I explained to them what he did, and they said that they would be more than happy to take him off our hands. How much did we want? I said the only thing we want is for him is to suffer for what he did, suffer every day. They said not to worry. They would take care of that. We don't like people like him, and we know exactly what to do with them."

Vanessa told me the night that she would be handing him over. I asked where and at what time. She said he'd be waiting in the back for us. Vanessa said she would tell them when she was coming out.

*****

Vanessa

David was sitting by himself in a booth, already looking like he was getting drunk. I walked up to the table and asked if I could buy him a drink. After looking at me, it wasn't hard for him not to agree to that invitation. He asked what I was doing there. He'd never seen me before. I said that I was visiting from Flagstaff and that I was thinking about moving here. I was looking for a job, so I thought I would check this place out and see what it was like. I asked him if he came here often. He said he was here so often I would think that he owned the place.

He said, "So if you're looking for a job, I know the owner. I might be able to help."

I told him that would be great. He told me to hold on. He would be right back. After a few minutes, he came walking back to the table, and he told me that the owner looked over and saw me and he was interested, but that, usually, I have to audition for the job. I said that I understood and when could I do that. He told me that it's my lucky day. He convinced the owner to let him do the audition and that we could do it in a private room in the back.

I said, "That would be great." I went to go grab a couple of more drinks to take back there. He told me where the room was, and he would meet me there. On the way to the room, I dosed his drink and walked in. When I opened the door, the owner was there too. He had decided he wanted to sit in for the audition. Okay, well, this wasn't something I was expecting. I would just have to improvise. I asked the owner if he wanted a drink. He said sure he would take it. I had them both sit on the couch, and I told them I had to get ready. I walked behind the couch and dosed the other drink, walked back in front of them, and handed them the drinks. They drank at least half of them before I got started. I thought this isn't going to take long. I turned on some music from my phone and started to dance. I slowly opened my coat and revealed that I had on nothing but lingerie. You could tell by the looks on their faces they weren't expecting that. I let the coat drop to the ground, turned around, and started shaking my ass in front of them. They both reached out and grabbed my ass more than once, totally making me want to puke; but again, it's for a good cause. I turned around, and they were still holding their drinks.

I reached up and grabbed the front clasp on my bra, looked at them, and asked, "Do you want to see these now?"

They both let out an enthusiastic yes.

I said, "Well, if that's what you want, then you need to drink the rest of those drinks now!"

They gulped down the rest of their drinks and waited. I started dancing again, grabbing the clasp to my bra, undoing it, and slowly taking it off. I started dancing closer to them, and they both reached over to grab my legs, pulling me closer. As they pulled me closer, they both reached out and grabbed my breasts. I pushed myself back and asked them if they wanted to see me take the rest of it off, and again, an enthusiastic yes. I turned my back on them and slowly started to take my underwear down, I got them around my ankles, turned around, and they were both passed out. *It's about fucking time*, she thought.

I got my clothes on and called Aaron to let him know what was going on. Aaron asked the guy if he wanted to take two with him. He said it wouldn't be a problem. She opened the back door and let them in. They taped their hands, feet, and mouth; bagged their heads; and took them out to the van. They started to wake up a little as they were being put into the van. Right before they closed the door, Roni walked up to David and pulled the bag off so he could see her face. His eyes opened wide. She looked at him and said that she just wanted him to see who was doing this to him and where he was going for the rest of his existence.

"Good riddance, asshole."

She closed the door, and the van drove off. We all got in the SUV and started heading back to Tucson. Roni started crying, and Lizzy reached over to comfort her. As Aaron drove down the freeway, the rest of us fell asleep. It was a long day, and he was glad it was over.

CHAPTER 19

Forming a New and Lasting Alliance

Aaron

We got back to Tucson late, so everyone just stayed at our house and went to sleep. I woke up the next morning and started making breakfast for everyone. They were all still sleeping, so I thought I would let them sleep for a bit longer. I thought about the night before and how Lizzy and Roni were not only all in with what we were doing, but they were really good at it. It always seemed like women were the angriest when it came to this, and it's understandable why. They are the ones that are the most taken advantage of, the ones that are the most abused. They're the ones that we're most fighting for, and maybe that's where we need to make the switch. We can still fight for all the ones that are and have been abused, but maybe we focus more on the women, the ones that have been always abused and harassed by the assholes in their lives, boyfriends, husbands, bosses—it didn't really matter. For some reason, I felt like we could really trust them. I don't know why, but I do. Definitely need to get Vanessa's thoughts on all this. I heard showers going, so I figured everyone was getting up. We had a lot to talk about.

Vanessa was the first to come into the kitchen. I gave her a hug and kiss and asked her how she was feeling. She said she was feeling good, like she had taken out more garbage, and she was fine with it. I asked her how she felt about Lizzy and Roni and their involvement in all this. She said that she thought they were great, perfect with what they did and how they did it.

"Yes, they were invested because it was people that hurt her, but they kept their cool. It was really impressive. We can talk to them about it, and then we need to move onto the business and get that all straight, or we're going to lose it all."

Vanessa agreed. Lizzy and Roni both came into the kitchen and sat down. They were both looking a little down, so we asked them if they were okay. They said that they were a little scared about everything that happened last night. Vanessa asked them what they were afraid of.

"Are you afraid of us?"

Roni said, "No, not at all. We're afraid that we liked it way too much."

I said, "What you liked was getting the revenge on someone that deserved it, not for the actual kill. There's a difference."

Roni got up and went to the bathroom, and Lizzy looked at us and asked if it was okay to tell her that she's already done this before. She felt like she needed to know. We both agreed that if it was what she wanted to, go ahead and do it. She's already into it, so might as well tell her that she'd been there before. Roni came back, and Lizzy told her she had something to tell her. Roni got a really worried look in her eyes.

Lizzy told her, "No, don't worry. It's just something that I felt I needed to share with you. We didn't want to have any secrets."

Vanessa and I told her to not worry. We're all pretty much tied to each other now. Lizzy went on to tell her what they had done, what Vanessa and I had done to protect her, how her boss was trying to take all her commission from the sale and that she was just fed up. Roni wasn't aware of the level of sexual harassment she had endured, and when she was told, she started to cry, like really loud and hard. Lizzy held her tight until she started to calm down.

Roni picked her head up and said that, "men suck," then she stopped and looked at me and said, "I'm sorry, not all men."

I told her that I totally understood where she was coming from. I didn't take offense to it at all. I just wanted to help as many people as

I can. That's my only goal, and it always has been. Vanessa asked Roni if she was okay with what she just heard. She said she was more than okay and that she wanted to help more people out, people like them.

I said, "That's great to hear, but remember, we still have the other business that we're working on."

Lizzy and Roni had gotten so caught up in stuff that they forgot. "Yes," they said, "we need to start working on that."

I felt bad for them. They basically just went through a very traumatic experience, and I was telling them that it's time to get right back to work. Let's get moving! What a heartless asshole. I looked at them and said that I realized last night was a pretty traumatic experience and I should've thought more about that. I was very sorry for that. Roni and Lizzy told me that I didn't have to be sorry, that I've done so much for them.

I told them, "Here's what we're going to do today. After we finish eating, we're going to go for a nice hike, spend some time outdoors, then come back home, go for a nice long swim. I'll make us a great dinner, and then we can get a great night's sleep and start over again tomorrow with this project, okay?"

They all loved the idea. The look of relief that came over their faces was immediate. I had to keep telling myself, *If you wanted to keep them in the game, you couldn't burn them out. You needed them fresh.* Something that a lot of chefs I worked for never learned. We finished breakfast, got dressed, and headed up to Reddington Pass. It's a gorgeous area with great places to hike. I didn't want to take them on a long hike, didn't want them to get too burned out. They still needed energy to swim and eat. We got done with our hike and headed back home. Once there, we changed into our suits and went swimming. Vanessa made them a pitcher of prickly pear margaritas; they had no idea what prickly pear was, but they sure loved the way it tasted. I thought that this is exactly what they needed—they needed to unwind from all the crap they just went through. I brought out some steaks and chicken to start grilling for dinner, along with some grilled vegetables and freshly made pico de gallo—it was easy and simple. I also brought out some red and white wine and some very old tequila just in case they wanted some. I had not had a drink for years, but I sometimes tried to live vicariously through others. I never caused anyone else harm, and as long as I never touched it, that's all that matters. I called them out of the pool. It was time to eat.

We were all sitting around the table, eating and laughing, having a great time when Lizzy brought up what had happened. She said that she and Roni had talked, and they wanted to know if they could keep doing this with us. They wanted to help make a difference. Vanessa told them they basically already are, but she and I required total loyalty and trust. Could they handle that? They both said that they were totally loyal to us and that we could trust them with our lives because they trust us with theirs.

I said, "Okay then, we can continue with this, but do not cross us. We're in this to help people just like we helped you. Please don't forget that." I told them, "Now that we have that taken care of, we need to get the legitimate business taken care of first, then we can move on to more, but everything will start in the morning."

They decided after eating, they would spend some time in the hot tub. They took a couple of shots of tequila, grabbed their wine, and got in the hot tub while I stayed behind to clean things up. They were all really excited about the future and what they were about to do both with helping people and with the gym concept. They thought that both would be extremely successful, and they couldn't wait to start. Lizzy and Roni had grown even closer since all this had happened, but Vanessa wasn't feeling worried like she was about Jody and Brian. These two weren't as mysterious or as damaged as the other two were. They were just two people that had been abused and needed help. Vanessa had gotten out of the hot tub to go and see if I was okay, and when we got back, Lizzy and Roni had their tops off, and they were making out with each other. I guess they were closer to each other than I thought. They heard us coming, and they stopped and apologized. They said this was a first for them both. We told them not to worry.

"We don't have a problem with what you're doing and who you are."

I told them to make sure they get some rest. "We're getting up early in the morning, working on the gym project, and then we're leaving for Kauai."

The thought of going to Kauai really excited them. They said they would be out in just a few minutes.

The next morning, I woke up, and I could smell coffee brewing and bacon cooking. I got out of bed and went to see what was going on. Roni and Lizzy woke up early, filled with excitement, and started making breakfast. They looked down and then up at me again and asked me, "Is that for us or Vanessa?"

I looked down, and there I was, hard as a rock. I covered myself and apologized. They both said that there's no reason to apologize.

"Just because you saw what we were doing last night, it doesn't mean we don't still like that."

I went back to the bedroom and woke up Vanessa to tell her what they were doing and what had happened. She started laughing and looked down. I was still hard as a rock. She grabbed me and pulled me in bed. As we made love, I could've sworn that they were watching.

I whispered that to Vanessa. She said, "Follow me." Vanessa threw off the covers, got on her hands and knees, facing partially away from the door, just enough so she could still see the door, and then she told me to slowly take her from behind. I started slowly and then built-up speed, massaging her tits, and spanking her ass. We both finally came at the same time and rolled over onto the bed. We gave each other a kiss and got up to take a shower. As the water was warming up, Vanessa whispered in my ear that when she looked over at the door, she could see them watching, touching each other and themselves while they watched. I asked if they had seen her looking.

She said, "No, they didn't."

She was looking through her hair, and they couldn't see her."

I asked if that bothered her, and she said, "No, it didn't. In fact, it turned her on."

"Did it bother you?" she asked.

"No, it didn't, and as long as you're okay, that's all that matters to me."

We got done with the shower, got dressed, and went to the kitchen for breakfast. When Lizzy and Roni saw them, they got big smiles on their faces and said good morning. They said they're looking forward to going to Kauai today and looking forward even more to everything in the future. I agreed. I said it was time to go over the plans and get an update on what's happening. Roni said that the build-out at Park City was about halfway done. It would take longer for the bunker to be built. She's been having the construction company send her pictures and videos of the progress, which she showed to the group. She's been dealing with small issues, which she hoped was okay, and anything larger, she would bring to them. Vanessa told her that was fine, and both she and I said it all looked great and if she had a time frame on when it would be done. Roni told us that that above ground should be done in the next four weeks, bunker 6–8. We both said that was good, and then we turned our attention to Lizzy.

"How's it coming with the equipment that you want?"

Lizzy told us that all the things she wants so far had been ordered, and it's all on its way. Her sister was handling it and keeping an eye on everything. She was also able to get a discount because they said they would be doing at least three locations.

"Is it okay to do that?"

I looked at her and said, "Well, you're a part-owner, right?"

Lizzy said "Wait, what? I thought I was just going to pay you back by living in Utah?"

"Vanessa and I spoke last night and decided that since we were all going to be traveling a lot that we would just go ahead and make you an owner. Actually, we're making both of you owners. You will each be receiving 20 percent, and you don't have to pay anything back. Oh, and that's 20 percent of the entire company, meaning everything we open up."

They both couldn't believe what they were hearing. This just kept getting more and more amazing.

"Everything that you all have done for us, we're forever indebted to you."

"We take care of each other. That's what we're all about. Please don't forget that. Now what about here?"

Roni said, "Things here are going well. Obviously, it will take longer because we started later, but it's all coming along nicely."

Lizzy said that all the equipment has been ordered and was awaiting delivery. Roni asked why he didn't want a bunker at this site. I told her the ground was as hard as a rock, and it would take time. She said she could speak to the foreman before we leave and see how hard and how much extra. I told her if the cost was reasonable to go ahead and have it done. Now it's time for everyone to get packed and be ready in two hours to go to the airport. Lizzy and Roni asked if we were taking the private jet. Vanessa told them that yes. We are taking it. It's the only way to go now. Roni got done giving the foreman some final instructions, and we took off for the airport. We were all really excited to start a new adventure.

CHAPTER 20

Off to Paradise

Aaron

Once we were in the air, we had some food and drinks and talked about the gym ideas for Kauai. This one would be a bit different. There would be a lot of higher-end clientele on the island because of the side we're on. We have gotten to know some locals that can help us with employees for the gym, but they also get paid a lot more on the island than they do on the mainland. Roni said that her friend in Park City gave her a construction company on the island to use. We can talk to him when we get there.

I said, "It sounds like we have things lined up and ready to go. You all are going to love the place, but things definitely work in a different time. The whole vibe will be so different with all this. Lizzy, here's what we're going to need to do. Your sister, what's her name again?"

Lizzy said, "Jenny."

"Okay. Jenny is going to have to get it set up there, get it open, and then move through the rest getting them staffed with responsible people."

Lizzy said, "She's got two kids, remember?"

I told her, "That's fine. Bring the kids. Tell her to hire a tutor for them, and we can put them on the private jet, and they can go where they need to go. Kids are the most important thing in all this. Vanessa and I will make sure they're taken care of."

They really couldn't believe what they were hearing. It just keeps getting better and better. She said she would call her and talk to her. Tears started welling up in Lizzy's eyes. Vanessa asked her what was wrong. She said that she's never felt so loved and cared about, never in her life.

Vanessa told her to get used to it. "This is who he is. He'll never let you down, and he will forever spoil us all."

I told them, "We still have a while before we land. We should probably try to get some sleep."

Lizzy and Roni were way too excited to sleep, but they thought they would try. They cuddled up in the seats in the back. They had both grown really close to each other since all this has happened—traumatic experiences can do that. They'd known each other for a long time, and right now, all they have is each other.

I woke everyone up about an hour before we were supposed to land. They swore they were in a dream, but lucky for them, they were in reality. So when we land, we will show you around the house so you can get a feel of the place. We can contact all the people that we need to for the construction end of it, then we can take a trip around the island. There are so many places to see, but we will give you a quick tour, and then you can take some day trips on your own if you want to."

Vanessa looked at them and said, "It's time for us to continue what it is that we do. Aaron was basically abused by a lot of people that he worked with or for. That's how this whole thing started. He was doing this before he knew me, and then he got me involved. Now the two of you are here. We need to continue what we've set out to do, which is to help people, but we need to know if the two of you truly still want to be involved."

I told them that if they wanted to stay behind and work on the business, we totally understood, but we need to keep going. Roni and Lizzy both said that we have them for life. "Where you go, we go, and we will help you with whatever you need, no questions asked, and as far as trust goes, you can always trust us, for life."

"Okay, when we get home, we will talk about creating a new recipe."

"One piece of business we haven't talked about, Lizzy, how are the investments coming along?"

Lizzy opened up her laptop and signed into the brokerage site where the money was invested. She started showing us where the money was invested, seriously great job with great returns, very impressive. I told her to make sure that she takes her commission for the work. She told me that she would rather not. They've done enough for her.

I told her, "We pay people for the jobs they do. You've earned that commission."

Lizzy said, "I get it, but for now, I would rather just hold off doing it."

Vanessa said, "How about this. Jenny has two kids. How about you take the commission and you invest it for them?"

I thought that was a great idea. Lizzy's eyes started welling up with tears again. I looked at her and said, "You better start getting used to this, or you're going to run out of tears." Everyone started laughing.

Lizzy and Roni said that in time they would. It's just very different, but they would never take anything that's done for them for granted. The plane landed, and we had an SUV waiting to pick us up to take us home. Lizzy and Roni were in awe of what they were looking at. This was going to be fun!

We got to the house, and we gave Lizzy and Roni a tour. It was way more than they could ever have imagined. They had seen three different climates in such a very short period. Eventually, they would have to slow down and stay in one place so their bodies could have time to catch up or they would have some serious jetlag. Vanessa told them that they could have one of the master suites. Not trying to assume anything, but there were also three bedrooms. They told her that they would share the master suite. They all got settled in, and I took them on a tour of the property. They saw a lot of great spots where they could build-out. They could add onto the studio for the workout area. Lizzy asked, "Would you all be opposed to using the tree house for the massage area?"

Vanessa and I said that it was a great idea, and we didn't mind it a bit. Lizzy and Roni wanted to take a swim. They asked if we minded. We told them no, that we would probably join them later. We could look out the window at them, and you could tell they were falling for each other. I asked Vanessa if we need to worry. She said no. They're not falling for her, and their personalities were way different. While they swam, Vanessa and I were planning for the next recipe. The person that they needed to go after was one that wasted a lot of my time, money, and energy. He was an investor that I got involved with, and when everything was going well, he pulled the rug out from under me. He left a lot of people high and dry—vendors, landlord, and worst of all, employees. He might be tougher because I always thought he was a bit on the sketchy side, has a ton of money, but very sketchy. Never knew who he dealt with. He never told me and then one day, like Keyser Söze, *poof*, he was gone. Left everything behind, and we never saw him again.

Vanessa said that he sounds a bit scary.

I said, "True, but he's also a lot older."

Vanessa said she needed his name so she could do a deep dive on him.

"Mauri Tombs is his name."

Vanessa said, "Even the name is scary."

I told her, "This one might have to be done from a distance. Not sure if we want to lay hands on this one."

Vanessa found him. "He's living in Austin, in a large house with nursing care. Basically, he's living in a long-term care facility for one."

"Well, that's interesting. Maybe he pissed so many people off that no one wants to take care of him. We're going to need to go out there and do some recon work."

Vanessa looked at me and asked me why I'm trying to sound so GI Joe. "Why can't you just say we need to go check it out?"

"Okay, fine, let's do that."

Roni and Lizzy were coming inside from swimming. They looked like they were so fucking happy. We didn't want to break up that fun, but we told them we would include them in what we were doing. I asked them if they wanted something to eat. They both said they were really hungry from all that swimming and playing. I gave them a pulled pork sandwich with a spicy mango BBQ sauce and some papaya iced tea. They were in heaven. The last time I heard moaning like that was when Vanessa and I made love before they left Tucson.

I looked at them and said, "Are you ladies okay? You feeling okay?"

They both smiled and rolled their eyes. "We think we just had an orgasm."

"Well then, I guess I succeeded."

They both said to him, "Oh my god, yes, you did."

So while they were all eating, I looked at Lizzy and Roni and asked them if they'd ever been to Austin. They both said no and what was there.

We told them, "We were going to create another recipe, and we told you both that we would tell you if you wanted to go along. You both looked like you were having so much fun out there we didn't want to disturb that."

Lizzy looked at Vanessa and me and said, "What's Charlie without his angels?" Everyone burst out laughing. Lizzy said, "No, really, it's you and three beautiful ladies, right?"

Vanessa said, "She's right. Okay, I guess that's what we are then."

I said, "I'm going to insist on a few things then."

They all said, "And that is?"

"You all need some training, self-defense, hand to hand, weapons, and someone else needs to learn how to fly the jet because if something happens to me, you have to be able to get out." I said, "We can delay Austin a few weeks and bring someone in to train you here. The jet, we can do in a simulator at the airport so we can at least give some experience."

They all wanted to learn how to fly. That was fine by me. The more, the merrier.

"Now do we need a theme song?"

When I was doing the security, I met some former military, special forces guys. I had them come out to train them in everything they needed to defend themselves. I made sure to remind Roni and Lizzy that the training was completely business. Do not strike up friendships, relationships, anything. They both told me not to worry.

All they're interested in was each other and Vanessa and I—that's it. I also made sure to remind the trainers of that as well, but these guys are beyond reproach.

Besides the fact, the money and the professional relationship meant more than anything. They wouldn't jeopardize that. I had guys from the same group in Tucson and now Park City. They would go wherever I ask them to go, and we would always be protected. It's like we had our own private army. Even though I had already been trained, we all went through it together. There's nothing wrong with learning more especially since there were things we all could forget. Same with the flight training, we all went through it together although I had enough hours not only for my license but to be able to fly solo. I could always have them come up and learn as we go places too, but they all have the basics down. They could handle it if something happened to me. I stretched all this training out to four months, which wasn't a bad thing because everything in Park City was finished and waiting for us to open it, and Tucson was coming up right behind them. Everyone was seriously in the best shape of our lives; it was a great feeling. It would be great to get Tucson finished and then go from Austin to Park City, Tucson, and then open on Kauai. I asked everyone if they were ready to go to Austin. They were already packed, and Vanessa packed for me.

"Okay, let's get to the airport and be on our way. I'll be doing the flying with help from my angels."

On the way, we talked about what the plan was going to be.

"We're going to be staying at the Lake Austin Spa Resort. I got us two suites right next to each other. Both have hot tubs on the patios, bedrooms with fireplaces, and a whole bunch of stuff that we will all like even though it's not what we're here for. After we check-in, we will drive by the house and see what it's like. Check to see if there's any live security that we need to take care of. Anything that's electronic, Vanessa will take care of once we get there. Then based on that, we will decide how to proceed." I asked them if they brought enticing things to wear. "This guy is a total ass, and I don't think it matters how old he is. He'll always be that way."

All of them at the same time asked, "Do you really think that we didn't?"

"I guess I really don't need to ask that question anymore. It's a little over seven hours to Austin. You all might want to get some rest."

Lizzy and Roni curled up in the back and went to sleep, and Vanessa stayed up front with me. Eventually, she fell asleep, and I was left to my own thoughts. *The cynicism that I usually feel toward people left with Vanessa, and it's leaving with these two as well. There's just something about them. I feel like this whole thing is going to go on forever, or at least until we get caught or we choose to stop. Meeting Lizzy, starting the gyms, all those help to make us legit. Okay, Vanessa hates it when I talk like a gangster—legitimate. So if we want to make ourselves seem like we are legitimate, then we need to keep expanding, which means we need to get another place to expand to. I've always loved Austin, so why not here? It's a great place to be, and they have lots of ranches where we could do the same concept. I will ask them once they wake up. In the meantime, I need to stay awake.*

Vanessa eventually got up and went to the back to sleep, and Lizzy made her way up front. I asked her how she was feeling about everything that's been happening. There's been a lot of changes that have come her way in the last few months. She said for the first time in her life, she felt calm, and she felt safe—something she hadn't ever felt and that it's because of me. I came into her life, and everything changed for the better. I told her that everything happens for a reason, me coming into her life was for a reason. It was to help her get out of all the crap she was in; and in the long run, I have a partner for life in both businesses that we're in.

She asked me why. "Why me? Why did you decide that I was the one that you were going to help?"

I asked her if she would get offended if I told her. She said nothing that I do could offend her.

"Okay, when I first saw you walking toward me, I thought you had to be one of the most gorgeous girls I had ever seen. Multiple scenarios went running through my mind, and yes, I've told Vanessa that. We don't get jealous or hide things from each other. But then I started talking to you, and yes, you still are one of the most gorgeous girls I've ever seen, but then I could see how much pain you were in, and all I wanted to do was help you."

"You've done so much to help me, more than any man ever has."

"Well, you're in a better place, and you need to understand that it's not going away. We're not going away."

She asked me if there was anything that she could say that would offend me.

I said, "Nothing. I don't get offended easily."

She asked me when I saw her walking toward me, what multiple scenarios went running through my mind.

I asked her, "Are you sure you want to hear this?"

As she closed the door to the cockpit, she said if she didn't, she wouldn't have asked.

"I wondered what it would be like if you were slowly buttoning down your shirt and slowly taking it off. I was wondering what you were wearing under your skirt and if it matched your bra. I was wondering what you smelled like, what you tasted like. I was wondering what those gorgeous breasts looked like. I kept thinking of you being in front of me half-dressed and what I would do to you. Does that give you a general idea of what I was thinking?"

"Yes, it does make it pretty clear what you were thinking about. Does Vanessa know what you were thinking about when you saw me for the first time?"

Yes, she does. I tell her everything."

"Roni and I were talking about how open the two of you are and what a great relationship it was."

"We've worked really hard to make it a good relationship, and we will continue to do so."

Right about then, the cockpit door opened, and it was Roni. "Am I interrupting anything?"

Lizzy said, "No, babe, we're just talking, and we didn't want to wake anyone."

I told them to wake Vanessa and get buckled in. "We're going to be landing in a few minutes."

CHAPTER 21

Welcome to the Best City in Texas

Aaron

We took a car service to the resort, very different from the other places that we've been to. It's on Lake Austin, and the views are just beautiful. You would think that with how much time we spend in these places that we would not stay in such a nice place, but we needed to keep appearances up. We all got checked in, and Lizzy and Roni came to our room.

I said, "Our first piece of business is, do you want to expand to here?"

Everyone was a bit confused. I asked if they wanted to buy a place here and expand the gym business here. I told them that I was looking at ranches while we were flying, and I thought it would not only be a great idea but a great cover. They all wanted to go and look and see what it looked like. I figured everyone should have a say since we're all involved in the business now. He told Lizzy and Roni to go back to their room and get ready and we would go and check it out. I told Vanessa about the conversation in the cockpit on the way in.

She said, "With all the things that you had to endure with Jody, don't worry about it because I'm not. I just wanted to make sure I told you. She told me she appreciated that. You remember I told you when they were watching us how much it turned me on, right?"

"Yes, I definitely remember that."

She said, "Good, maybe we'll have to arrange it so that happens more."

I didn't disagree. I asked her if she had looked into Mauri's finances. She said she had, and he has quite a bit, and he has even more hidden offshore.

"Is it easily accessible for us to get?"

She looked at me with that look.

I said, "Okay, I'm sorry. If there is any opening, anyway, to access the money, you'll get it, right? That would be correct. Okay, well, let's get it set up then, and let's go and check the ranch property and his house."

We got an SUV from the resort and started toward the ranch. The agent was waiting for us when we got there. The house was a five-bedroom, five-bathroom, 6,750 square feet on a little over forty acres. It had an arena with a horse stable, perfect to build out for the gym, saltwater pool, waterfall, and on and on. Like all the properties, when the weather was good outside, there was so much Lizzy could do outside with the clients. We all gathered by the pool and talked about how this is the property we wanted. I had looked at a lot online, and this was the best one I felt for what we wanted to do. Roni said that there was a lot that she could do with the place. We just needed to find contractors. I said I was already working on it. We all loved the property, and we decided that we should go for it. We called the agent over, and we made a cash offer to her. She couldn't have been happier. I know it seems crazy that we keep buying in cash, but we have a lot of it. It's coming from a dummy corporation, and it's basically helping to launder what we've got. Plus, it's for the business as well. The agent was going to bring all the paperwork to resort later on in the day for us to sign. Vanessa got the bank info so she could transfer the money. Now it was time to go and check out Mauri's house.

I needed to see the inside, so I had the girls bring something really distracting to wear. Vanessa and Lizzy were going to pose as realtors and they would ask to speak to the owner. Someone wanted to make a cash offer. Mauri cared about one thing, money, and that was it; and if he had two extremely hot women making the offer, he would at least listen to it. Short skirts, no underwear, tight button-up shirts, tiny bras, high heels, you had him at hello. Oh, and let's not forget the cameras for me to look at the place and see what kind of security he has inside. I gave them both chokers that had cameras in the medallions in the front and earbuds so we could communicate. There was no outside security, so he must not be that worried. He did have cameras, but anything of an electronic nature, Vanessa would handle it without a problem.

"Okay, are you two ready to go?"

They both looked at Roni and me, dressed the way they were, with their cute hoodies on, and asked us, "I don't know. Are we?"

"Yes," we both replied, "you are more than ready."

We watched them walking up to the house, and out of nowhere came a guy and a girl that we hadn't seen before. Apparently, there was a little hidden guardhouse right by the front door. We were going to have to deal with them before we started. They asked us what we wanted. We told them who we were and what we were there for. We worked for a private investor that was interested in buying the house, full cash offer. They told us to wait while they checked to see if he wanted to see us. We could see through the girl's cameras that the woman security guard was looking them up and down.

I said, "Now there's an advantage."

Roni agreed. The man was on the phone talking to someone. When he stopped and told the girls to move toward the cameras, they stepped in front of the cameras. The man hung up, and they walked them inside.

*****

Vanessa

The inside was definitely not as good as the outside. It wasn't that it was rundown—it was just outdated. The guard told them that he was instructed to show them the house and then they could go and make their offer. They looked in every room and closet. No one but this guy lived there, and there were no other security guards but them. The whole place looked like it was shut down. When we were done, they took us into a room that was by the front door. They opened the door, and there, Mauri was, sitting in a chair. He really didn't look that bad. He was frail, probably couldn't fight off a six-year-old but still not too bad. He sure perked up when he saw Lizzy and me walk in the door. He welcomed us and asked us if we liked the house. We both said we loved it, and we wanted to make an offer. He said that was good news, but he was sure they couldn't give what they wanted.

We said to him, "Well, tell us what you want."

He said he wanted $1.1 million for the house. Seriously, the house was worth about $750K, but I looked at him and said that he's in luck because they're authorized to go that high. He couldn't believe it. He thought for sure he had just pulled one over on these two dumb girls. We told him that we would go and get the paperwork and cashier's check and be back later tonight to give it all to him. He said that he couldn't wait. He walked us to the door, and before we left, he gave us a key and told us to let ourselves in when we get back. We said to give us a few hours and we would be back.

We got back out to the SUV and asked Aaron, "Why do you think he did that, gave us a key?"

Aaron said, "Well, knowing him the way I do, he's giving the guards the night off because he expects to have some fun with the two of you."

Lizzy said, "So then we'll have some fun with him. Should we bring Roni too?"

I said, "With three of us, he might wind up dying of a heart attack."

Aaron said, "No, not this guy. Plus you need to keep him alive long enough for me to take care of him. You need to bring two bottles of champagne just in case the guards are there and enough drugs for all of them. We need to go get a few things back at the resort, different outfits for all of them, and the stuff that I need."

We forged some documents and a cashier's check and started heading back to his house. Again, we had on the cameras, the earpieces, and enough drugs for three if needed. We were dressed in such revealing clothes he would never be able to resist. We got to the house, and as soon as we let ourselves in, Aaron killed all alarms and camera feeds. I also set it up so it wiped all of the recordings from earlier in the day. We checked the house, and there was no one there. We got to his room, and we opened the door. There he was, sitting on the couch. Next to him was the woman security guard. Both of them had nothing but robes on.

He said, "While we were waiting for you to get here, we thought we would make ourselves comfortable. You don't mind, do you?"

I said, "Not at all. We were going out after, and we brought a friend with us. Do you mind?"

Mauri said, "Not at all. The more, the merrier."

Lizzy asked, "Did you want to take care of business now or toast our deal first?"

The security guard, Allie, said, "Why don't we toast the deal first?"

Mauri nodded.

Roni told them that we had brought champagne for the celebration. "Do you have glasses somewhere?"

Mauri told her they were behind the bar. Roni went behind the bar and poured the champagne. In their glasses, she put the drugs in and took them out to them. She grabbed the rest of the glasses and gave them to Lizzy and me.

I held up her glass and said, "Congratulations on making a cool million today!"

Mauri looked at us and asked us if we wanted to earn some of that money back. I asked them how we could do that. He said to us that he's an old man now, probably not much time left, and he would love to see all of us beautiful ladies party together.

"What exactly does that mean?" asked Lizzy.

Mauri looked at Allie, and she stood up, walked over to Lizzy, and started dancing slowly with her. Lizzy was wearing a short strapless dress that zipped up the side. As they were dancing, Allie slowly unzipped the side of the dress and let it fold down to expose one of her breasts. After she did that, she untied her robe to reveal that she wasn't wearing anything underneath. She unzipped Lizzy's dress the rest of the way and let it fall to the ground. She then pulled her toward her and started slowly dancing with her again as she was rubbing Lizzy's ass and back.

Mauri looked at me and said, "That's what I mean. Why don't the two of you join them?"

I walked over to Roni and walked her toward Lizzy and Allie. Lizzy and Allie turned around and slowly started to take my and Roni's clothes off. After we were all naked, we started to dance and stroke each other's bodies. I looked over at Mauri. He had opened his robe, and he had started stroking himself. After this went on for what seemed like forever, I looked over again, and he was passed out. Allie saw that, and as she walked over to him, she stumbled onto the couch, and she also passed out. All of us got our clothes back on and let Aaron in the house.

"Jesus, we thought they were never going to pass out, and as much as we were all enjoying that, we needed to get this moving. What are we going to do with her?"

Aaron said, "She made her choice to help him, not to mention to treat you three like you're fucking whores. What do you think we should do with her?"

All of us said, "She deserves whatever she gets. We don't need anyone else in this group. Don't you remember what happened when they added the fourth angel?"

I said, "This was the time when Aaron gives you a choice. You can stay or go. They all chose to stay. Give her some more drugs to keep her asleep, not dead but asleep. I need to tape Mauri up and prop him up in his recliner over here."

*****

Aaron

He started to wake up, and the first thing he saw was me. He couldn't believe his eyes. I reminded him of all the bullshit he caused, stealing from people, not just money but reputations as well.

"We all sold our souls to the devil because we thought we would get something out of it and what we got was you."

To this day, all he could say was the same thing: "It's business, and in business, people get hurt."

"That just doesn't cut it anymore. For your sins, for your evil, you'll burn in hell, but I have something special for you. You're going to burn from the inside out."

Lizzy and Roni had never seen me this way. Vanessa told them there were a lot of people that hurt him, and he was going to pay them back for what they had done. They were all here for whatever he needed. I taped his mouth shut and cut a round hole in the tape. I poured pure grain alcohol down his throat until he started choking and he stopped. The booze made its way into his system. When Mauri took a deep breath, I lit a match and dropped it in the hole. His entire mouth lit on fire. It was like he was burning from the inside out.

"Burn in hell, you bastard!"

I took off Mauri's restraints and left him in the chair. I turned on the gas to the fireplace and the stove and oven in the kitchen. While I was taking care of that, the girls started to clean up any traces of us that we might have left behind. I lit candles in both rooms, and we left. As we were driving away, everyone was really quiet, and then there was a huge explosion and fire. Whatever there was of us left in there was gone now. Burn in hell. We got back to the resort, and we went to our room. Lizzy asked me if I was okay.

I said, "I am. I don't feel bad when people get what they deserve for the pain they've caused. Sad thing is, I see them again, and I think that maybe something inside them has changed. It hasn't. People like him don't change. They go through life thinking that they can take and have whatever they want, and it's fucking sick, and it's fucking sad, and that's why I do what I do. I have no remorse for what I do at all. I'm sorry if that bothers you all. I really am."

Lizzy and Roni told me that it doesn't bother them at all. They get it, and they actually respect what he's doing. He's right. People deserve what they get.

"The agent for the house should be here in the morning to sign the paperwork. We need to clean up and get some rest."

*****

The agent showed up the next morning, and Vanessa and I signed the papers and transferred the money. Time to move out of here and into our new fourth home. We all packed up and headed toward our new home. Although nights like last night could take a toll mentally and emotionally, we still felt justified and satisfied with what we did, and we always will. We all got settled into our rooms, and we turned our attention to business. I told them we need to get started here and what were the updates on the rest.

I looked at Lizzy and said, "It's time for the million-dollar question. What's the name going to be?"

Lizzy said that she wanted to get our opinions on the names.

Vanessa said, "No, this is your baby. You tell *us* what you're going to name them."

Lizzy said, "Okay, for the gym side, Achieve Your Balance, and for the massage side, Unbelievable Touch."

We all asked, "What about the We Beat You one?"

Lizzy said, "Since all these places are so elegant that the names needed to fit, and she felt that those do."

I said, "Okay, then it's settled. Let's start getting the marketing going and all the collateral printed. Have you all come up with the programs, promotions, all that you need?"

Lizzy said, "Yes, we have all of that lined up, but I need to tell you something. Please don't be upset with me."

Vanessa said, "We would never get upset with you. What's going on?"

"When I decided what I wanted the names to be, I got the ball rolling on all the stuff that we needed, signage, all of it, so it's pretty much all done."

I looked at Vanessa and looked back at Lizzy and told her, "That's fantastic! It's your baby. I'm glad you took the initiative and got it done. For Tucson too?"

Lizzy said, "Yes, that's also complete. The phone lines and stuff were already in, so that was easy. All the new staff is waiting for us."

"Okay, so let's get a good night's rest, and we can start in the morning. The rest of the day, we can swim and relax. Map out exactly what we want to do here."

Vanessa and Lizzy stayed behind to make some lunch, and Roni and I went to drive around and look at the property.

Roni and I hadn't spent as much time talking as the rest. I knew that she was good friends with Lizzy and that they were growing closer. She asked some of the same questions as Lizzy did, why her, why did we help her, and I told her that it was mostly because of what people had done to her but also because she was friends with Lizzy, that you meant something to us and protecting you is something we will always do. She wanted to know why I never asked for anything in return.

I said, "Do you mean things like sex?"

"Yes, sex. Whenever any man does something for a woman, that's exactly what they're looking for, sex or some version of that. Sex, pictures, something they can use to control."

I told her, "I'm sorry, but that's not who I am. I don't expect to get anything for what I do. I do it to help you, to help you have a better life. Look at what we did for you with those three people. Well, four if you count the owner. Did we or have we asked you for anything? No. We haven't. In fact, all we've done is given to you, correct?"

"Yes, that's true. I'm sorry I brought anything up."

"You don't need to be sorry. You just need to believe, that's all." I said, "I'll give you one more example. Before we left Tucson, when Vanessa and I were making love to each other, we knew you two were watching. Did we get mad or say anything?"

Roni looked at me, turned bright red, and said, "Oh fuck." Roni said, "No, no, you didn't, correct."

"We didn't, and that should tell you something. You all are one of us now, period, end of story, and nothing is going to change that."

Roni said nothing.

"Only one thing. If you betray us."

Roni said, "That will never happen."

Roni said that she and Lizzy did enjoy the show they were getting.

"Well, we enjoyed giving it to you. It seriously turned Vanessa on."

Roni turned red again and looked away from me so I couldn't see her. We got done looking and went back to the house for lunch.

The lunch they created was really good—cheeses, meats, fresh tomatoes, fresh berries, infused olive oil, and a sweet and tangy balsamic syrup and French bread. I looked at Vanessa and said that I taught her well.

She said, "Uh, we went to the store."

"Well, it's still beautiful."

After lunch, we all went for a swim. It definitely helped to relax us, which was something we desperately needed. We all climbed into the hot tub, and Lizzy asked me who or what is next.

Vanesa said, "You know, Lizzy, it's interesting that you should ask what is next."

I agreed. "We've never gone after corporations before, only individuals, but what about the corporations that have enabled them? That would be a much larger takedown, don't you think? That would require more of your skills than mine, Vanessa."

Vanessa said she would research it further. I circled back to the original question: who is next?

"I haven't really thought about it. There are plenty of them out there, and it usually just hits me in a moment when I'm not thinking about it. You know what, if you two have any ideas as to who, feel free to bring them up. You're in this just as much as we are."

They both said that there were plenty of people they could put out there. "We will let you know the worst of them."

Vanessa and I told them about our idea of getting jobs at some of the worst places and dealing with those people as well. They liked it, but we would be busy until we die.

"Might be easier to scour social media and see if we can find them there. You know how people are always complaining about work and bosses."

"That's a hell of an idea, Roni. That might actually work."

Vanessa said, "We all make a great fucking team. The ideas that flow so easily between us. We care about each other. Take care of each other. We're not going anywhere." Vanessa asked me if I wanted to go and take a nap.

I said yes. I was tired and needed some rest. As we walked out of the room, Vanessa turned around, looked at them, and said, "Showtime, ladies."

We got into the room, and I looked at her and said, "Showtime? Really?"

She said, "Yes, showtime. I told you how much it turns me on when they're watching."

I asked her, "What are you going to do if they try to join in?"

She said, "We will cross that bridge when and if they come to it." She made sure to leave the door halfway open so they wouldn't miss a thing.

I grabbed her from behind, and I started rubbing the front of her body. I took off her shirt and pulled down her shorts, biting and grabbing her ass. I pushed her on the bed. I took off my clothes and climbed on top of her. She rolled me on my back and got on top of me. As she slowly started to grind on me, she looked over, and Lizzy and Roni were sitting on the floor, up against the wall, shirts pulled up and shorts down around their ankles. Vanessa leaned down and whispered in Aaron's ear, "You want to ask them to come in and sit and watch?"

I enthusiastically said yes.

Vanessa sat back up again, turned her head, and looked directly at them. They stopped, wondering if they did something wrong. They were starting to stand up and walk away when Vanessa said, "The couch in here over by the bed is a lot more comfortable."

They looked at each other in amazement. They were about to speak when Vanessa put her finger up to her lips, making the "be quiet" sign, and motioned them over toward the couch. They finished taking their clothes off, and they sat on the couch, legs up and holding each other's hand. Vanessa continued to grind on me until she got off, got on her hands and knees, and I started fucking her from behind, massaging her breasts and spanking her ass. But this time, Vanessa wanted something different. She told me to tell her when I was ready to cum. When I did, she lay on her back and let me cum all over her chest. Right about the same time, both Lizzy and Roni came one right after the other along with Vanessa. That was the most amazing orgasm, for all of them. Lizzy and Roni got up quietly and walked out of the room, closing the door. Vanessa asked me what I thought.

I said, "It was really good, but I think that was more for your benefit, right?"

She agreed and asked me if I was okay with it. I said as long as it makes her happy, that's all I care about. Lizzy and Roni got back to their room, looked at each other, and said almost simultaneously. "What the fuck just happened"

Neither one of them knew, but what they did know was that what just happened was the most amazing thing that's ever happened to them in their lives, and they hoped it happened again really soon.

*****

We all decided to lay down for a while and take a nap. We had never felt so happy and safe. It's a feeling we never wanted to stop. We all woke up and hopped in the shower. We all met in the kitchen so we could decide what to do for dinner. We decided to go to this BBQ place called Salt Lick—some of the best BBQ around.

Vanessa asked, "What about if we go and pick it up and bring it back to eat by the pool for our last night here?"

We all thought that was a great idea. We would still all go and pick it up so that they could see some of the sights. We ordered online and went to go pick it up. We were really happy with everything that we were seeing. We were really going to enjoy this place. We got back home, took it all out to the pool, and enjoyed the BBQ. The sounds we were making while we ate weren't orgasmic this time, but we loved what we were eating. By the time we were done, we were a mess.

I said, "Only one way to solve this." I got up and jumped in the pool.

They all followed right behind me. After swimming and laughing for a while, we all got out and cleaned the place up. We decided that we were going to leave early for Park City, so we all said good night and went to our rooms. It was a great time in Austin, and we're glad that we're expanding here. I got up to grab a bottle of water, and as I walked by their room, I heard noises that I could only associate with orgasms. I went back to my room and told Vanessa what I had heard.

First thing out of her mouth was, "Hey, how come we weren't asked to watch?"

I said, "Right?"

We both started laughing, gave each other a kiss, and fell asleep in each other's arms.

CHAPTER 22

Time to Open the "Legit" Business

Aaron

We all woke up feeling really refreshed and ready to get on with the day. We grabbed our stuff and headed to the airport. I was still going to fly because I needed to teach them how to do it. It's a little over two hours gate to gate, so we needed all the time we could get. I wasn't a licensed instructor, but I could still get them training time, and then by the time they got to an instructor, it would be a piece of cake. I wanted them to learn more so that if something happened to me, they would have a way out. I was going to let Vanessa take off and land. I would be there right with her, but she was actually going to do it. She's had more time than the rest, so she should be okay. I mean, what's the point of teaching them to fly if they don't know how to take off and land? I'm not teaching them to be terrorists. She was so very smooth on the takeoff. It was almost as good as me—almost. I'm a competitive person, but not when it comes to Vanessa. We've never felt the need to compete with each other. We would rather help each other than compete. Once in the air, I went in the back to relax, and Roni went up front to get some airtime in. I sat across Lizzy. and she started talking about the gyms and what we needed to get done. Jenny has hired all the staff, including a manager to handle things when she's gone. That's fine because no matter who is hired, the security team has been tasked with making sure everything runs smoothly while we're gone. Us and Jenny have authority over them—it's just in place for when we're gone.

"As much as I hate to ask, do the trainers and masseuses look like you? Well, no one will ever look like you, but you know what I mean."

"Yes, I know what you mean, and yes, they do. Not as nice, but they do. I had Jenny send my pictures and videos of them training someone. I figured it was the best way to get around the law."

I said, "I totally agree. So everything there is ready to go. I figured we could take Jenny and the kids with us to Tucson."

"She hired a tutor already, so that's ready to go."

"Is the tutor going to have issues with traveling?"

Lizzy said, "No, she was young, just graduated college, and has no attachments."

I said, "That's perfect."

I told Lizzy to walk with me to the cockpit. Vanessa and Roni were talking about flying when I stopped them and said, "Before we land, we need to talk. Vanessa and I have been getting away with what we're doing for as long as we have because we've been really careful and really secretive. You see how we are always trying to cover our tracks whether it's wiping security cameras to our DNA. We never create a recipe the same way. That way, there's nothing to connect to anyone. Then the two of you came into our lives, and we loosened up on what we do and how we do it."

Lizzy asked if we are regretting what we've done.

I told her not at all. "That's not why I'm saying this. I'm telling you because when we land, we are going to be surrounded by all kinds of people, from family to friends to workers. These will be the most people we've been around in a long time, and when we're around them, we can't talk about or insinuate anything, and I'm not just talking about the recipes we create. I'm talking about *everything* we do. Do you understand? People can't know about any of that. I'm not talking about the two of your relationship. That's a personal part of your life. I'm talking about the four of us and anything we do together."

They all completely agreed with me. "We're all in it, and we can't make any mistakes at all, or we all go down. If you have an idea, a thought, if something just pops into your head, think before you say anything. If we're all alone in the house and we know that no one is around, okay, talk, but talk quietly. No texting or emailing either. No trails."

They understood. I told them we were going to need to get ready to land. Roni went in the back with Lizzy, and I stayed up front with Vanessa to land.

*****

We got back to the property and were amazed by all the improvements that had been made: the signage for the gym and massage studio, the way the roads led to the different areas—very impressive, all of it. We got to the house and got settled in. Jenny made sure that all the staff was there, ready to meet us. We went down to look at everything, and it was amazing—all of it. The workout equipment was some of the most modern you could get, brand-new shiny weights and benches, TRX bands hanging from metal bars, treadmills, rowers, and spin cycles. They also had decided to add a juice bar with coffee drinks and healthy snacks, all displayed on big-screen monitors. After looking over everything, we went over to meet the staff. Lizzy was correct. They were all incredible, and they all looked just as good as she did. Everything was ready to open for business the next day. They had already scheduled training sessions and massages. They would hold off on group training for now since the personal training was booked, and we could utilize all the trainers doing that. If we needed to hire more for that, we could. We sat down with Jenny and her manager to talk about the opening tomorrow. Everything was set up, and they were even having food catered in for the grand opening—another nice touch to add to the day.

We went back to the house because we wanted to meet the tutor and get to know the kids better. The kids were Alexandra, ten, and Scarlett, eight, adorable and very well-behaved. The tutor's name was Emmanuelle. She had just graduated from the University of Utah with a master's degree in childhood education. She was perfect. The kids loved her. She was beautiful, unattached, and had no problems traveling. Even the kids were excited about traveling. I decided to take everyone out for dinner. I asked everyone where they wanted to eat. They all wanted steak, so we decided to go to a local steakhouse.

Vanessa and I were talking while we were getting ready, and she said, "This all started with you, then I came in. Now we have us, Lizzy, Roni, Jenny, Alexandra, Scarlett, and Emmanuelle all getting ready to get on a plane and go traveling. Do we need a bigger plane? I mean, we're only leasing. Can we get something else?"

"Believe it or not, I already thought of that. I traded the lease on that for a Gulfstream that seats twelve."

She asked about all the flight training we had done. I told her a lot of it was the same, so it shouldn't be an issue. I had the SUV pull around, and we started out of dinner. Dinner was really great. We got to know everyone. They were all nice, and Vanessa and I had a great feeling about the business and what we started. It's all going to work out really well. The kids needed to get to bed. It was getting late, so we drove home so we could all get to sleep. We had a busy day tomorrow with the opening.

Before we went to bed, Roni told us she had one more thing to show us. She took us into our bedroom and into the closet. She pushed a button underneath the ceiling to the floor shelf where I had my shoes and the shelf slid open. Behind the shelf was a heavy-duty solid metal door that had a biometric lock on it. It hadn't been set yet so we could just pull the door open. Behind the door was a stairway that when you started to walk down, a light came on. It led to the underground bunker that we had wanted. It was about three thousand square feet, with a kitchen, bathroom, two bedrooms, fully furnished, monitors, and controls for the security system. There was electricity on a separate line that was also hooked into a generator if the power went down. There was also a separate room that was on another biometric lock where we could store more private things. Vanessa and I were floored by all the work Roni had done. We told her that she just earned a huge bonus for this, at least $100K, but we would discuss it. She and Lizzy just smiled and said they were both happy that we're so pleased. I told them that

I wanted them to be able to access everything, the biometric locks. I wanted them to have the ability to get in as well if needed. We all went back upstairs and said good night. Vanessa and I both thought that we made a great choice with those two—just amazing. We climbed in bed and fell asleep, happy with the day and what the new business was going to bring.

I got up early and made breakfast for everyone—eggs, fruit, bacon, and pancakes for the girls. Everyone had a good breakfast and was going to get ready for the day when Lizzy stopped everyone. She told us to all wait because she had a gift for all of us. She went to her room and brought out bags that had Achieve Your Balance in a half circle and Unbelievable Touch making up the other half. She handed the ladies and girls different color leggings and tank tops with the logo on them, and for me, she had a pair of shorts with a T-shirt and a polo shirt. Lizzy said she wanted to give these things to us for the opening. She thought it would look great.

I told her, "You just get better and better."

We all made our way down to the gym and welcomed our first guests. The day was laid out so well. It went incredible we couldn't have asked for it to go any better. It was obvious Lizzy knew what she was doing. We needed to go over what we needed to get done for the Tucson property. We all sat down to discuss how far that project was. We had Clarissa and Jake, the assistant manager and the head of security, sit in on this meeting since Jenny would be gone. We told her that although she would be running the gym while we were gone, Jake would be in charge of the overall security of the property. She had already been spending a lot of time with Jake since they were both on the property, and they got along well. Vanessa told her if she needed to stay on property, she could. Roni told them that Tucson was almost complete. One of the last things we needed to do was get down there and hire the people we need.

I said, "All sounds great. We'll leave first thing in the morning. Let's make sure that everything is ready to go by eight."

*****

We had to get two SUVs to take our large family to the airport. With all the people and luggage, one would never have worked. We climbed aboard the Gulfstream, and it was so much bigger than the last plane. Everyone was so excited to be riding in a private plane—well, everyone but the four of us that had been spending so much time together. Gorgeous leather seats, XM/Sirius radio, worldwide satellite phone, Wi-Fi—it was incredible. We had a pilot and copilot on this trip. We didn't need to fly solo on this one since we weren't going to be creating any recipes this trip. The flight to Tucson was not a long one, so people didn't settle down too much. They were all too excited about their first ride and visiting a place they had never been before. We started making our way out to the ranch. On the way, they all fell in love with the mountains and the cactus everywhere. The fact where they were was a desert, and with a short drive, they could be in the same climate as the home was just fascinating to them. We pulled into the ranch, but it wasn't complete yet—a lot of it was. I had Roni fashion the gym office like they did in Utah, with the extra rooms for Jenny and the kids, which would come in handy with all the extra people. Some staff still needed to be hired, equipment installed, and utilities turned on. Everything else was in place. One of the things that was completed and built exactly the way we wanted it to be was the bunker, same spot, entering through the bedroom closet and completely furnished and ready to go. I told Roni, Lizzy, and Vanessa while everyone else was getting settled in to meet me in the bunker. I needed to talk to them about something. They made their way to the bunker, and I told them to close the door behind them. I told them Tucson was going to take some time, so I think that we have time for another creation. They all agreed. They asked who and where. I told them I had someone very special in mind—one that really deserves it more than the most.

We left the bunker and told the rest that the four of them were going to scout another location for the gym. Since it was all going so smooth, why not keep going? Jenny asked where we were going. I told them that we would be heading to Boulder to look at a ranch in that area and that we would only be gone for a few days. While we were gone, Jenny was in charge, and she would have the full support of the security team that was there. The four of us spent the day in the bunker, going over what we were going to do. The person in question was a former human resources director. Her name was Leslie Winkle. We used to say that she was so cold and so tightly wound. She would wear a turtleneck sweater and an ankle-length wool skirt on a hot summer day. The place where we used to work together was a country club, and we were a really tight-knit family until she came in. She broke up everything that we had put together. She made people's lives miserable. She got our GM fired, got me suspended, and even after I left and tried to get a job at a new resort, she blackballed me there as well. We had always suspected she was gay, which we wouldn't have had a problem with, but the way she came down on other people's lifestyles, it was totally hypocritical. I did some research and found her living in Boulder with a lady named Sharon. She was someone that worked as a lady's locker room attendant at the country club. She was one that started complaining about all of us to Leslie the moment she walked in the door. The two of them became great buddies, and now I can see where that led. They're seriously horrible people that caused a lot of damage to people's lives, including mine. I found out that Sharon recently lost her job, but that didn't really matter. Leslie was divorced, and she seriously made out with a lot of money. Here's the problem, two women, not a man involved, not sure how to reel them in.

Vanessa said, "We're talking lesbians, right?"

I said, "Yes, we are."

She said, "Well, look at us?"

I said that I completely understand that, but they are cold, extremely cold, living in a freezer cold, and it will be hard to excite them.

Lizzy said, "You need to leave it up to us. We will lure them in, and then you create your recipe for them."

Roni agreed. "They need to go, and we will get it done for you, Aaron."

We came up from the bunker, and everyone was busy running around getting things done. Emmanuelle was busy teaching Alexandra and Scarlett math and English in the kitchen. I've never seen kids so happy to learn. Then again, if I was learning from her, I would be happy too. She was seriously gorgeous. It was all working out so well Vanessa and I couldn't have been happier. So strange that I am actually thinking that maybe we get out of writing recipes and just do this, maybe have our own kids and raise them in a few different places. All of us could just grow old together, but deep inside, I knew it wasn't time. There were still too many people out there that needed to be dealt with. I went and found Vanessa with Jenny, Roni, and Lizzy in the gym going over where they needed the equipment to be set.

I told them all, "We will be leaving for Denver in the morning early, so let's make sure we get some sleep. We have a lot of places to look for."

Everyone continued on the rest of the day getting things set up for the opening. We decided that it would take four more days to get the place open. I asked Jenny if she had all the staff she needed. She told me she needed only a couple of more, but when I told people who we were, pointed them to the website of Park City and what else is opening soon, it was amazing how fast they wanted to come and work here, not to mention we pay well. That was a great piece of news to hear. To know that it wasn't going to be a chore to get people here made me happy and not just people but quality people. We can trust quality people more to get the job done, not to mention perfect for promotions to the other properties, maybe even rotate them around. Can you imagine, we will rotate you around to our properties and we will get you there on our private jet, who wouldn't want to work for us? I had dinner waiting for everyone when they were done. We were all eating out by the pool. The kids were swimming, and we were finishing up any last-minute things we needed to talk about before we left. We told Lizzy and Roni to sleep in the bunker with us so we didn't wake anyone when we left. All the bunkers had a separate entrance/exit to the outside no one would hear us leave. We all said good night and then went downstairs.

Vanessa told me that they had been talking, and they had come up with a couple of ideas for how to lure them in.

"From everything you told us, they're pretty cold, conservative, and they're definitely lesbian, correct?"

I told them that was correct.

"Well, we're going to go away from our normal barely wear nothing attire to a more conservative approach, something that would be more attractive to them. We're going to need to scout where they're hanging out and go from there. Do you remember what they looked like?"

"They weren't very cute at all, so the three of you will be a breath of fresh air for them."

Lizzy said that they're definitely going to have to buy some more, well, some different clothes when we get to Denver, more suited toward them.

"Whatever conservative clothing we wear, we're wearing nothing on underneath it. I guarantee that as much as they come off as cold bitches, they're not wearing anything on underneath all that."

I said I never had a desire to find out. They all asked me if I had thought how I was going to take care of them. I told them I was still thinking about it, but if they had any ideas, let me know. They smothered everyone until we all left. We can all sleep on it. We need to get some rest so we can get out of here early. We got ready and climbed into bed and went to sleep, or at least we tried to sleep. There was a lot of tossing and turning, probably because we had a lot of things going on, a lot running through our heads. We finally got to sleep. We woke up, gathered our things, and headed to the airport. We had a pilot for the trip since the recipe creation was almost one hour away, plus we really needed the rest. We could get some food and coffee on the plane.

CHAPTER 23

Time for a Trip to the Mile High City

Aaron

I got us rooms at the Brown Palace Hotel. It's been in Denver since 1892, historic and impeccable service. Under any other circumstances, it would be a great place to stay, I'm sure, but we really weren't there for pleasure—well, maybe a little pleasure. The first thing we did was find out exactly where they were living and working. Sharon had been fired from her previous job—not a surprise if she was the same person with the cheese grater attitude that I knew—and Leslie was working as an HR director for a hotel, working nine to five, Monday through Friday. She still had a ton of money from her divorce, and Vanessa started doing her thing, figuring out how to hack her system and take what we wanted. She told me that she had all she needed. We just needed to push the button.

The next step was getting the outfits we needed. They went shopping while I stayed in the room, going over what I was going to do. They both slowly smothered people so much they made it unbearable to work there, like being in a sauna with a locked door, steam constantly building until you couldn't breathe anymore. Maybe that's what they needed. Maybe they needed to be slowly smothered until it was just too unbearable to live anymore. It definitely got me thinking about some different ways to take care of them. They got back a few hours later and asked me if I wanted them to model the new clothes for me. I said of course I did. First was Lizzy. She came out in a floor-length skirt, boots, a button-up shirt with a sweater vest over that. I've never seen her wearing so much clothing before. Next up was Roni. She was wearing a Hilary Clinton type of pants suit with a button-up shirt, sweater, and a coat—very sexy. And finally, it was Vanessa's turn. She was wearing a floor-length long-sleeved button-up to her neck dress—again, *sooo* sexy.

I told them all, "Great job on picking out things that would appeal to them, and it really would." They all asked if I wanted to see what they had on underneath. Of course, I did. All of them had on extremely sexy lingerie, something I'm sure they would love. I needed Roni and Lizzy to go back to their room because I really needed to make love to Vanessa. Lucky, we had adjoining rooms because they didn't have far to go. They went back closed their door but left ours open.

"Are they wanting to watch again?"

Vanessa said, "I don't know, but I'm sure they do." She added, "Personally, I think they're missing having a dick in their life, but they fear getting involved because of the situation we're in."

I told her that I totally understood but that I feared them getting involved, and if they did, this would all have to stop.

She agreed. "They would have to stop because we can't take the chance. We've built way too much to let it go down. We can talk to them about it tomorrow. Give them the choice of what they want to do."

We made love to each other before we slept. We knew they weren't watching this time. They were tired, and they needed sleep. Big day tomorrow.

*****

I ordered room service for everyone the next morning. I went into the next room to wake them up. They were both sound asleep. I bent over to Lizzy and whispered that it was time to get up. She reached up, pulled me down, and gave me a hug and kiss. Then she opened her eyes. "Oh fuck, it woke Roni up." Lizzy said, "I'm so sorry."

I said, "It is fine. You all get up and come into our room. We got some breakfast for everyone."

Lizzy and Roni made their way into the other room. Lizzy was still embarrassed by what had just happened. I had told Vanessa what had happened. Vanessa told her not to worry, but we did want to talk to them about something.

"We feel like you all are missing something in your life. Would that be the case?"

Roni asked, "Are you sure you want to talk about this?"

Vanessa said, "Yes, we do. We feel that both of you are missing something in your life. Is that correct?"

Lizzy asked, "Are you talking about dick?"

Roni said, "Yes, we are both missing dick in our lives. Why do you think we want to watch the two of you?"

I said, "We understand, and our biggest fear is that you will get involved and things will start to unravel, and we can't let things unravel."

Roni and Lizzy said they would never let that happen.

Vanessa said, "We didn't think that you would, but we wanted to give you a choice. If this is what you all want and need, after this next creation, we will stop and just carry on with the gym business and never talk about this again."

We thought that Lizzy and Roni were both going to explode. They both took deep breaths and looked at us with tears welling up in their eyes.

Lizzy said, "We love you both more than you know. You were there for us when we needed someone the most."

Lizzy looked at Roni, and Roni said, "You took care of us and protected us when no one else would. There are no two people on the face of the earth that we love or care about more."

Almost in unison, they both said, "Do you really think that having a dick in our lives is more important than you two? We appreciate what you're doing and what you're offering to us, but we're not done yet. We need to keep this going. We will find a way to satisfy ourselves. Don't worry. Keep offering your shows, and we'll be okay."

Vanessa said, "Okay, we can do that, but please let us know when this gets to be too much. We will understand, and we will move on from all this."

"Okay, so what we need to do is scout out where they live and where she works."

We found the house. It was tucked away on a street, not a lot of houses or foot traffic around it. We could definitely get in and out very easily. It was surrounded by trees and bushes no one could see us going in or coming out; plus the dark SUV with blacked-out windows tends to help. Sharon came outside for a short period to do a bit of gardening and then went back inside. It was time to head toward the hotel. My plan was for Lizzy and Vanessa to go into the hotel and ask for Leslie.

"Once you get in front of her, tell her that you're from a new property in Denver, a B&B, and that they would like to speak to you about the two positions, HR director or general manager. Give her a range of salary, and she will bite on it. Ask her if she will meet you at the bar down the street when she gets off. Did you all bring your clothes with you?"

They did. They started to get changed when, all of a sudden, there were moans and groans coming from the back. I asked what was going on. They told me they were all seriously struggling.

I asked them, "Why, what's wrong?"

They said they weren't used to having to put so many clothes on. I couldn't help but laugh. They finally finished getting dressed, and they were ready to go. I asked Vanessa if she had everything she needed, and she said that she did. I gave them earbuds and told them to get going and let me know when they're all set to go. We would be waiting for them.

*****

Vanessa

Lizzy and I made our way through the hotel to Leslie's office. We found her there by herself, and we asked if we could have a moment of her time. Leslie instantly had the utmost respect for us. We were dressed like we were ready to go to church, and that impressed her. Leslie led us into her office and offered us a seat. She asked what it was we needed to talk about. We told her that we represented a small group of owners that were opening a high-end B&B in the Denver area, and we have been authorized to offer her a position as either the HR director or the general manager. It would be her choice as to which one she wanted. She asked all the relevant questions, which we answered. She asked about the salary for each position. She was impressed and excited at the amount, and then she asked who it was. We told her we weren't able to give her that information until she accepted the offer. I suggested to her that we meet at the bar down the street and talk about it. "Say in thirty minutes?" She agreed, and she said she would meet us there in thirty minutes.

Lizzy and I got to the bar, and we waited. Leslie showed up exactly thirty minutes later. She saw us sitting in the back in a booth. I got out and let her sit between us. I told her that I took it upon myself to order some champagne and shots of tequila to celebrate.

Leslie said, "You're pretty sure I'm going to say yes, aren't you?"

Lizzy told her, "Yes, we were. It's a great corporation, and you will really enjoy working here."

Leslie told them that they were smart because she's accepting the job as the general manager.

I said, "It was great to hear that you're coming aboard. It's time to celebrate!" I had already poured the champagne, and I had already dosed the shot of tequila. We all took a sip of champagne and then did a shot. I had another round of shots brought to the table. Lizzy said that she was feeling a bit warm. I agreed. We asked Leslie if she cared if we got a bit more comfortable. She said she had no issues with that at all. We could tell the booze and dose were starting to take effect. Inhibitions tend to loosen up. Lizzy removed her sweater vest and buttoned down her shirt. She could see Lizzy's nipples poking through the shirt. She wasn't wearing a bra.

Acting surprised, she stopped and said, "Oh my god, I forgot I wasn't wearing a bra."

Here was the big test. Lizzy reached for her sweater to put it back on, and Leslie grabbed her arm and stopped her.

She said, "Don't worry, I don't mind at all."

She passed that test with flying colors. It was my turn. I started to unbutton my dress all the way down until it reached right between my breasts. Leslie could see that I was wearing a bright red bra that pushed my breasts up so that it showed really deep cleavage—deep enough that Leslie's eyes were trained there for a good five seconds. We asked Leslie if she wanted to get comfortable. She got a really shy look on her face. Lizzy picked up on that and told her that she was a beautiful woman.

"It's just us here. There's nothing to be shy about."

After a few more seconds of thinking, she said, "What the fuck."

She took off the sweater vest she was wearing and unbuttoned her shirt down very low as well. We had her; this was definitely the beginning of the end for her.

I told her, "See, you are a beautiful lady." I reached my hand inside Leslie's shirt as I cupped her breast. I used two of my fingers to rub the material of her bra, and I asked her, "Who makes this? It feels fantastic. It's beautiful." Leslie turned red but didn't stop me. She just took hurried shallow breaths. I could feel her heart beating faster. Leslie was wearing a skirt that buttoned up the side.

Lizzy asked her, "Does the underwear match the bra?"

Leslie slowly nodded as Lizzy started to unbutton her skirt. When there was just one button left, Lizzy reached her hand under the skirt, and she started rubbing her belly and between her legs.

She said, "You're right, Vanessa, this does feel fantastic."

I told Lizzy that she needed to feel the bra to make sure. Lizzy told me the same about the underwear. Lizzy reached her hand inside Leslie's shirt and started rubbing her breasts while I reached inside her skirt and started rubbing between her legs, spreading them so that I could feel it more. Leslie closed her eyes and put her head back. We could tell she had never been here before, and if it wasn't for the drinks and the drugs, she probably wouldn't be. At the same time, both Lizzy and I asked her if she wanted to take this back to Leslie's house. She nodded, she did, then she mentioned that her girlfriend was there. I told her not to worry. She can play too. We got everything buttoned up and headed out the back way. Roni and Aaron were in the far back of the SUV, it was dark, and they couldn't be seen. Lizzy drove, and I sat in the back with her, continuing to rub her body. I needed to keep her interested so she didn't say no. She was almost out from the drugs; it wouldn't be long now.

As we got closer to Leslie's house, we stopped a couple of hundred yards before so that Aaron and Roni could get out. We continued the rest of the way and pulled up front. Aaron and Roni made their way into the backyard. They saw Sharon sitting on the couch watching TV. They told Lizzy and me that they were in position and to go ahead and go to the front door. We helped Leslie out of the car and started walking her to the door. We knocked, and when Sharon answered, the look on her face was one of total shock. Lizzy and I tried to introduce themselves, but Sharon already knew who we were and why we were there. That's probably why she didn't throw a fit when she saw us. This would be a great payday for her as well. She figured it was best to keep the peace. I told her we were so sorry.

"We were celebrating her accepting the GM job, and she might have had a bit too much to drink."

As pissed off as she was inside—and she was pissed off—on the outside, she said that she totally understood. She had a great reason to celebrate. Lizzy said that she would go into the kitchen and get her some water. As she went in, she opened the door for Aaron and Roni, and she took the water back to the living room. Leslie was barely coherent. She kept rambling on about wanting to be touched more, and Sharon had no idea what she was talking about.

Sharon asked us both if we knew, and I said, "We had no idea. She was rambling on about that when we were driving home. We thought she was talking about something between the two of you."

Sharon said she had no idea. She thanked us for bringing her home, but she needed to get her to bed. Lizzy said that she would help take her into the bedroom. As they sat her down on the bed, Aaron came up behind Sharon and stuck her. This woman was a pig, so using the term pigsticker would be appropriate.

*****

GILBERT-ALAN SANCHEZ

Aaron

We laid them both down on the bed. Now it was time to get this one done and over with. The girls were wondering what I had in mind, what was I going to do. I liked what they had done a couple of other times, let me tell the story to them, do what I was going to do, and then burn the place to the ground—it leaves no traceable evidence behind.

Vanessa agreed with that. "But what would be the end for these two?"

I told them, "They smothered everyone that they came in contact with, and they deserved the same."

As I was doing it, I started to explain what he was going to do. "I am going to hog-tie them, well, because they were basically hogs, and attach something that goes around their nose and face and is connected to their ankles. They get a ball gag in their mouths, and their nose and mouth are covered with a towel and heavy-duty plastic wrap. Each time they move the ankles, the mask gets tighter around their faces, and it, well, basically smothers them, just like they did everyone else."

They were all amazed that I did that all while explaining it to them.

"The next step would be to set the place ablaze. I've always loved fire. I wouldn't cook if I couldn't start fires. This might turn into a thing going forward. We need to look for any lingerie that they might have." Vanessa found some. "Now we need to get them out of their clothes and try to get at least some of the lingerie on them. Baby oil is very flammable under the right conditions."

Lizzy said that she didn't see any.

I said, "It's okay. I brought some. I actually had a mixture of baby oil and Sterno gel. The gel will burn for a long time, and I needed it to get hot enough to ignite the baby oil."

They both started to come to, and the first thing they saw was my face, and they both tried to scream, but nothing could come out. They kept pulling their legs; and the more they did, the more the ball gag in their mouth and face-covering tightened, smothering them just a little bit more. I looked at them and told them that by the look on their faces they remember exactly who I was. They both nodded.

"Well, then you remember all the problems you caused to people, all the damage to their lives. People getting fired, suspended, having to quit, and move on losing their livelihoods, and the two of you just ride off into the sunset, with a shit load of money, like nothing was wrong, and to make matters worse, you blackballed people from getting jobs. Why, why did you have to be that way? Because you never got your own birthday cake? After all these years and all these people, your time has finally come. Your time has finally come to pay for everything you've done. Time for you to be smothered just like you did to others. An accidental fire will be set. You will struggle, and you will smother yourselves just like you have smothered others although yours will be final."

I spread the mixture all over the bed around them. I spread the mixture in the middle parts of their bodies, and I spread baby oil all around them. I lit the outside part and watched them squirm. I had already told the girls to go and wait down the street in the car and keep it running. I stayed long enough to make sure that they passed out from smothering themselves and they wouldn't be able to get away. I walked out the backdoor and made my way to the car. I got in, and Lizzy drove away. They all asked how it went. I told them I stayed long enough for them to pass out. They couldn't survive that. We looked back, and we could see the blaze growing bigger. Another recipe was created and executed—it was done.

As we were driving back to Denver, they all asked me how I was doing, how I was feeling. They asked me if there was ever a point where I just got tired of what I was doing.

I said, "In the moment, it's exciting. I feel alive, and it feels like I'm doing good and helping people. But after, yeah, I do feel tired, and after each time, I get more tired than before."

I lay down in Vanessa's lap and fell asleep. They had never seen me like this before, and they were worried about me. Was all this starting to take a toll on me mentally and emotionally? Vanessa believed that maybe it was time for a break.

We got back to the hotel and decided to order some room service. I asked Vanessa if she had taken care of the money. She said she had and that it was, again, a lot of money. She said we could stop if I wanted to. We have a lot of money, and with the new business, we could just live and do that and not worry about doing this again. We all sat around eating, and it was probably the quietest we've ever been. I could tell they were worried about me. I don't really know what was going on in my head. I knew I was tired from all this, but I don't think I was ready to be done yet. There was still too much to do. I still had people that needed to be taken care of.

Roni finally broke the silence with an update on Kauai. She said that it was all pretty much completed and that as soon as we got back, we could go there and get that one open. Lizzy said that she had spoken to Jenny and that Tucson and Park City were doing really well. We were getting tons of clients, and they're all way beyond happy. Without saying a word, I got up and said I was going to go take a shower.

*****

Vanessa

Lizzy asked me if she's ever seen him like this before.

I said, "Never, and it is starting to worry me. One thing that he hasn't done in a very long time is cook, like in a restaurant, being a chef."

Lizzy said, "Maybe that's the answer. We get him a place of his own where he can cook what he wants, when he wants."

I said, "That was like his therapy. Whenever he needed to get away, he always went and cooked or baked. He had always dreamed about opening something on Kauai. Maybe we can look while we're there."

I told them that I was going to go and talk to him. "Go back to your room, but leave the doors open. You might get a show tonight."

They both smiled, put the room service outside, and went back to their room.

I went into the bathroom. Aaron was standing under the hot water. I got undressed and got in the shower with him. I told him that we were all really worried about him, and we had an idea that might help.

I told him, "The idea is to open a small restaurant on Kauai, where you could cook and bake and do whatever you want, your brand of therapy. What do you think? We've spent a lot on the gyms, so why not something like this?"

Aaron told me that it was a great idea, maybe it's something that he needed because he truly has missed cooking. "Cooking for you all is great, but I'm talking about for the masses."

I totally understood. I said, "So when we go back to Kauai, let's start to look."

He told me, "We would definitely do that, but we need to look at a ranch here tomorrow that I've been checking out."

I asked, "Maybe we should put a hold on this one, get Kauai open, and find a place for a restaurant. How about if we just go look and not make any decisions yet?"

"That will work. We have to go and see the ranch and leave, so we better get to bed."

We got out of the shower, and Aaron started to put some shorts on. I stopped him and said, "No," and I led him into the bed. I laid him on his back and started stroking his hard dick with covers off. I looked up, and I could see the girls looking through the door. They stepped in and sat on a couch away from the bed. They had actually gotten themselves a pair of vibrators to help, not a bad idea. Not a dick, but not a bad idea. I knew that there might come a time when they would not be satisfied with vibrators and they will need what I was stroking right now. When that time comes, we would have to decide how far this would go. I climbed on top of him and started to slowly grind, then faster and faster until we both came at the same time. I looked up, and they finished slightly after we did and walked back into their room. We rolled over in each other's arms and fell asleep; it was going to be a busy day tomorrow.

*****

Aaron woke up feeling really refreshed. He decided he would go and walk around the city and grab some food for breakfast. I woke up, and Aaron wasn't there. I went into Lizzy and Roni's room and asked if they had seen him. They said they had not. I climbed into bed with them and told them that I had mentioned to him their idea for the restaurant on Kauai. He said he loved the idea. He still wanted to look at the property in Eagle River, close to Vail, but we won't decide on it right away. They were really happy to hear that he liked the idea, and they wanted to thank me again for another great show. It helped them.

I said with a laugh, "Live porn helps you?"

They both laughed and said, "Well, yeah, it does."

I told them I noticed they got something to help themselves with their "no-dick" situation. They both told me that it's not the same, but it did help. We heard the door in the other room open, and we got up and went over. Aaron had brought coffee and breakfast burritos from a café down the street. The smell of coffee, smoky bacon, and eggs—you can't beat that in the morning. Lizzy told Aaron he looked really happy and refreshed. He told her that he slept really well and just felt like it was going to be a good day.

Aaron said, "Let's eat our breakfast and get going. We can fly into Vail Valley Jet Center and go from there. It's a pretty short distance."

We finished breakfast, got packed, and left. We barely had time to settle in before it was time to land. This area was so gorgeous. They always seemed to pick the most beautiful places to go, and Aaron found one of the most beautiful properties we've ever seen. It's a total of 173 deeded acres with river frontage and mountain lands. It's hidden away along a bend on the south bank of the Eagle River. It has a 14,000-square-foot house. That includes a large master wing, movie theater, game room, wine cellar, professional prep kitchen, four guest rooms with en suite bathrooms, three offices, numerous porches, four-bay garage, outdoor entertaining areas that spill out to the Eagle River. It has soaring ceilings, walnut beams and finishes, and walkout porches. It has a riverside guest house and a large custom garage. Both buildings are set back from the primary residence but connected to it by short walking trails and a private paved driveway. There's also a mountain cabin, which is sited on a separate 111-deeded-acre parcel. Tucked among an aspen grove at the top of a mountain ridge, the 1,900-square-foot cabin, and detached garage.

There is so much to work with here. It's just amazing, but the question is, Do we really want to wait or make the offer now? We don't want to lose this. We decided that we would make an offer on the property, cash of course, and for less than the asking price. They accepted, and we were the proud owners of another house. We needed to get back to Tucson, so they were going to messenger the paperwork there and we would wire the money. Time to head back to the airport. It was a short flight back to Tucson. We needed to get back and get the gym open, move on to Kauai, and then start working on Vail. We all noticed that Aaron was walking with a spring in his step. That was good to see.

On the flight, we started talking about what they were going to do with Vail. There were more structures to work with, so it will make it easier. Everything was set up so well throughout the property it was going to be a real experience for the clients. There were going to be people from all over the high-end places, and they would expect a lot. Lizzy said she was thinking of incorporating local traditions into the programs, incorporating the landscapes, and using the weather to our advantage. We all thought that it was fantastic ideas.

Aaron said, "All the ideas you come up with are incredible. He stood up, picked her up, and gave a huge bear hug and a kiss, and said, "Thank you. I appreciate you."

We all just looked at him and then looked at one another, and we didn't really know what to think. He turned around and walked to the bathroom.

I said, "What the fuck was that all about? He was acting so strange."

We were hoping he wasn't breaking, breaking down. We landed in Tucson and started making our way back out to the ranch. We got there, and everything looked so amazing. They had finished everything, and it was just perfect. They were welcomed by Jenny and the girls. Jenny said, along with tutoring, they were training Emmanuelle to be a trainer and a masseuse.

Jenny said, "She asked, and I didn't have an issue with it since she would always be traveling with us. We could always use her if needed."

They were opening the next day, and they were booked all day and into the early evening. We sat down with Heidi, Jenny's assistant in Tucson, and Johnny, the head of security. We explained to them the same thing we did in Park City. We would help get it open, work it, and then take off for Kauai right after that. We all ate dinner, and Aaron headed straight for bed. It was so strange. By the time I made it into the bedroom, he was already passed out. I guess we'll see how he is tomorrow.

I woke up the next day, and Aaron was gone again. I got dressed and went into the kitchen. Maybe he was making breakfast. I heard splashing in the pool. I went out back, and he was swimming laps—all very strange because he doesn't usually swim laps. He saw me and stopped. I asked him if he was okay. He told me that he was. He just felt like he was living outside of his body the last couple of days, very strange, but he was working his way back. Aaron told me that even though what we were doing was helping people from further abuse, he felt that we were taking in a lot. He wanted to give back somehow. I asked him how he wanted to do that.

"Maybe just randomly pick people to give to. Let's start with Emmanuelle since she's straight out of college, and since she knows people that are still there, she could help us with that too. We could set her up with the ability to donate to people that really need it. What do you think?"

I thought that it was a great idea. "Let's talk to her about it, but it needs to be kept between us, Lizzy and Roni, so we'll take her down into the bunker after breakfast."

*****

Aaron

I made us a big breakfast. We all needed a lot of energy for a busy day. We also invited all the new staff to eat on the first day. We had a great conversation with all the expectations, the management tree, all of it. By the looks on the employees' faces, they had never been treated this way. That was a very good thing for everyone.

I told Emmanuelle to send the kids out with Jenny. "Just tell them that you need to make a call to your family and you'll come and get them in just a bit. We want to speak to you privately."

She got a really scared look on her face and asked if everything was okay. I apologized for scaring her.

I told her, "Everything is fine. We just needed to get your opinion on something."

A huge look of relief came over her face. I told her to follow me. The girls were already down in the bunker. Again, she got a scared look on her face.

I said, "Look, we all love you. The kids love you. No one is going to hurt you. In fact, we will all protect you going forward for the rest of your life."

She said okay, and we walked down into the bunker. When we got there, she saw Vanessa, Lizzy, and Roni sitting there. A wave of relief came over her.

Lizzy said to her, "Emmanuelle, we're not here to hurt you. You take care of my sister and my nieces. We love you. We just want to know if you'll help us with something. If you want to, Aaron will explain what we need."

She said she felt fine, and she was interested. "What do you all need from me?"

I explained to her, "We wanted to start a program where we could give back to people like yourself, to help people that need help with school, bills, with whatever they need. The reasons why we want to talk to you are twofold. First, how much do you owe on your student loans or anything else you have?"

She said she had $175K in student loans and about $55K in credit card bills and car loan. She looked over, and Vanessa was writing it all down.

I said, "You need to give Vanessa all the account info so that we can pay all of it off for you."

She couldn't believe what she was hearing. Tears started welling up in her eyes.

Lizzy looked at her and said, "I know how you feel. They helped me when I was in a bad place. There are no strings attached. They truly want to help."

I told her, "There's one more thing we would like for you to do, and the first one isn't contingent on the answer to the second."

Lizzy looked at her and told her to get that worried look off her face. "It's okay."

I told her, "We want you to manage a fund that will distribute money to other students or younger people that need the help, but only people that truly need it and deserve it. Would that be something that you would be interested in doing?"

Emmanuelle told us that she would be honored to oversee something like that for us. Just tell her what she needed to do.

"Vanessa will set up an account for you to distribute the money. We will be able to see where it's going, but we have trust in you to distribute it correctly."

Emmanuelle said she would make a list of names and situations for them to look at, and when they approve, she'd get started. Emmanuelle gave them all a hug, and they went back upstairs so they could help get everything open.

*****

The opening went off without a hitch. Everyone was on point, and all the clients couldn't be happier. We stayed for a few more days to make sure things went smoothly, and we got ready to go to Kauai. We got Emmanuelle set up to start distributing, and she started bringing us some great candidates. Most of them she knew, people she went to school with, and the rest she was finding through her friends that were still at school. One of our stipulations was that she never told people where the money was coming from—that was the most important thing. We weren't looking for recognition. We just wanted to help people. She agreed to keep it quiet. Everyone was really excited about going to Kauai. It was hard to believe that we actually had stumbled into all this, but it was reality—a really good reality. You know when it's something good, people can never believe it's happening to them—they're much more used to bad always happening. We wanted to change that for some people. Night came, and the last clients left. I made dinner for the staff and explained to them that we would be gone for a few days trying to get Kauai open. The looks of jealousy from the people sitting there were actually kind of funny. I told them all that they had an opportunity to travel to all locations and work and help open when needed. I told them the Vail location was next after this one and that more would be coming.

"We will utilize all of you to get things done, but that depends on you and how you work."

They all understood, and they told us that they wouldn't let us down. Everyone finished packing, and it was time to go to sleep. We were leaving early tomorrow, and we needed the rest. When we got to our room, Vanessa asked me how I was feeling, if having Emmanuelle take on that project helped me, and if getting the restaurant on Kauai was going to help as well. I told her it was a start and that it will definitely help me in the long run.

Vanessa told me, "We will get you right again. Kauai will be good for you and us. Let them get the gym open, and we will concentrate on the restaurant."

We climbed into bed and went to sleep.

CHAPTER 24

A New Venture in Hawaii

Aaron

We all woke up excited to get going to Hawaii, new business, and all on a private plane. How much better could it get? We loaded up the SUVs and took off for the airport. We could feel the excitement build as we got closer to the airport. Once in the air, we started getting caught up on how things were progressing on Kauai. It's almost complete. Once there, staff would need to get hired and trained. Lizzy and Jenny had already placed ads and spoken to people via Zoom so they could get to know them. Jenny wanted to fly some people out from the other two locations to help and maybe stay permanently. Vanessa said that was a great idea and to get them out as soon as possible. Attention turned to what area we should be looking at for the restaurant, which would be the best side of the island. I always liked the south shore, especially because it's where we met, but Vanessa suggested staying closer to home might be a better idea, especially if I was getting out late, and I didn't want to drive that far. Everyone else had fallen asleep, and it was just the two of us. I looked at Vanessa and asked her if we felt like we were growing too quickly, too many businesses, and too many people.

Vanessa told me that she didn't think so. "The more we do, the more it legitimizes us, and the more cover it gives to us while we're out doing other things."

I agreed and told her, "This is the reason why we're so good together. We can help to calm each other down. We make each other feel better and make each other better."

We both decided that we needed to get some sleep. It didn't take long and we were out.

They woke us up before we landed so that we could all see us coming into the island. I'll never get tired of the sight of coming into the island, especially the north shore. We landed and were met by two SUVs to take us back to the house. When we pulled up, those who had never seen it were just in amazement by its beauty. All the additions that had been made for the gym looked awesome, including turning the tree house into the massage area. Everyone started getting settled in. Vanessa and I would sleep in the bunker so that everyone could spread out everywhere. Roni went to check with the contractor and security to see how things were going, Emmanuelle took the girls outside to play, and Lizzy and Jenny started making calls to get people in to get them hired. Jenny told us that she had two people each coming from Park City and Tucson to help with the training and the opening.

I told her, "Do not buy them tickets. We'll just send the jet back for them. Actually, have Park City fly to Tucson, and we'll grab them all from there."

We walked the property to see how things were going. Everything was set and ready to go. There were some minor issues, but for the most part, it turned out great. We had face-to-face interviews set up for the afternoon, and if everything went well, with the arrival of the other four from the mainland, we should be able to start training tomorrow. It was all coming along great. We haven't had any issues, and that said a lot about the people that are involved, but I always was waiting for something bad to happen—all part of my skeptical attitude that I'd gained over the years. All you could do was move forward and keep doing what you need to do. Our next step was the restaurant, so that would be what we're moving to next. It seemed like a lot, but it's one thing that would make me happy. We decided to start on the north shore first and see what we could find.

One of the local hotels was looking to have someone take over their restaurant on the beach. The cost was too great for them, and they needed to move on from it. It was actually a great deal because since it was attached to the hotel, we didn't have to buy any property. We could just take over the existing restaurant. It even had a staff and all the equipment that I would need. Although things like tableware, glasses, and even tables and chairs, we would probably want to change. The GM knew my work from the hotel, and he was more than happy to have me take over the restaurant. We went into his office and worked out all the details. After signing the contract and paying the deposit, the place was ours. I spoke to the staff and told them that in one week we would be shutting down for renovations. I had to get the gym open and that I would still keep them employed if they wanted to stay and help with what we were going to do. Everyone wanted to stay and help. No one wanted out. I was going to need Roni for this project. She was going to help with renovations, furniture, all of it. Vanessa suggested that we call in Lizzy to help as well.

"It's always the four of us with everything, right?" Vanessa said.

"I agree it is always the four of us, but right now, we need to get back the house to help get that moving."

*****

Over the next few days, we spent our time making sure that everything was exactly the way we wanted it. We brought in new staff, got them trained, and got everything ready to go. We needed to sit down with Emmanuelle to see how she was doing with the fund. She told us it was going great but that she was feeling bad because Jenny was asking questions and she didn't know what to say. She was afraid that it was going to compromise her position with her and the kids, and she didn't want that. Vanessa told her not to worry. She and I will take care of it. We asked Lizzy to grab Jenny and Roni and bring them to the bunker. We needed to talk. When they all got down there, Vanessa explained to Jenny what we were having Emmanuelle do. It wasn't her fault. We told her we needed her to stay silent with this project. The fewer people that know, the better since we didn't want to draw any attention to ourselves. Jenny totally understood. All she said was that we could trust her like we trust Lizzy. The four of us knew that wasn't true with everything and that we can't tell her anything. Vanessa told her that we appreciated that, and the next time, we would be more honest with her.

"Emmanuelle is doing some great work for us, the cause is great, and we would like to keep it going." I told Emmanuelle that she would be getting a bonus on top of the salary she's getting paid for watching the kids.

I told them I wanted to make an announcement to them all. "Vanessa and I decided to take over a restaurant here on the island. It was on the north shore, close to home. We would be taking over an existing restaurant in a hotel, and in one week, it was going to get shut down for renovations."

They all could not have been happier. Some of them knew how much I needed this to help me get my head straight again. I told Roni I was going to need her to help with the renovations and design, and I wanted everyone's help with coming up with a name for it.

"Since Lizzy came up with so many good names for the gym and massage, how about helping with this on too?"

Lizzy got a smile on her face and said, "How about Outta My Head?"

Everyone loved it. For those who knew what had been going on, it fit perfectly with what they'd been going through. That's why they loved it so much. I told Lizzy that I knew she would come up with something good.

"Now we needed to work on the concept and design, but we need to get the gym opened first."

We emerged from the bunker tighter and stronger than before we went in. We went to go and check on everything. It was all together and ready to go for tomorrow morning. We had already booked clients. Things were coming along great. Now it was time to open a restaurant.

Working on the restaurant was a blast. We got the gym up and running smoothly, so I was getting a lot of help, and opinions from people, even Emmanuelle was out on the patio tutoring the kids and coming in to help in between assignments. Vanessa, Lizzy, and Emmanuelle were working on the bar menu. I don't drink, so I figured they would be the best choice. Roni and Jenny were working on the furniture. The type of decor was fairly obvious given where we were, and I was working on the menu. I called back in two cooks to help me, Jimmy and Isabelle. Jimmy did really well with savory, and Isabelle did well with pastry. I was going to need two strong people to help and keep this place going. They were both really good, but again, wherever I wasn't, my security was, that's how much I *don't* trust some people. When you pay people, especially professional people, they will do anything for you, including kill, although that's the part I didn't need them for. We made some dishes for people to try. Everyone was hungry from all the hard work. As I explained each dish in detail, people could see the smile on my face. They knew how happy this was making me. Vanessa could see me coming back, just like the day she first met me, when she started to fall in love with me. Lizzy and Roni both came in the kitchen and told me it was great to see me back. I looked happy and satisfied. I told them this was who I am, it's my art, and it's what I need and love to do.

I asked Jimmy and Isabelle what they thought. They said they loved what they saw, and they couldn't be happier that they stayed, but they did have a question: would they have any freedom to create? I told them that I have no problem with people creating but that they would have to show me loyalty.

"I will have to be able to trust you 100 percent, no exceptions, and no one will be able to change the concept of this place when I'm not here. Even when I'm not here, there will be people here that I trust 100 percent that will make sure nothing changes. Are you both okay with that?" I said.

They both told me that they would earn my trust and that they would do whatever it was that I needed for them to do. I told them that was what I was hoping would happen. I left them to finish cleaning the kitchen, and I went out to see where we were at with this project. Service and bartending staff had all been rehired and trained. We just needed a bit more training on the menu. We had already repainted and renovated the inside and outside patio area. It overlooked the ocean and the beach—some of the best views on the island. The furniture had arrived and was put in place. All the smallwares, china, glass, and silverware had also arrived and were being unpacked, cleaned, and polished. Equipment for the front and the back of the house had arrived along with all the equipment that needed to be set and hooked up. All the liquor and wine had arrived, and tomorrow I would start receiving all my food and for the employee tastings. Once done and if everything goes off without a hitch, we would be ready to open. I had Emmanuelle working on the social media campaign, Facebook, Instagram, and every other place that would help get us out there. She had a working knowledge of all of it, so she was a great candidate for it. She was turning out to be more than just a tutor for the kids.

After a few more days of training, we were ready to open the restaurant. We did an invite-only soft opening, consisting mostly of gym clients, the gym employees and significant others, concierges from the resorts, and a couple of food reviewers and bloggers. Emmanuelle had put together a fantastic guest list for the opening. It was the right blend of important people, ones that could really bring us the exposure that we needed. She was working the door greeting and seating people when this asshole couple that was staying at a house down the street tried to crash their way in. They were the kind of people who had a lot of money and absolutely no class. They figured their money would get them whatever they wanted. Not in my place it didn't. They started to become verbally abusive to her. I saw it and walked to the front and asked them what the problem was. They told me that they wanted to come in, but she told them no. I informed them that this was a private party, but we would be more than happy to have them another time. They told me they were leaving in the morning. That wouldn't be good enough. I told them that I would be more than happy to bring them some food to their house tonight if that was acceptable. They said that would be great.

I told them, "Please let Emmanuelle know what they want, and I'll get it right over to them."

They told me she was rude and they didn't want to deal with her. I called Vanessa over and had her take the order. Emmanuelle looked at me with this stunned look on her face, like she couldn't believe what was happening, where was the person that said he would always protect them. He told Lizzy and Roni to take her into the office. When Vanessa was done, she followed me into the office as well.

When they got there, Emmanuelle was crying.

Vanessa said to her, "Hold on, there's no reason to be crying."

She said the man said some pretty shitty things to her. They were rude and nasty, and she thought that I was there to protect them from stuff like that. It was just disappointing. I looked at the girls, and they nodded, and then I looked at Emmanuelle and said, "Look, how much can we trust you?"

She told us that we could trust her with anything. We could trust her with our lives.

Vanessa said, "That's really good to hear because what we're about to share with you, only the four of us know, not even Jenny knows, and it can't get out. The consequences would be great for everyone."

I looked at her and said, "So we'll give you one more chance. Understand that I do take care of you all. I do protect you all, but I do in my own way, and I will continue to do so, so do you want to leave it at that, or do you want to know more?"

Emmanuelle looked at me and said, "I told you all that you can trust me with anything. Whatever you want to tell me, it stays with me until the end."

We all four looked at one another and then her and said, "Okay, here goes." We started to explain to her everything that we had been doing, in detail, and the look on her face didn't change. When we finished, we asked her what she thought.

She looked at them and said, "I fucking love it! Why hasn't someone thought of this before, so we just lure them in and Aaron takes care of the rest?"

Vanessa said, "That is correct. We bring them in, but there are times when we decide to stay, we want to stay because we understand why we're doing it, and leaving it to just Aaron doesn't seem right, and it's taking a toll on him. We all help in writing the 'recipes.'"

Emmanuelle wanted in. She wanted to help. She would be willing to do anything, and she would never say a word, even to Jenny. She was in, and we couldn't be happier about it. I looked at them and said, "Okay, now we deliver the food and a message that you just don't fuck with us."

I told Vanessa and Lizzy to take Emmanuelle back to the house and show her what she needed to wear.

She said, "What I need to wear?"

Vanessa said, "How do you think we lure them? It helps to get them off guard, kind of like shock and awe. We knock them off their game, and we have them."

Roni and I stayed and got the food ready. When they got back, we all left for the house, and they wanted to know what the plan was.

"Well," I said, "I think that this one might seem a bit out there for you all, but it's something that I think some people deserve."

That piqued their curiosity.

Vanessa said, "Okay, tell us what it is."

He told them, "There are way too many assholes out there to even deal with sometimes, so why not feed them some of their own medicine?"

Lizzy said, "What the fuck are you talking about?"

"These people are supposed to leave tomorrow. We go there, we seduce them, knock them out, and take care of them. We clear the house of all their shit, clean it up, and everyone will think they left. The owners will send someone by to deep clean, and that will clean up anything that we may have left behind."

Lizzy said, "Okay, what about them?"

"Well, this would be the crazy part. I want to bring them back to the restaurant, break them down, wrap, freeze, and label the packages as special meat, only to be used by me. I can break it down to where no one would ever know what it is. Then when assholes come in, we feed them another asshole."

They all just stared at him with their mouths open. I said, "Can I guess by the looks on your faces that you don't like the idea?"

Emmanuelle said that she couldn't speak for anyone else, but she loved the idea. The rest of them followed. They loved it too.

It always fascinated me how much it *didn't* take to bring out the darkness in people. It's there. You just needed to give them a good reason—I gave them a good reason.

We loaded the food and started heading toward their house. It wasn't very far from the restaurant, so it didn't take us long to get there. On the way, I explained to them what the plan was.

"Vanessa, Lizzy, and Emmanuelle will go inside the house. Emmanuelle, you will tell them that I wanted you to come along and apologize and that if there is anything that you can do to make up for it to please let them know. That will really get them thinking, trust me. Lizzy and Vanessa, you start setting the table for their dinner, and, Emmanuelle, you're going to have to react to whatever they ask you for."

She asked, "In what way?"

Vanessa said, "Well, you know how to tease and flirt with people, how to make people want you, right?"

She said that she knew exactly what to do. They all asked Roni if she was okay staying behind, that she's been behind the scenes the last couple of times. She told them she was fine with it. She'd always do what's needed of her.

I said, "That is good to hear, but please tell us if it ever bothers you or if you ever start feeling any animosity, anything like that."

She said, "You never have to worry about that. I'm fine with it, but I will let you know if I ever do start feeling that way."

*****

Vanessa

We got to the house. We pulled a foldable cart out of the back and loaded up the food. Aaron asked if we remembered the champagne and tequila—always the tequila and of course the asshole medicine. I told him not to worry. It was all under control. We rolled it all up to the front door and knocked.

He answered the door, and the first thing he did was look at Emmanuelle.

He said, "What are you doing here?"

Emmanuelle stepped to the front and said, "Sir, I was told to come here by my boss, apologize to you for my behavior, and tell you that if there's anything that I can do to make it up to you, please let me know."

That stopped him from going on. He figured since she was being forced to be there, that he could seriously take advantage of this situation. He and his wife were already slightly drunk, so he wouldn't have any issues saying what was on his mind. He told them all to come in and get it all set up. The plan was for Emmanuelle to take the champagne over and serve them. I asked them to have a seat on the couch and we would get it all set up. The house they were staying at was in a very secluded area of the island—no houses around for as far as the eye could see, and it backed up against a grove of eucalyptus trees, some that were at least three hundred feet high. Needless to say, it was a well-hidden house, so we had very little to worry about. Emmanuelle grabbed the champagne and glasses and went over to the couch. She set the glasses down on the table and asked if they would like to start with a glass.

The wife looked her up and down and asked, "Aren't you going to join us?"

Emmanuelle said she would be right back.

She told me they wanted her to join them. "Is that okay?"

I said, "That's exactly what we want, but just remember, no matter how disgusted you may get because of their behavior or with what they ask, the end game is what we're after."

She said not to worry. She totally understood why we're there.

She went back out again with another glass and told them that she would love to join them. Emmanuelle was wearing a short leather skirt that buttoned up the side, no underwear, a strapless black bra, and a very sheer white silk shirt, buttoned down low; and because of the island breeze, she had on a thin zip-up jacket with a hood. He told her to take off her jacket and stay awhile. She let out a giggle, faced them, slowly unzipped her jacket, took it off, and tossed it on a chair. Emmanuelle could tell by the looks on their faces that they had them. She finally got what the rest of them were talking about, and she was loving it.

Emmanuelle said, "Wait, just a minute," and she ran into the kitchen, grabbed the three shots of tequila, two of which were dosed, and went back out.

She told them, "I forgot the most important part, celebrating your vacation, and I am sorry it is ending tonight because if you have more time, we could've gotten to know one another better."

The wife said, "Well, we do still have tonight, right?"

Emmanuelle agreed. She said, "Let's drink the champagne first." She bent over to pour the glasses of champagne. Her shirt was so sheer and buttoned down so far there wasn't much to leave to the imagination. She noticed them both staring at her as she poured the champagne. She handed both of them their glasses and grabbed hers. She toasted their vacation and them meeting each other even though it was under not so good of circumstances. As she took a sip of her champagne, she pulled it away from her mouth a little too soon and on purpose and spilled some down the front of her blouse. Not that it needed to be anymore see-through, but the wet T-shirt effect didn't hurt.

The wife said, "Oh, sweetheart, come over here and let me help you clean that up."

Lizzy and I were looking on from the kitchen.

Lizzy said, "She's pretty damn good at this."

I said, "I couldn't agree more. She's going to be really helpful to us."

*****

Emmanuelle walked over to the wife's side of the couch and sat on the arm. She took a cloth napkin and started to slowly wipe Emmanuelle's shirt with one hand while she took the other and started to rub her skirt.

She asked her, "Is this real leather?"

Emmanuelle said, "Yes, it is. Doesn't it feel great?"

She started rubbing the buttons and asking her what it was like having these on there. She said it was great and very convenient. As she rubbed the buttons, she grabbed one and popped it open.

"Aren't you afraid that they can easily be unbuttoned?"

Emmanuelle said, "No, not at all. That's what's convenient about them."

She started to concentrate on drying her shirt. She said, "I'm so sorry that you got this beautiful shirt all wet." As she wiped, she grabbed the open part of her shirt and pulled. It popped another button open. She told Emmanuelle, "Why don't you come and sit down between us and we can all can get to know each other better?"

Emmanuelle looked at the husband. He was so licking his chops to get her there. She said, "Okay, but first, it's time to do your shots of tequila."

They both downed the dosed shots and asked for one more. They said, "Don't forget yours."

Emmanuelle grabbed hers and did it too. She went to go and sit down between them, and the wife put her arm around her. When she did, he just sat and watched. You could tell by looking down at his crotch that he was enjoying all this. As Emmanuelle was drinking more champagne, she did the same thing, pulling it away from her mouth too soon and making sure this time that some spilled on her skirt.

She said, "I just don't know what's wrong with me. Maybe it's just been a long day."

She said, "That's okay, sweetheart, I'll help you clean it up."

She took her arm away from being around her, and she started wiping her skirt. As she was wiping, she started tugging at the buttons again, popping open enough of them to see that Emmanuelle didn't have any underwear on. She was sitting up on the couch a bit facing Emmanuelle. She got a huge smile on her face.

She told her, "It looks like you got some on your legs too, sweetheart."

Emmanuelle could feel her hand shaking as she started wiping her legs, working her way down in between and up.

She stopped for a second and said, "We can't forget this beautiful shirt."

While she started to dry it with one hand, she slipped the other under the napkin and started to unbutton her shirt, spreading it open as she went down until she reached her waist where the shirt was tucked in. Emmanuelle knew what they were doing here, but my god, this was turning her on. She told Emmanuelle that she needed to untuck her shirt the rest of the way, but rather than pulling it out, she unbuttoned her skirt the rest of the way until it completely opened. She unbuttoned her shirt, then reached up and unhooked her bra from the front. Emmanuelle's breasts popped out into her hands. They both looked over, and he was passed out on the couch. Emmanuelle thought, *One down. Now it's her turn.*

She looked at Emmanuelle and said, "Oh well, his loss."

As she started to put her hand between her legs and kiss her neck, Emmanuelle could feel that she was starting to pass out as well. Emmanuelle pushed her back on the couch and told her, "Just rest and let me do the work."

By the time she stood up and turned around, she was passed out on the couch. She put her clothes back on, and Lizzy and I came out of the kitchen. We looked at her and asked if she was okay. She said she was perfect.

We both said, "Yes, you are. Time to let Aaron and Roni in."

I and Lizzy never unpacked anything; in fact, they didn't really have much food, just enough to put a nice smell in the room. Aaron came in, hugged Emmanuelle, and asked her if she was okay. She said she was good. He told her that she did a great job.

"It is my pleasure," she said.

He told us, "The goal wasn't to do anything messy here. We would drug them enough so their hearts would slow, but they wouldn't be done yet. I needed the hearts to still be beating so that it would help him with draining their blood. We could get them back to the restaurant, and I would take care of the rest."

He told us all that we didn't need to stay for it, but we all said we wanted to help and learn. He told us that it was going to get a bit messy. We said we were fine with it. He told them he wasn't going to keep it all. Whatever he wasn't going to use, it was going to get taken out to sea. He had a boat that he rented for the morning. What he's not keeping, he'll tape up in bags, put them in an ice chest, and load them on the boats. We all wanted to go, but we had to remind Emmanuelle that she had kids to tutor. We shot them up one more time, wrapped them up in plastic, and loaded them up in the SUV along with all their luggage and other belongings. We all made sure to take everything we could think of and took off back to the restaurant.

By the time we got back, all the employees had already left. Even though the restaurant wasn't attached to the hotel, it still wasn't far enough away that we still needed to keep a lookout for the hotel security. We pulled up close to the back door, got them both in the kitchen, and locked and barricaded the door. There was a massive floor drain in front of the equipment in the back kitchen. It ran the length of it and had a metal grate over it so that people don't step into it. He laid them both down on the ground with their heads on the grate over the drain. He checked their pulse, and they both had a very weak one. He inserted a needle connected to a tube into the carotid artery in their necks, placed the tubes in the drain, and watched the blood slowly drain out. He covered the rest of the floor, tables, and equipment with plastic. As much as he could get away with blood in a kitchen, he didn't want to push it.

*****

Aaron

I unwrapped them and started to cut their clothes off. I handed them to the girls, and they started to cut them up into smaller pieces and put them in bags. I started first by taking their feet off at the ankles. Using an electric saw made it easier, but I had to make sure I kept everything well-covered to stop body parts from flying everywhere. Enough blood had drained, so there wasn't a lot of mess when I did it. I placed them in the bags, then I worked my way up the rest of the way. They were all looking at me like they couldn't believe how fast I was doing it. What they couldn't believe more was that it didn't bother them what I was doing. I was skinning and carving off what I was going to use and putting it in a pan, and the rest went in bags to be dumped. Breaking down two full-size bodies took some time, but in the end, the result is definitely going to be worth it. I removed the kidneys, heart, and the liver and put these in a separate pan. They needed to be broken down into smaller pieces.

When I got to the heads, some of them left, but Emmanuelle and Roni stayed. They were curious. I cut the top of the skull off and popped out their brains, I figured they could pass as sweetbreads. Once everything had been broken down, I doubled bagged what was going to be dumped along with the plastic, put some heavy bricks into the bags, duct-taped them tight, put them in ice chests, and put them in the freezer. The parts that I wanted to save, I broke them down into smaller pieces, vacuum-sealed them, wrapped them in brown paper, taped them up, marked them "Only to be used by Aaron," and stuck them in the freezer. We all cleaned up the kitchen and started for home. Once there, we unloaded their luggage and personal belongings and put it all down into the bunker, we all showered and climbed into bed. We had an early morning tomorrow. Vanessa asked me how I was feeling, that was more than she's ever seen me do, and she was wondering if I was okay. I told her to remember, I was doing this before I met her, and back then, I wasn't as refined as I am now. She helped me get that way, so yes, I'm feeling fine.

*****

The next morning, we got up early and went upstairs. Lizzy, Roni, and Emmanuelle were there waiting for us, dressed like they were ready to go to work.

Vanessa looked at them and said, "We are just going out for a day on a boat, is that how you would dress?"

They looked at one another and realized that they might just be a bit overdressed. They went back and put their bikinis on instead. They got to the restaurant and no one was there yet. They went inside and quickly loaded the ice chests into the SUV and then started their way to the dock. It was really quiet when they got there. It was too early for anyone else to be around, so loading the boat was easier than expected. They started heading north of the island. They didn't want to take the chance of anything else coming back. The packages were weighted down enough, and if something got ahold of them, it would all be gone before it reached the shore.

I told them, "Get comfortable. It was going to be a while. The bridge, wheelhouse, or whatever you want to call, the steering area sits at the top of the boat, so people sit below that on the deck."

They all decided to go down there to relax. The way they were going on down there, you wouldn't think anything had happened, drinking, sunbathing. When they lay on their bellies, even their tops came off, but I guess that's a good thing. I really don't want or need anyone freaking out about what we just had done. I just wanted to unload these ice chests and get back to the restaurant. I needed to go over everything and make sure that we left nothing behind, then I would feel a bit safer.

After going for about an hour and half, I decided it was time to stop and unload what we had. I didn't need to tell them. They could feel the boat coming to a stop. They got their tops on and started walking up to the top of the boat. I told Emmanuelle and Lizzy that they needed to stay up top and keep an eye out for any other boats. I handed them some binoculars and told them to scream if they saw anyone. I went down to the deck and grabbed the ice chests, pulled them to the side of the boat, and opened them up. Everything was still frozen solid so it would help aid in the sinking along with the bricks.

Once the paper started getting wet, it would start to fall away. Eventually, something would come and get what's left. I had a good feeling that we wouldn't have anything to worry about after this was done.

After I dumped it all, I stopped, looked at them all, and asked them, "Based on our behavior out here, you wouldn't think that any-thing had happened."

They all told me one by one that they understood why we did what we did and they're okay about all of it. They all couldn't be happier with what's going on, and they want to keep going. Even the newbie, Emmanuelle, was more into it than we thought she would be. It was like she was made for it. We started back to shore. We never saw another boat. It couldn't have been easier. We got back and drove home to get cleaned up and changed. Clients weren't arriving quite yet, and the girls were just getting up. Emmanuelle made them breakfast and started getting their lessons ready for the day, and the rest of us went about our days doing what we do. It almost seemed less than exciting when we weren't out plotting against someone, almost like we were living a normal life. That was a bit scary. Is this what we needed, to just start living a normal life, definitely a conversation I needed to have with Vanessa. We really needed to make sure Vail got open and then they could decide what to do from there.

The days went on like normal—nothing happening out of the ordinary. Everyone was really happy with the restaurant, the gym, and the massage services. I wanted to sit down with everyone and get an update on what was going on in Park City and Tucson and how Vail was coming along. Everything in Vail was coming along really well. The construction was almost done, and Lizzy and Jenny had been working on interviewing people for the new spot. Jenny said that the people she brought in from the other locations were a great help, and she wanted to take the two to Vail as well. We were going to start needing a bigger plane. The bigger it gets, the more focus it puts on us; and the last thing we want is to have that focus on us, but then again, if it's time to go legit, then it's not so bad. Park City and Tucson were doing really well. Clients were happy and spreading the word. Word of mouth is the best form of advertisement. When it was time to open Vail, I sent Vanessa, Lizzy, and Roni to get it started. I needed to keep working the restaurant to make sure that everything was being done correctly and that we were building the clientele that we needed. Besides the fact, we had already opened three of them. Vanessa was more than capable of opening the places and making the decisions that needed to be made. We were fifty-fifty, and if it's one person I have totally faith in, it's her.

Emmanuelle was still working the door every night at the restaurant. She knew what to do, and now that we all had something in common, she was someone that we could trust. It was a Friday, and it happened to be a particularly busy night. Everything was going very smoothly, and then it happened, in came an asshole and his wife, already complaining because they had to wait for a table, and it just went on from there. Emmanuelle came in the back and told me that she was having a problem with a couple, and she was sure that I would want to deal with them. One of the things that I had created was a chef's table off the kitchen for special groups of people to sit so I could personally take care of them. Well, this was about to come in very handy based on what I had decided I was going to do with what was left of the assholes in the freezer. I told Emmanuelle to bring them to the chef's table and I would take care of them. Once they got back there, you could just see them dripping with entitlement. It was just unreal that they thought they were owed something and that we were nothing but pieces of shit that were put there to wait on them hand and foot. I greeted them and told them that I apologize for the wait and that Emmanuelle and I would take care of them now and would they have a problem with a chef menu created especially for them. They loved the idea.

I asked them if there was anything they didn't like. They said absolutely not. They loved it all. I told them that was great to hear. I called Emmanuelle in the office and told her I needed her to be a distraction for me. She said that wouldn't be a problem. She reached under her shirt, unhooked her bra, took it off, and put it on the desk. Then she reached under her skirt and took off her underwear, grabbed them both, and put them in her purse. She unbuttoned a couple of buttons, looked at me, and asked how she looked.

"Enough of a distraction?"

I told her she looked perfect. There was something about her. She seemed to enjoy this more than we thought she would. It was like she had something inside that she was needing to get back at, an emotional score to settle, nothing unstable like Jody, but there was something there; and eventually, I would get it out of her.

I started to prepare their appetizer, veal sweetbreads—well, more like asshole brains, but they'll never know that—made in a traditional way with capers, brandy, lemon juice, and whole butter.

Emmanuelle started to pour their wine for them, bending over just enough to get them both wondering what was under her shirt, dropping the cork, and doing a half kneel, half bending over just to get them thinking even more. I brought them their appetizer, explained to them what it was, and stayed there long enough for them to take their first bite, they loved them! It's amazing how much people don't know about food, but I was going to keep going. Emmanuelle was trying really hard to contain laughter, but she knew that wouldn't be appropriate.

Next up, grilled ostrich steaks—both Mr. and Mrs. Ostrich—served with brown sugar mashed taro, kabocha squash, kula onions, and Hawaiian chili pepper demi-glace. Emmanuelle went back to offer them more wine. They both asked if she wanted to join them. She said she would ask me and let them know if it was okay. She came and told me what they wanted. The restaurant had emptied out, and staff was almost done cleaning. I told her to tell them that she could sit down with them for dessert. I came out with their dinner and explained it to them. They were very impressed with it all, but if they only knew. They finished every bit of their dinner. They loved all of it. The four of us were the only ones left in the restaurant, and it was time for dessert.

Emmanuelle asked if they wanted an after-dinner drink, they both wanted a nice brandy to go with their dessert. She brought them each a glass of Louis XIII, some of the best they had ever had. I finished off their meal with a nice chocolate pate, laced with candied poblano chiles, honeycomb, and finished with a crystalized ginger, mango, pineapple, and strawberry salsa. They were in heaven. They asked me if Emmanuelle could sit down and have a drink with them. I told them sure. She had time to sit for one. She went and grabbed herself a drink, and as she went to sit down in the booth, he got up and had her sit between them.

As she went to sit in the booth, her skirt slid up a bit, showing more of her legs. I was cleaning up, watching as this all was starting to go down. She seriously looked like she was enjoying all this. Emmanuelle pulled the same trick she did with the last couple. She took a sip of her drink and pulled the glass away from her lips too soon, making sure to spill some down the front of her shirt and skirt.

The woman grabbed her napkin and said, "Oh, sweetheart, let us help you with that."

She started to rub the front of Emmanuelle's shirt while the man grabbed his napkin and started to rub her skirt. I was watching. She just sat there, letting them do it to her. Emmanuelle was going on about being a klutz, and she apologized for that happening. They both told her that it was no problem at all. They didn't mind helping her one bit. As she was wiping her shirt, she started tugging at her buttons, and some of them started to pop open. As he was wiping her skirt, he noticed it zippered up the side from top to bottom. He grabbed the zipper and slowly started to zip it down. She noticed a couple of drops on her chest, so she reached into her shirt and started to slowly dry them off. She dropped the napkin and kept rubbing with her hand, working her way down and around her breasts, caressing and squeezing them. He finished zipping down her skirt until the skirt was completely separated. He pushed the skirt to the side, reached in, spread her legs, and started rubbing between them.

I looked around the corner, and I couldn't believe what I was seeing. They were all over her rubbing her body. Emmanuelle had her arms over her head. Her head was laid back, eyes closed, taking short shallow breaths, not stopping them at all. As arousing as this was, it needed to stop, I said distract them, not fuck them. I pretended like I accidentally dropped something, and it snapped her out of it. Startled, she put her arms down, buttoned up her shirt, zippered up her skirt, and asked to leave the booth. They let her out, and she came and got me. I didn't let her know what I had seen. I thanked them for coming in for dinner and told them that the evening was on me, to not worry about it. They thanked me but asked if they could leave Emmanuelle a tip. I told them that I didn't have a problem with that. He reached in his pocket, pulled out a thousand dollars in hundreds, and gave it to her. She thanked them both, and we walked them out of the restaurant and locked the doors behind them. I looked at her and told her that we needed to talk.

"I had seen everything that had just happened, and we needed to talk about it."

She started getting teary-eyed, and I told her, "I'm here to help you, but I need to know what's going on. I'm also concerned about whether there was something we needed to worry about."

She said, "No, there is nothing to worry about, but I wanted to tell you what is going on with me. I need to get it off my chest."

We grabbed a drink and went back to the scene of the crime, the chef's table. We sat down, and I told her to explain what was going on with her. I'm here to help her with whatever she's got going on.

She told me, "It really started when I was younger. I have a seriously abusive father, not physically but emotionally and mentally, and my brothers, two of them and both older, played right along with it. Always putting me down, telling me I was worthless and that I wouldn't amount to much, telling me that I was the ugly duckling of the family. My father hated me showing my body, so he always had me dressed in long sleeves and long skirts or dresses. It didn't matter what time of year it was, and do you think I ever tried to change after I left the house?

"No way. He had my brothers follow me everywhere to make sure I was following the rules."

I asked her where her mother was during all this. She told me that her mother was always trying to protect her, but she died of cancer when she was very young. After that, she had no one. She figured her only way out was to keep her head down, study hard, get a scholarship, and get out. They couldn't stop her from doing that.

"They somehow found out what I was doing now, working for you, and all of sudden, they're trying to get money from me."

I looked at her and said, "Tell me you're not sending them money. Please tell me that you're not."

She said she had thought about it. They were giving her some sob story about how her dad was sick and he needed it. She looked at me and told me she needed to tell me something, something I wouldn't like, but she had to tell me. She said that even though she thought about it, she never followed through and she would never follow through.

I said, "Okay, tell me what you're talking about!"

Tears started welling up in her eyes. She told me that for a split second, and only for a second, she thought about using the fund to give them some money. "I didn't tell them that I was in charge of the fund, and I never would've followed through with it."

I just sat there looking at her. She kept wanting to know what I was thinking.

I told her, "Okay, here's what I'm thinking. I'm glad you didn't do that, and even if you did, I would've understood it, to a certain point. We take really good care of you, like really good care. We trust you with Jenny's kids, we trust you with our money, and most importantly, we trust you with our deepest secrets. Why couldn't you have trusted us with yours? We told you that we're here for you, always, but you have to give back to us. Another reason why I would have understood, you're not a common thief. You're being governed and guided by your shitty past. You're still letting your abusers manipulate you, and that's understandable, but you understand what we've been doing, right? We help people break that cycle. We help to empower people."

She thanked me for all of what I had just said. She didn't expect me to go so easy on her.

I asked her, "What did you expect, to end up in the freezer?"

She just kind of looked up at me… "I don't really know."

I told her, "When we told you that we loved you and that you are part of us, I meant that 110 percent. I wouldn't do that to you!"

She understood and thanked me for being so understanding.

She told me that it didn't end there. When she got to college, some of the garbage continued to carry over.

"As soon as anyone I dated saw how easily I could be manipulated, they took full advantage of me. It usually took something drastic to happen to get me to wake up. Even friends screaming at me to get out didn't work."

I asked her to give me some examples. She asked if I really wanted to hear them. I might lose some respect for her. I told her there's no chance of that happening.

She said, "Well, there was this one guy I was dating. He used to make me masturbate in front of him, not a bad thing when you're by yourselves, but when he saw how easy it was to get me to do it, he used to make me do it when we were in restaurants and bars. He would make me wear some really skimpy clothes with nothing underneath and have us sit in booths in the back. But the one thing that finally got me away from this one, he started making me do it in front of his friends, and the last time, when I opened my eyes, they had their pants down around their ankles, and they were standing in front of me trying to jerk off onto me. That was the end of that guy. I left and never came back."

I looked and her and said, "Jesus Christ, what the fuck is wrong with people!"

She said that wasn't the worst one.

I said, "There's worse?"

She said, "Oh yeah, there's worse."

I told her, "Okay, I'm ready. What was the worst?"

She said, "The last guy I dated. Everything was going really well, and then he started realizing that he could tell me to do things and I would do it. It started out kind of small and innocent, a little role play, a little choking, and then he started wanting to tie me up and blindfold me. I said okay, no problem, so we started doing that every once in a while, and then it started becoming more frequent, and then it turned into every time. And each time, he started lasting longer and longer and he was having multiple orgasms. I know because each time, he was having them on me or in me."

I looked at her and said, "Please don't tell me what I'm thinking is right."

She said, "Okay, well, I guess you will have to wait and see."

She continued, "I got smart, and I got a different blindfold, looked the same, but I could actually see-through this one. Nighttime came, and he wanted to do it again. I took my clothes off and climbed in the bed. He handcuffed my hands to the headboard and tied my legs spread wide open to the foot of the bed. He then put the blindfold on me. It worked really well, almost like there was nothing there. He took his clothes off and went down on me to get me wet. As soon as I was, he climbed on top of me and started going at it. After some time, I could hear him start to cum. When he did, he leaned over and whispered in my ear that he still wasn't done. He still felt hard, and he wanted to go some more. I told him, 'Okay, baby, I'm here for you.' Then my worst nightmare came true. I watched him get off the bed, and behind him was one of his friends. He climbed on me, and he started going until I started to hear him cum. He pulled out and came all over my belly. He got off me, and my boyfriend wiped it off me.

"He leaned over again and whispered in my ear that he wanted to go one more time. Am I okay with that."

I asked her what she said.

She asked me, "What was I supposed to say? He's tying me up and doing what he's doing, don't you think if I started freaking out, screaming, or yelling that they wouldn't have taken care of me right then and there? It would've been a lot meaner and a lot rougher."

I told her that she was probably right. "Please continue."

"When his friend got up, there was another one standing behind him. He went down on me to get me wet again, climbed on top of me, and started going at it. But this guy, he was a bit rougher with me, choking me, squeezing my breasts hard, and the whole time, my boyfriend was just looking on, doing nothing, and then to just finish in a more degrading way, he pulled out of me and came all over my tits and my face, making sure to hit my face more. He got up and walked out. My boyfriend cleaned me up, undid my hands and legs, took off the blindfold, gave me a kiss, and told me he was going to sleep. That was a lot of work, and he was tired."

I asked her what she did next.

She said, "I climbed out of bed, waited for him to go to sleep, got my clothes on, and left, and I never looked back. That's when I got the call from Jenny, and now I'm here."

I told her, "That's one hell of a story, and I'm sorry that you had to go through that, and I promise you that we will take care of your demons for you."

She asked what I meant.

I told her that we needed to get home. I'll explain more to her later on at home.

CHAPTER 25

Testing Our Bonds and Solving More Problems

Aaron

We got home, and everyone was sleeping, so we went down into the bunker. We grabbed a drink and sat down on the couch. Emmanuelle apologized and thanked me again for being so understanding. I told her that she didn't need to keep thanking me. She asked me if I was going to share what had happened with everyone.

I told her Vanessa and I had a very open and honest relationship with each other, and since the rest of us were so close, they would need to know as well. "You can tell them, or I can tell them. It's up to you."

She said she would be there, but she asked if I would tell them. I told her that I wouldn't have a problem with that. She asked me if I was going to tell them about the fund.

I told her, "Of course, I was going to tell them. I have to tell them. We're all a part of that. That tells your story, Emmanuelle. It tells them how you've been treated and what you're about. They might be pissed at first, but they will understand. Trust me, I know them. We're all in this together until the day we die."

She understood. She was scared, but she understood. I told her that we needed to go to bed. It was late, and they were all coming back tomorrow. It would be a long day. She asked if she could sleep down here with me so she didn't wake anyone up. I told her to go ahead and crash in the other room, but I would be waking her up early.

I woke up, made some coffee, and just sat. It always seemed like everything was moving 110 miles an hour, and I just needed to stop and sit, collect my thoughts for a bit before it all started again. I went in and woke Emmanuelle up. She was in a deep sleep, and it took a minute to get her there; but she finally opened her eyes. I told her that it was time to get up. They would be landing in an hour, and we needed to get things going before we all sat and talked. She didn't want to get up. She was scared for what was about to happen. I told her there was no need. I would take care of her. We went upstairs and started making breakfast. Just as we sat down to eat, they all got home. Scarlett and Alexandra ran up to Emmanuelle, gave her a huge hug, and told her that they missed her. Jenny decided that they would take one more day of no studies and head to the beach. Vanessa gave me a huge hug and kiss. We told each other that we missed each other tons. We're not separated very often, and we don't really like it. So I told them all to get settled in, that Emmanuelle and I had something to talk to them about. Once settled in, they all came and sat down to hear what had happened when they were gone.

I told them all that Emmanuelle had asked me to tell them what has happened and what's been happening.

"I gave her the choice, but she's afraid of you all's reaction to it. I told her that I believed initially you all would be upset, but that in the end, you would understand."

Roni said, "Okay, what is it!"

I proceeded to explain to them everything Emmanuelle had told me. With all the details added in, there was a lot of crying and holding from all of them, and then I saved the fund for last. The three of them just stopped and thought for what seemed like a very long time. Emmanuelle looked at them and told them that she would leave if that's what they wanted, and she would never say a word about anything that they had done.

Vanessa told her, "It wasn't that simple. You're a part of us now, and we don't just dump people like that. It's not who we are."

Roni and Lizzy agreed. Lizzy said that they all have done shit that they weren't proud of, and I didn't get rid of any of them. We fight for one another, and we take care of one another—period, end of story. Vanessa did say that it concerned her that she was going to take money that was for a good cause and send it to her asshole family.

"I get that they still have certain control over you, but how will we know that you won't give in the next time? It's a huge amount of money with a huge responsibility."

I said, "Well, going forward, until we're sure of it, there won't be any distributions without our approval. We can set it up that way. Emmanuelle, do you have a problem with that?"

She said she absolutely didn't have a problem with that at all.

I said, "But really, how is it that we've all solved our issues from the past, what have we done to break that hold that people have had over us, how have we gotten them out of our systems?"

Vanessa said, "By getting rid of them."

The rest of them agreed.

So having said that, I asked Emmanuelle who had caused the most damage to her, who was the most responsible for causing her the pain that caused her to hate herself as much as she does. She said it was definitely her father and brothers. I asked her where they were and what were they doing.

She said, "They were back in Utah, living in some backward-ass cabin in the forest. It was a place where we went when we were kids, but when life started to spiral down for them, they all decided to disconnect and go there."

I said, "Okay, it's time to make our plan. Let's fix this for her."

Emmanuelle couldn't believe what she was hearing that we were so ready to take care of her no matter what was blowing her away.

"Side note, taking care of people is one of the best things that we can do. It breeds loyalty. Family and people will never leave you. I was stomped on and treated like shit by so many people, and it bred this, me wanting to eliminate you from existence, me eliminating you from existence and giving you what you deserve, me taking everything you've ever earned away from you and your family. You either get a life sentence, living the rest of your life destitute with your reputation destroyed, nothing to your name and not a pot to piss in, or a death sentence and not one that the state gives to you, a shot in the arm, but one that I will give to you. I'm judge, jury, and executioner, and with your execution, I will break you down. I will make you suffer. I will degrade you like you have done to so many people in the past, and I will tear you apart. You will get no mercy from me, your death will be harsh, and it will be ugly. Just hope we don't show up at your door."

Now back to the plan. We asked Emmanuelle if her family had guns, were they into guns, explosives, anything at all since they were so far out into the woods. She said they had them for protection and for hunting, but other than that, it's not like they had a stockpile of them; and as far as explosives, most of the time, they were drunk, so they didn't care for them much.

"Okay, so here's the plan. We will use you, Vanessa, Roni, and Lizzy to go into the house. You will communicate with them before-hand and tell them that you have money for them, a lot of it. You and your friends took it from me, and you wanted to give some to them."

Emmanuelle said that it would drive them crazy waiting for us to get there.

I said, "Good, tell them it's time for a family reunion. It's time to party. That'll get them in the mood."

They all asked where I would be.

I said, "Where else, in the back of the SUV, waiting for you to do what you do." I told them, "We needed to get $100K in cash. We would split it between two bags. We would leave half in the SUV, and you would take the other half in. Once you get inside, show them the money and start to party. Apologize for staying away. We'll make sure and put some top-end booze, champagne, and single malt scotch in there for you to give to them. They'll like that. Emmanuelle, your job is going to be very important. Since you obviously aren't going to be flirting with your family, you're going to have to basically direct the show. You won't be flirting with them, right, or did you leave something out?"

237

Emmanuelle said she didn't leave anything out. One of her brothers had tried to make some moves on her one time before she left, but she shut that shit down.

I said, "Well, maybe we can use that to our advantage. You'll have to gauge that as you all go along."

They all asked what was my plan and how was I going to take care of them. I told them that I was angry, seriously angry, not just for what they put her through because of all this shit. It just kept happening over and over again, and I was just tired of it and how long could we keep this up.

Vanessa said, "Maybe we need a break?"

"Maybe we do, but the way they're going to go is going to be violent. I will show no mercy on them, at all."

What really surprised the girls wasn't how I was going to take care of them but how calm I was. It didn't scare them, but they knew that it might be time to slow down or stop, maybe focus on the businesses for a while.

"All the businesses were running smoothly. Let's just try to stick with that. Focus on that, and maybe open some more, restaurants included."

I said, "I wanted Emmanuelle to tell them that she had more money in the car. I just wanted to see how well you all got along first, then one of the other girls flirt him out to the outside toward me, and I will take care of him. After he's done, I will take care of the rest. Let's get packed and get some rest so we can leave in the morning, but before we sleep, Emmanuelle, I need for you to call them and let them know we're coming."

She got ahold of her father. His name was Zeke, and her brothers' names were Sam and Joe. She told him that she felt really bad for ignoring them and that she and three of her friends had stolen a bunch of money from me and left. She wanted to give some to them. Zeke told her that it was about time she came to her senses. After all that he'd done for her, she was worthless until he made her a some-one. She was on speakerphone so we could hear him. We all were getting pissed off, and then we looked at her, and she was tearing up, saying, "Daddy, I'm so sorry."

I put the phone on mute and told her to snap out of it. "Get tough and fuck him!"

I unmuted the phone, and she told him they would be there in two days. We would be there earlier because I wanted to check the place out to make sure they didn't have traps set up anywhere. We all went off to get some sleep. We were going to need it for the next couple of days.

We got up the next morning, grabbed a walking breakfast and coffee, and headed toward the airport. The flight time was six and a half hours, so we would have time for more rest and more planning. I told them when we get to Utah; we would get the one hundred thousand for her family. Vanessa said she had already alerted the bank, and it would be ready for us when we got there. She said she also rented an SUV, so we don't have to take ours out there.

"I know I don't have to tell you all what to wear anymore."

Lizzy said, "No, you don't, but with this group, we were told to kind of country theme it, cutoffs, crop tops, and cowboy boots."

Good thing is, we have our place to stay, so it's just like we're going to check on our businesses—no hotel and no reason to not travel. Vanessa took me to the back of the plane to ask me how I was doing.

I told her, "I am tired again. I've been doing this for a while, even before I met you, and as much as I keep pushing myself, I believe that it might be time to take a break and we can just focus on our businesses for a while. I'm not saying that I want to stop forever, but I think after this, it might be time to take a break."

She agreed with me. She could tell it was taking a toll on me. The person that she met and fell in love with wasn't there anymore, or at the very least he is, but he's buried because of this shit.

We went and sat with the rest of them and explained what we had just talked about.

"Sometimes we get tired and burned out, and when that happens, we can make mistakes. We need to make sure that with this next one and possibly the last one for a while that we're extra careful and we watch each other's backs."

All of them agreed with what they were told. As much as they want to bury these people, parts of them felt like they needed to take a break and concentrate on life and running the businesses because they felt like they're neglecting it in some way. I understood and agreed.

"So this one will be the last one for a while. Let's exorcise Emmanuelle's demons and then take a break. We still have some time, so let's try to get some rest."

CHAPTER 26

One More Recipe to Cook, For Now...

Aaron

We got to Park City, and the first thing we did was stop at Lizzy's old bank. A lot of people were really happy to see her. It had been quite a while. She and Vanessa stepped into the back and got the money, stuffed it into the bag, and said our goodbyes. They had Emmanuelle direct them to where her family was. It was a very remote area without anyone else around.

I stopped short and got out to take a look around. I wanted them to stay because I didn't want them to be seen if they saw me. I made my way around most of the property, and I didn't see anything unusual—no traps, cameras, or security of any kind. It doesn't mean there isn't, but I'm pretty good with noticing that stuff having done so much of it. I even made it closer to the house, and sure enough, they were all in there getting drunk. I heard them talking about tomorrow. Zeke was telling them that it was about time she came back. He was saying that he should punish her when she gets here, but since she was bringing money, he might just let it go. Sam and Joe were going on about the friends she was bringing and what they looked like. Sam said that if they were half as hot as Emmanuelle, then they would be gorgeous.

Zeke looked at Sam and said, "You always had a soft spot for your sister, didn't you? I think you wanted her to be more than your sister, didn't you, boy?"

Sam said, "Maybe, just a little."

Zeke told him, "Well, maybe that will be her punishment. We will make her have to be with you. What do you think about that?"

Sam's eyes just lit up. Could his dream actually come true?

I had heard enough. If I had actually had a weapon on me, I would've killed them all right there—problem solved—but Emmanuelle had to do it. The only way she would exorcise this demon from inside her was to be a part of the process, doing it for her lets her off easy. I got back to the car and told them everything that I had heard. They were all pissed, including Emmanuelle. She was ready to take care of the problem. She told me that Sam would be the one that she would lure outside with the chance to get what he's wanted for so long. Then I could do whatever I wanted to do to him. I said that we needed to be particularly careful.

"These guys are drunks. They're mean and ugly, and they really want to punish Emmanuelle for what they feel she's done to them. No matter how full of shit they are, they truly believe it."

I told them, "I think you should drug them to keep them off-balance, unable to overpower you all. They might try to take a swipe, but it probably wouldn't hurt even if they could connect, but hopefully, it won't come to that. When we get back, we're going to take you to a part of the bunker you haven't seen yet. We will give you something out of there to take with you."

*****

When we got back to the house, we dumped all our shit and headed down to the bunker. I led them to the room they had never seen and opened it up. They couldn't believe their eyes—the security systems, weapons, explosives, so many things they've never seen before. They didn't know whether to be impressed or afraid of me and Vanessa. I told them that they needed to have a weapon on themselves, nothing bulky and easy to hide in their boots. They all took stiletto switchblades, small and easy enough to put in their boots. I told them I was going up to make them dinner. I led them out and closed the door. While I was cooking dinner, we all decided to go for a swim and relax. It felt like such a long time since we had relaxed. I brought dinner outside for them, and we all talked and laughed about anything and everything *not* related to all this bullshit. Jenny and the girls had joined us, and it was really nice to have everyone together again, like a big family. After eating and swimming some more, Emmanuelle and Jenny took the girls and got them ready for bed. It was back to Charlie and his angels again. It had seemed like forever since we weren't so busy with everyone around—just us— and it felt good. Emmanuelle came down and told us she was really wiped out and if we cared if she just went to bed. We told her we understood and that it was fine to go ahead. I told her that I would be getting us all up early to get ready to go tomorrow. We told them that we would be there by two or three at the latest so we had some time to gather and talk in the morning. Emmanuelle thanked all of us again for helping her out and she would see us in the morning. Right behind her was Jenny and the girls to say good night. Lizzy said she would walk them back up to say good night. The rest of us got out and decided it was time to get ready for bed.

Vanesa and I decided to take a nice hot shower to help relax us. It felt so incredibly good—the water beating down on us, soaping each other's bodies, and helping each other rinse off. It had been so long since we'd been with each other, longer than ever before. We got out, dried off, and jumped into bed. As we started making love to each other, we saw the other two angels at the door. I looked at them and told them to come in and sit down. They looked at Vanessa, and she told them the same thing.

"Come in and have a seat."

I looked at them and said, "You know since we're stopping this for a while, the two of you could theoretically go out and find yourselves someone to be with, right? Maybe that would also stop us from starting again. I don't know, but anything is possible, I guess."

They both looked at me and said, "We will *never* stop helping you do this. We will want to continue this forever because if we don't, way too many people out there will suffer. We can't take care of everyone, but we can help make some people's lives better right? That's why we do it, right?"

Vanessa and I totally agreed with them. "If you all don't want to stop, we won't. We were just giving you the option again."

Lizzy and Roni asked, "So do we still get a show?"

Vanessa and I had a very large bed with a huge headboard. Venessa told them to go and sit up against the headboard and just watch. Vanessa and I proceeded to make love to each other like we hadn't in a very long time. They didn't know why. Maybe it's because they were going to stop all this for a while. After tomorrow, they could just relax and live their lives. They all finished at what seemed like the same time. They were getting ready to leave, and Vanessa told them to stay. The bed was big enough. Vanessa and Lizzy slept in the middle. She didn't really want to put me in there, and they all fell asleep.

It all may seem a little strange what we were doing, but we all have grown so close to each other; and with everything we've been through, we were even closer than most people—okay, probably almost all people because I'm sure that there aren't a lot of serial killers out there. But I don't know if there's any like our group anywhere. We all hit it off from the beginning, from the moment this whole thing started with just Vanessa and I to the family we've become. No matter what happens, the four of us, and maybe even the five of us—if Emmanuelle sticks it out—will never leave each other. We have thriving businesses in multiple locations along with multiple homes and more than enough money to last us for the rest of our lives. There's nothing to worry about. Would I be able to last for a long time without doing what I do? I think I can, and I think that for my sanity, I have to at least try. It's time to sleep.

*****

We got up early and started getting everything together. Emmanuelle made her way up to the house and grabbed some breakfast with us. We made our way into the bunker and changed into the clothes we were going to wear. They all looked like they were ready for a line dance. They each grabbed their weapon of choice, and we went over the plan one more time before we got on the road. The drive out there was very quiet. It didn't bother me because I knew we were all going over mentally what we needed to do, what our roles are going to be, and maybe even getting a little hyped. We were almost there, and I had to warn them again to not get lazy. Just because this would be our last one for a while, we needed to stay alert. I moved into the far back of the SUV before she pulled onto the property. They pulled up to the door. Vanessa looked at all of them and said, "Are you ready? Let's do this and do it right for Emmanuelle."

They grabbed the bag of money and booze, got out of the SUV, and went to the door. Before they even had a chance to knock, Sam swung the door open and screamed Emmanuelle's name and gave her a huge hug. As he hugged her, his hands went down and grabbed her ass. She introduced everyone to her father and brothers. The brothers looked like they were in heaven. Her dad took an immediate liking to Vanessa. Emmanuelle put the bag on the bar, pulled out the champagne and scotch, and then showed them the money. Zeke's eyes opened wide. He'd never seen that much money in his life. He told her that it was about time you became worth something.

Emmanuelle said, "I know, Daddy. I should never have gone away, I'm so sorry, please forgive me. I brought you all this money. Will that help?"

Zeke said, "It might. If you go and get me a drink, I'll think about it. In fact, get us all drinks. Sam, go and help her."

"So let's set this up."

All of them were wearing low-cut tank tops, no bras, some of the shortest cutoff jean shorts I've ever seen, just short enough for you to wonder whether there was anything on underneath them, and cowboy boots with socks and straps where they had their knives. They have all been trained, and I have no doubt that they can't protect themselves, but that didn't matter. We needed to be careful.

Sam walked into the kitchen with her to help get the drinks. She popped the cork on the bottles of champagne, and some came shooting out of the top. Sam got a big smile on his face and told her he liked the way she grabbed the neck of the bottle.

She told him, "You like that trick? I've got a ton of them."

Sam wanted to take a shot with her to celebrate her return. She went to go and look for shot glasses, and they were dirty in the sink, along with what seemed like every other dish and glass in the house. She told him she'd have to wash the glasses. He walked up behind her, grabbed her ass, and said, "Why don't you wash all of them for us? I know Daddy would be happy if you did."

Emmanuelle started washing the dishes while Sam just sat there and watched her, waiting, so she figured, *Why not? Let's give him a show.* She turned the water on and started splashing—accidentally, of course—pressing her hand up against the water coming out of the faucet. She made the water spray all down the front of her, wetting her tank top down. Since it was thin and white, it didn't leave much to the imagination, and the look on his face, he was like a kid in a candy store.

They took their shots and took the champagne into the other room. Zeke asked what took them so long. Emmanuelle told him that she had done all the dishes for them.

He said, "Look at you, soaking wet. You can't do anything right, can you?"

She said, "I guess not, Daddy."

He walked up to her and gave her a slap on her ass and told her, "Next time, it will be across your face."

She just stared at him, a look Zeke had never seen before; and truth be told, it worried him more than he was willing to admit.

*****

Vanessa

I saw what was happening, so I took a glass of champagne over to Zeke to break the tension. I got between him and Emmanuelle and started flirting with him. It helped to pull him away from her. Lizzy and Roni were busy flirting with Joe, and Sam was still paying attention to Emmanuelle's wet shirt although it was drying. Emmanuelle interrupted all of them and told them that she was really sorry for leaving them. She figured out she was wrong, and she wanted to make it up to them. That's why she came back with gifts for them. Zeke asked what kind of gifts was she talking about.

She said, "First, we're going to get us all some shots. I want the three of you to sit on the couch and wait for us."

The three of them sat down on the couch and waited. The four of us went into the kitchen to get the shots. We all commented on what pieces of shit they all were.

Emmanuelle said, "Now you know why I got out."

I pulled the dose out of my pocket and added it to their shots. Emmanuelle said to just follow her lead. She's got it from here. We all nodded.

We took all the shots and the bottle out into the living room and gave it to them. The three of them downed the shots quickly and asked for another one. Lizzy poured them another, standing in front of them, and making sure they had no problems seeing what was down her shirt but still wondering if there was anything under her shorts. As she was standing up, Joe grabbed her ass and then spanked it—spanked it hard.

I brought the girls together and said, "It is obvious these guys liked to play rough. What they don't know is that we can play a lot rougher. Let's show them how."

Emmanuelle told them that she wanted to come back and make it up to them, make it up to them for running out on them.

"I have felt like shit for a long time for what's happened, and it is time to make it up to you, and I want to start with Daddy." Emmanuelle told Sam to put on some dancing type of music. She went over and grabbed Zeke's hand and then grabbed my hand and walked them over to a chair next to the couch. She moved the coffee table and told Sam and Joe to move apart from each other. She put Lizzy in front of Sam and Roni in front of Joe. Sam asked her what she was going to do.

She told him, "Don't worry, I still have surprises for you."

She walked back over to me and said, "Okay, now show him what we can do for him."

I started swinging my hips around, squatting down and up, reaching over and grabbing my ankles, and standing back up again, like I was dancing on a pole. Zeke tried to grab me, and I slapped his hand away, hard, and said in a really loud voice, "Bad boys don't get fed. Just wait."

Emmanuelle went and tapped Roni on the shoulder, and she started doing the same thing although Joe wasn't stupid enough to try to grab her, then she went and tapped Lizzy on the shoulder, and she started dancing. Again, Sam wasn't stupid enough to try to grab her. They were all so engrossed in watching them dance they didn't even notice Emmanuelle pulling the knife out of her boot, she opened it up, walked in front of Vanessa, and started to cut down her shirt from the top, stopping mid breast so there was still some guessing involved.

She whispered to her, "So much easier to remove now."

I smiled. She walked over to the other two, did the same, and told them the same thing. Sam was still asking what was she going to do.

Emmanuelle told him, "I thought I told you not to worry, didn't I? Enjoy the show you're getting now, boy!"

He nodded and went back to watching. You could tell how much he really wanted Emmanuelle.

The girls were all dancing like they were giving lap dances in the club. It was a thing of beauty. Emmanuelle decided it was time for her to get involved in the party. She pulled the coffee table over in front of Sam and climbed on top of it. She told Lizzy to move over, and she started dancing for Sam. She took the knife and started cutting her shirt from the bottom up, leaving a couple of inches of shirt, letting the bottom of her breasts pop out. She picked up the bottle of tequila and started to pour some down the front of her shirt until the shirt was clinging so hard to her breasts you could see her areolas perfectly outlined. Sam couldn't stop squirming.

Zeke couldn't take his eyes off me as I was slowly tearing my shirt open more and more, and Joe, well, Joe had Lizzy and Roni in front of him doing the same thing, slowly tearing their shirts open. Emmanuelle unbuttoned the top button of her pants and unzipped them about halfway down. You could tell by looking that she was very well-groomed down there.

She looked at Sam, grabbed one side of her shirt, lifted it up to expose her breast, and asked, "Is this what you've been wanting all your life?" Sam very enthusiastically nodded. She said to him, "Why don't we go outside and I can give you all that you've been dreaming about?"

He started to stand up, and she yelled at him to stay, "I'll tell you when I want you, boy. You just wait." She walked over and said, "Daddy, I'm going outside with Sam. Are you okay with that?"

He asked if I was going to go and play with my brother. I nodded yes. He kept staring at Vanessa's tits. I said, "Eyes up here, Daddy. I've also got another surprise for you."

He said, "Okay, baby. I'll see when you come back."

She walked over to Sam and said, "Come, boy," and waved her hand toward the front door.

They walked outside to the SUV. She opened the back passenger door and told him to get in and sit down. It had captain's chairs in the back, and the third row behind that, she had him sit in the captain's chair. She knew that Aaron was right behind him, so she could easily signal him when it was time. She hopped in, unzipped her pants the rest of the way, let them drop to the floor. She thought he was going to die right there in his chair. He sat forward and reached over to try to touch between her legs, and she slapped his hand away and said, "Don't touch until I tell you it's okay."

She sat in his lap, facing him, tore her shirt the rest of the way, and took it off. She was completely naked sitting on him. She put her arms behind him with her thumbs up in the air, leaned over, and whispered, "Is this what you've been wanting, you sick piece of fucking shit!"

He picked his head up and said, "What?"

And with that, she turned her thumbs down, and when she did, Aaron popped up from the back and put a garrote around his neck. Because of the drugs, he was way too weak to struggle, and as he was strangling the life out of him, Emmanuelle looked him in his eyes and said, "You sick motherfuckers treated me like a piece of meat all my life, and you're still trying, but not anymore. You have no control over me anymore. I'm going to take from you everything that you've ever taken from me and more because I'll be taking your life from you. I just wanted to make sure you knew that when it was time to go, I would be the instrument that sent you straight to hell."

Aaron held it until he was lifeless and not breathing anymore. He was done. He asked her how she felt. She told him she felt fucking great. She felt relieved, and now it was time to finish it. Aaron gave her some clothes. She got dressed and went back inside with the second bag of cash.

When she walked back in, we were still dancing for them, topless and with their shorts almost zipped all the way down now, and the guys were getting anxious. They had their dicks out, and they were stroking themselves. I squatted down in front of Zeke again, and as I did, he grabbed me by the hair and tried to pull me forward, putting my head on his dick. I slapped his hand and pulled away, and as I did, he backhanded me across the face, knocking me to the floor.

He stood over me and said, "Now it's time get fed, bitch!"

As we were getting ready to fight back, Emmanuelle slammed the door, and it startled them all.

She walked over to Zeke and said, "Look, Daddy, I brought you another present," and as she threw the second bag down on the floor, she reached over and helped me up.

Zeke looked at Emmanuelle and said, "You really need to teach your bitch friends some manners."

She agreed and said that she was sure I was sorry. "Right, Vanessa?"

I looked at them and said, "Yes, I'm very sorry for what I did, and I will be sure to make it up to you."

He asked her what was in the bag. She told him to open it and see. When he did, he couldn't believe his eyes. He asked her what the fuck was this. She said it was the other half. She wanted to see how things were going to go before she decided to give it to them. Now that she can see how great it was, she wanted to go ahead and give it all to him.

He looked at her and said, "You wanted to see how great it was going to be?"

He half turned away from her and then turned around fast and backhanded her across the face hard. She fell backward and to the floor. Aaron asked if we wanted him to come in and end it. I and Emmanuelle both said no. We got this.

I went over and helped Emmanuelle up off the floor.

She said, "I apologize, Daddy, for making you mad. It won't happen again. We will all make it up to you."

Zeke said, "It better not, because if it does, you're going to get much worse than a hand across the face."

Emmanuelle told him she understood. She told him that there was $100K total in both bags. "That should help you all a lot, right?"

He told her that was great, but he wanted to know how much more she could get. He wanted more. He wanted all of it, and if he didn't get it, he's going to make things really rough for them. Through this whole thing, no one once asked where Sam was. Zeke was too into trying to get all he could, and Joe had two gorgeous girls all over him. They were topless, shorts unzipped and almost falling down, and they started dancing again to distract him; and this time, they were taking it a bit further. They were allowing him to touch them while they "helped" him out too.

Zeke said, "Well, how's this going to go?"

I asked him if he had a computer. He went into his room and brought out his laptop. "Is this good enough?"

I said that this will work. I asked Zeke what his account numbers are. He asked me why. I said I needed something to transfer money to.

He said, "Okay, well, I'm going to stand over you and watch you then."

Emmanuelle walked up to him and said, "Daddy, we can trust her."

Zeke turned around and slapped her across her face. It didn't knock her down, and you could tell that the drugs were taking effect because it didn't hurt as much, but it still stung. He said, "Don't you ever fucking question me, girl, do you understand?"

"Yes, Daddy, I understand." Emmanuelle said to herself, *God, I can't wait to kill this motherfucker.*

Zeke said he was going to stand right behind me while I worked. He was rubbing my shoulders and working his way down to my breasts, squeezing them and my nipples so hard at times it made me flinch. Zeke grabbed my hair and pulled my head back. As he squeezed my breast really hard, he asked me, "Is this too hard for you? You're feeding me now. Do you not like the way I'm eating?"

I said, "No, not at all. I love it. In fact, I like being choked too. When we're done here, I want all of it. I can't wait until I'm done, and I can do what I want to do to you."

Zeke got a big smile on his face.

Problem was, Zeke's not really bright. He voluntarily gave me his account numbers, and he has a lot of money—like a lot more money in the bank, more than anyone ever thought. None of them had a clue, not even Emmanuelle. Zeke leaned over and told me that if I told anyone what he had, he'd choke me right here and not for fun either. I told him not to worry. I wasn't going to say a word. I wanted the fun.

Lizzy and Roni had taken Joe into the bedroom. Emmanuelle walked in the back to see what was going on. Lizzy and Roni had been wanting a dick for so long they figured, *What the fuck, there was a dick here. He wasn't the only one that was getting aroused with all that dancing, and it wasn't like there was going to be a risk of anyone getting emotionally attached, right? He would be dead by the end of the day anyway.* Emmanuelle walked through the door, and she really didn't know what to think about what she was seeing. Lizzy was on top of Joe's dick, grinding away. Roni was on his face rocking back and forth, and they were both making out with each other. After some time, they switched places. They never even noticed her standing there, she just shook her head, walked out, and walked back to the living room.

When she got back there, she was a bit surprised. Again, it was like she was in some alternate universe she didn't know what to think. She went to the bathroom and started talking to Aaron about what's going on over here. She asked, "Don't you get jealous with all this stuff going on?"

Aaron told her, "The relationship that I and Vanessa have is a solid one, one that we both believe in, so no, I don't get jealous. All that we're doing and all that we've done is for you and for others that we've helped get out from under all their bullshit and to be free from it, it's for a greater cause, and we both understand that. The difference is, with all these situations, you all are the ones that the people are attracted to, not me, but I do what I do unless you would like to trade places?"

She said, "No thank you. I'll keep doing this."

He said, "Okay, so believe in what we're doing and go out there and do what needs to be done."

She said okay, and she was off.

*****

I walked back into the living room, and Vanessa was still working on the computer. There was a gun sitting next to the computer, and this time, Zeke had made Vanessa sit in his lap with no shorts or top on. I wasn't sure if Zeke had his dick inside Vanessa or not, but the way she was slowly grinding on him, I was thinking it probably was. He was squeezing Vanessa's breasts hard, like really hard with one hand, and he was choking her with the other, not choking the life out of her but what you would normally do when you were fucking someone. It definitely made the computer work go slower than normal, and it was obvious that the gun helped to motivate her to be where she was sitting. I was about to say something, and Aaron spoke up and told me, "Stop. She knew what she was doing." She shook her head, turned around, and walked back into the bedroom. They had finished with Joe, or Joe had finished with them. Either way, he was passed out from all the drugs and booze. He wasn't waking up anytime soon. Just to make sure they taped his mouth, hands, and feet, now it was two down and the biggest asshole to go.

Before they walked back into the living room, Aaron told Lizzy and Roni what was going on. Emmanuelle was amazed that it didn't faze them.

They told her, "This is what we do. We're doing this for you. Do you get that? Do you think that we would be out here fucking these guys, your family for nothing?"

253

Aaron piped in, "I hate to interrupt, but you two did need some dick, right?"

Lizzy and Roni laughed. Emmanuelle was so confused.

Lizzy said, "Anyway, we all know what we're doing here. We sacrifice certain things for the greater good. We sacrifice for you. They sacrificed for me, and we just keep paying it forward. We're set for life with businesses and money, and we don't have to worry about anything ever again because even if we were to stop now, we will always be there, will always take care of each other. We are stronger now because of what we're doing. Does that make sense?"

Roni said, "Shit, Aaron has such a big security force that's filled with such badasses. We will *always* be protected."

Emmanuelle was starting to get it. She just wasn't used to having so much support. They all told her that she does now. "Okay, let's go get Vanessa and get this over with."

*****

They found a gun in the bedroom they were in with Joe, and Lizzy took it with her. They got out to the living room, and Vanessa was still sitting on Zeke's lap, still grinding slowly. His head leaned back, and his eyes were closed. Emmanuelle grabbed the gun from Lizzy, walked up to her dad, grabbed him by the hair, stuck the gun in his mouth, and said, "Fun's over, Daddy."

Roni brought Vanessa a big shirt from the bedroom for her to put on. She stood up, got dressed, looked at Zeke, and said, "Are you full yet?" Emmanuelle pulled him up out of the chair and told him to sit on the floor. Lizzy went and opened the door for Aaron. He walked up to Zeke and knelt in front of him.

Zeke said, "Who the fuck are you?"

Aaron told him, "I'm your worst fucking nightmare. Look around you, Zeke. This will all come to an end tonight. You and your boys will be coming to an end tonight."

Zeke started laughing and said, "But I have all your money. If you want it back, I stay alive. I don't care about my boys. In fact, I care less about my bitch of a daughter."

Aaron said, "Well, that's too bad, Zeke, because we all happen to love her very much."

Zeke said, "You still need me for your money."

Aaron said, "Oh yeah, that, well, the cash, I'll just take back. And as far as the rest, Vanessa, you want to explain?"

I said, "Zeke, you're really not as smart as you think you are. You gave me access to your accounts, which wasn't very smart. I may have transferred money in, but with the push of a button, I cannot only take it back, but I can also take your small fortune as well. Emmanuelle, would you like to do the honors?"

She walked over to the computer, saw the amount that he had, and just about shit "you wanted me to give you money when you already had this!" She walked over to him and struck him across the face with the gun, snapping his head back, and taking a couple of teeth for good measure. She walked back over to the computer, pushed the button, and told him, "Wave your money goodbye. You won't be needing it where you're going."

Zeke tried to stand, and Lizzy kicked him in the chest so hard it sounded like it may have cracked a rib.

Aaron said, "You know you just don't get it. There is no out here for you. There's no path for you to ever leave this cabin again, which of course led to cursing and threats." Aaron looked at him and said, "Do you not think that we've ever done this before?"

He told us that his sons would come after us. Aaron said, "Hold on just one minute, Zeke." He walked outside and came back in with Sam over his shoulder. He dumped his body right next to his and said, "Is this one of the boys you're talking about?" He asked him to hold on for one more minute, went onto the bedroom, and grabbed Joe and brought him in. "Is this the other one you're talking about?" And Aaron dumped him on the other side of him. "Understand me when I tell you that under no circumstances will you ever be getting out of this, that this here, will be your last night on earth courtesy of that daughter you refer to as a bitch." He turned toward Emmanuelle and started to plead with her to save his life. Aaron grabbed him by his bottom jaw and told him, "Once the ball gets rolling, I'm the only one that can call it off, and it's not getting called off. Sam is already gone, but he will still be part of the plan."

Joe started to wake up a bit. The shock and fear in his eyes told us that he knew this wasn't going to end well.

Aaron took Sam's body and spread it out like he was on a cross. He opened up the duffel bag he brought and pulled out four very large stakes and a short-handled sledgehammer. Aaron started telling Zeke, "In some societies, in order to exorcise demons or bad spirits, you need to offer up a sacrifice of some kind. In some societies, it's a human sacrifice. You three are the demons or the bad spirits that have been haunting Emmanuelle ever since her mom died, and you must be exorcised."

With that, he hammered the large spikes through Sam's hands and feet. Joe totally freaked out but couldn't move, and Zeke tried to get up again. Aaron swung the hammer and broke his jaw.

"You know Zeke, you need to really think before you do things in your life because, eventually, you're going to have to answer to someone. To me, it's usually God that you have to answer to, unless you really piss someone off enough and then there's someone like me that will make you pay before that. Eventually, we all have to pay."

Aaron told me to give them both another dose, not enough to knock them out but enough to make it so they couldn't really move. Joe was really the only one that tried to put up a struggle, but Roni kicked him in the face, and it stunned him long enough to be able to get a shot in his neck. Zeke received the same. It was hard for Zeke to talk, but he tried. Same old shit. Again, we're not going to get away with it and people will find us. Joe was asking Aaron what he was planning on doing. He asked if he really wanted to know. He said he did.

Aaron told them, "You're really far out here in the woods. There's nothing and nobody around for miles, except—"

He said, "Except what?"

Aaron said, "Except for the animals and the critters. I've done my research on you all. You've pissed a lot of people off in the time you all have been alive. No one is going to miss you, besides the fact you all are going to be bait for the animals out there that need something to eat. I've seen bears, big cats, hell, I've seen feral hogs out here. You all are going to make a good snack for them."

Joe looked at Roni and Lizzy and said, "I thought we had something. I thought we had a connection."

Lizzy said, "No, you had a dick, and that's what we wanted. Don't mistake that for anything else."

He turned to Emmanuelle. Before he had a chance to talk, she said, "Don't bother. Really, after all the hell you all have put me through? You were willing to let your brother fuck his sister. What kind of sick fuck would allow that?"

They had all run out of options. Aaron stuck a dirty pair of underwear in their mouths and duct-taped them shut.

"It was time. Do you have anything you need to say to them, Emmanuelle?"

She stared at her family. Tears started going down her face. She told them that she was sorry that it had to come to this. "This needed to be done. There are no people more deserving of this than the three of you, and I will never feel guilty for it."

Aaron finished nailing the rest of them to the floor. The pain was so excruciating they passed out.

I and the rest of the girls were busy going around cleaning everything up. There was a lot of DNA everywhere, and we couldn't leave any behind, and we can't burn it like we'd done before. Being in the woods, it might start a forest fire, and that's not the kind of attention that we needed. They picked up and sprayed, gathered sheets, basically anything they could find where there might be traces left.

*****

Aaron

So the final piece was to do some cutting, not a lot but enough for the animals to be able to smell the blood and come after it. Everything was bagged up and loaded in the SUV. I grabbed a rag and smeared some of the blood all over the front door and porch just enough to attract some of the animals. We all got in the car, and they were ready to go. I told them to wait just a few minutes.

"When I was out here waiting for you all, I saw the feral hogs wandering around."

No sooner than after he got those words out, they all saw a family of them wandering toward the front porch. I knew they were done for. Hogs can devour a human body—bones and all. There would be nothing left behind. Emmanuelle said she couldn't think of a better ending for all of them. With that, I took off for home.

CHAPTER 27

Time to Relax

Aaron

We got back to the house and got cleaned up. We all grabbed something to eat and headed down to the bunker. I asked Emmanuelle how she was feeling. She said that she was unusually calm, stress level was really low, and she felt seriously at peace. She thanked all of us again for all that we had done for her and that she was sorry that it had to go as far as it did. She did have a question.

"What was it about with the Lizzy and Roni wanting dick?"

Vanessa explained everything to her, in detail, including the shows that they put on for us and the reasons why—why they couldn't go out and get involved as long as we're doing this. Emmanuelle could totally understand the reasoning for it. She hinted that she might want to go to some of the shows. Vanessa just smiled and nodded.

Roni asked, "So what now? Where do we all go from here? It's going to be hard not doing anything to help the ones that need it. We run into them every day."

I said, "How about if we find ways to keep us distracted, how about if we continue to build the foundation and the infrastructure of our businesses and not just in gyms and restaurants? Roni, how about an architecture firm where you're in charge? Emmanuelle, how about a tutoring service, and, Lizzy, how about a financial consulting firm to go along with the gyms? How about if we work really hard to build the foundation and make sure it's rock-solid? Then once we do that, we can start all over again."

They all asked about not being around one another as much. We're used to one another, and we love being around. That's going to be hard to give up.

Vanessa said, "We won't give that up. We're so woven into one another's lives that we won't be able to give that up no matter what. We will need to help pick properties, help with design concepts, all of it. There's still a lot to do, but right now, it just doesn't have to involve getting revenge on people. They're not going to stop, and neither are we."

I said, "No matter what we choose to do, I'm never going to stop. I can't stop. Too much needs to be done."

Vanessa asked me if I remembered the conversation we had a long time ago. I said that I did and not to worry. This is not that at all.

So they wanted an explanation on what kind of infrastructure I was talking about.

I told them, "This is what I'm thinking about. We seem to have stuck ourselves on this side of the country. There are people everywhere that need to be taken care of. I still have people that I want to take care of."

They asked me where.

I told them, "Boston is a great starting place, and we can work our way through the country, but this time, we won't be going to a place seeking revenge and then decide to build something. We get the properties and businesses done first and then work our way out from there. It's building the infrastructure first, but the biggest question is still this, can we still sustain this for a long period, staying silent and not wanting to quit it all, and can we and will we always trust each other? Any long amount of time we take off is going to test that because once you're out there, you going to meet people, and you're going to want to do things. You might fall in love, want to start a family, and there's nothing wrong with that at all."

They asked, "What about you and Vanessa? Don't you want to have a family?"

Vanessa said, "We do want to have a family, but we will not stop what we're doing because it's way too important to stop. We will work it out. Do you all think that if you chose to do that you could keep this secret from your significant others?"

They couldn't answer that question because if they walk into a relationship, they want to do it with honesty.

I said, "Okay, I understand that, but you're in this relationship, right? If you use that reasoning, shouldn't you have honesty and loyalty to this one first, and don't tell me about personal because from the revenge to the 'shows' and everything in between, this is nothing but personal." It was hard for them to argue with that. "I want all of you to be happy. That's why I've done what I've done for you. If you want to be with others, then do so, but we have to make other arrangements for all this."

Emmanuelle said, "Okay, let's do it. Let's get it all built up. Take some time off and work on ourselves. Work on our time together with one another. Let's grow and become better."

I told them all that we need to come up with areas of the country to work on and then research places to buy. Even if we stop cooking the recipes, we're still going to be together.

"Let's get some long-needed rest, and then let's get started looking for our new homes."

EPILOGUE

Aaron

Honestly, this is something that I never wanted to do; it was something that I always felt was forced upon me. You can only push humans so far before they snap and start to get back at those that have hurt them. Too many people kill for no reason. That's not what we do. We do it because we feel obligated to help others. Look at the difference that we've made in people's lives. We've actually helped people move on and feel better about themselves. They can live their lives without fear. All the "family" that Vanessa and I have taken on, look at where it has gotten them and us. We're building businesses, a foundation for the future. We'll never want for anything again ever.

But we'll never stop. It's too important to not keep going. It was suggested to me that maybe we expand and make it bigger. Add more people, but that would be like a business. Where would the personal touch come from? People say that no two chefs cook the same. Well, can't that be said about this too? We each have our way of creating, of cooking, and even killing. People that we put down need to know the reasons why it's being done to them, and if some random person is saying to them, "Hey, you remember this guy, or this girl, and do you remember doing this X amount of time ago?" It doesn't have the same feel or meaning to it; besides, sometimes I come up with things on the fly. We've been lucky in that we have been getting away with what we're doing, adding more to the mix creates more risks for us, ones I'm not willing to take.

But honestly, it doesn't really matter because I will continue doing what I have to do to help people live without fear and without feeling like every time they turn around that someone is waiting to come and get them, hurt them, or even worse.

But people just need to know that as long as they keep harassing, hurting, or just treating people like shit, there's always going to be someone like me to make sure that they never have the chance to do it again; and whether it's a life sentence or a death sentence, I will make you regret the day you made the choice to treat someone like they were less than you.

Keep your eyes open and your head on a swivel because, someday, it will be your time, and I'm the creator of the recipes that you will be a part of.

About the Author

Gilbert is the father of two kids, and he's lived in Arizona, Colorado, and Hawaii. He's been in the restaurant industry all his life as an executive chef, food and beverage director, and general manager. One day, he decided to write a different type of cookbook, one that not everyone could use but one that brought him great satisfaction. Bon appétit!

CPSIA information can be obtained
at www.ICGtesting.com
Printed in the USA
LVHW101507030722
722675LV00005B/51